The Innocent Man Who Broke the Law

I0622398

James Berry

Acknowledgment

Judith

Your inner beauty and goodness matched the
exquisite elegance of your life.

"To the pure, all things are pure"
(Titus 1:15)

CONTENTS

Prologue

THE PLANE LANDED ON GATWICK runway with the usual sounds of screeches and vibrations, followed by relief—the flight was over. In a slow crawl, the aircraft moved to its arrival gate. A young, successful engineer sat still and reclusive, reflecting on where he had lived in the tropics for the last twelve months enduring the heat, humidity, and lack of sensory comforts. Overhead, the pilot's voice failed to penetrate what was rushing through his mind. The plane came to a stop; the flight from Freetown had taken seven hours. By the time he reached the baggage table, the cooler climate had already made a difference in his stride; the bigger world he had withdrawn from was reappearing. He cleared customs and followed signs giving directions to the nearby Hilton Hotel. With the use of his shanks mare and the close-by train, he arrived in short time.

Patronage at the Hilton was cosmopolitan. The short distance from the airport made it convenient for businesspersons and tourists from all over the world. The engineer's arrival was at a busy time of the day, and right off the plane after a long flight from the tropics made him look disheveled and underdressed. He gave no thought to his rough, down-dressed look. Even in the best-of-conditions, his appearance would be no better. Part of him was iconoclastic—he took pleasure in being different. When patrons gave stares at his rumpled look and beat-up luggage, it made him think they considered him someone who had washed up on a near-by beach and wandered into this place. It mattered little that he stood in contrast to the business suits and first-class luggage that surrounded him in a first-rate hotel. He smiled and took consolation knowing his inferior-made luggage matched the person holding it.

The desk clerk handed him the key to a reserved room. By the time he reached the elevator, he found it full but managed to do what his assertive nature was accustomed to doing: push until he had his own space. His room welcomed him to a silent and private world. No one knew where he was except his family back in the States. His only friend in this lonely place was his phone—his connection to the outside world.

Anxious to unpack, bathe, and change into fresh clothes before dinner, he threw his single piece of cheap, battered luggage on the bed and opened the case. With the case open in full view, something looked wrong. It appeared different from when it left Freetown. He lifted a few pieces of his personal effects from the top, ran his hands through the rest of the contents. Everything underneath was not his—it belonged to someone else. A thousand thoughts rushed through him in one sudden burst. He removed all the contents inside the case in an attempt to find additional articles of clothes; he found none. Among the things not his, were a rolled-up snakeskin and two ebony head carvings. Most of his personal effects, pictures, and a miniature chess set were gone. Before he left Freetown he had written his name on the underside part of the   luggage handle with a felt-tipped pen. He grabbed the empty case from the bed to examine the handle; it revealed no name. It was blank. Though the case contained his baggage-tag number and looked like the one he left Freetown with, this was not his case. He tossed the luggage piece back on the bed with a sound of clatter coming from inside. Upon careful examination, he found the case altered. He shook it with both hands. Again, he heard the rattle. The inside bottom cover was peeled back, revealing a hidden compartment. Intrigue now matched the engineer's adventurous nature. He removed the cover of the hidden section. Concealed inside were six, well-insulated bags. Lifting them out one-by-one, he could tell by the feel of the contents that they all contained illicit, uncut diamonds from the minefields of up-country Sierra Leone.

The young engineer's pulse quickened. Inner voices were telling him he possessed illegal contraband, a punishable violation. Then, other louder voices were heard with greater clarity: Middle East terrorists smuggled diamonds to sponsor terrorism. In his possession were several million dollars of smuggled rough diamonds he had just carried through customs in someone else's case. A veil of dark weakness gripped him. He stood to his feet, turned off the lights and hoped the hush of darkness would quell the voices coming at him. In his darkened room, he sat on the bed while his world spun in disorder. Though the darkened room quieted the voices, he knew somewhere outside there were eyes of smugglers searching for their lost plunder. He mulled over his acquisition of this luggage piece he had carried through customs. One thing was certain—it wasn't his.

Chapter 1

The Shuttle

WHEN JAKE STEPPED ONTO the shuttle bus for the twelve-mile trip to the Freetown airport, the overhead sky bore the usual marks of a tropical downpour. Humidity made everything clammy. He had never adjusted to the hot, sultry conditions in this country, though he had lived here for a year. Everyone and everything moved slower in the tropics and was noticeable in Jake's walk down the aisle clasping with a sweaty hand his single piece of luggage. It was in his nature to be first in everything, and it included boarding planes and shuttle buses. Being first onboard, he chose a seat next to an open window near the back of the transport, leaving his luggage on the floor alongside his seat. It held his entire wardrobe of three changes of clothes after giving the rest to charity. Clothes kept in the severe tropics over six months absorbed a permanent strong musky odor, noticeable only after departure from the area. A men's clothing shop was his first stop in London.

Passengers boarded the shuttle and suitcases filled the aisle. Some were identical, showing they were indigenous to the country and available in most shops. They looked like Jake's piece who had bought his at the travel agency where he purchased his airline tickets. Luggage made in the country had limited variety.

Solitude, in the midst of change, made Jake reflect about where he was in life and where he would end up. Right now, he was in the middle of change after spending a year as a civil engineer directing the construction of several large government buildings in the interior of Sierra Leone. New diamond fields in the area had created an economic boom. Now, that his project was completed, his schedule included England and his return to the States. It was his business he started several years ago, which his father now managed in his absence, that would consume the rest of his life. At the age of thirty, he would continue the challenge of searching for what was missing in his life. His venture of going to Africa was one of those pursuits. Jake mused over his remarkable short history of success. When he was twenty-one, before he completed his Masters in Civil Engineering, he gambled the inheritance from his grandfather on land speculation, then used the profits to launch into property development. His company had ownership of several new shopping centers and prime subdivision land in three major cities. Money never drove him to success; it was the excitement and challenge of walking on the edge making it. The drumbeat he had heard and marched to in life passed others in silence. His nature destined him to arrive at one of two extremes in life: a ne'er-do-well with friends, or success without them. In either state, his level of happiness would remain static.

Jake's reflections today were part of his on-going saga of sorting out the meaning of life. Tomorrow, he thought, he could lose everything, but his contentment would remain the same: very low. Happiness, as defined by most people, was an illusionary unreachable reality for Jake, even in his state of financial security. There were two reasons why he had gone to Africa: his grandfather, and boredom. Success had lost its sparkle and life its purpose. He needed change. The anchor of his life had been his late grandfather who had served as a medical missionary in this country. Though the recent civil war had left the hospital in ruins, he wanted to see and experience life in the country where his grandfather had lived and worked. His father, an accountant, made everything possible by agreeing to manage the business in his absence.

He looked down on the floor at the cheap, brown box of luggage purchased in Freetown two days before. It was a picture speaking to him: he had everything, but little to show for it. He sat alone on his bench seat with thoughts that continued to sink lower into the bowels of introspection. Real security, he thought, was what he possessed on his person and the contents inside the single piece of luggage on the floor. He knew security could be real, or imagined, but neither state allowed permanence. At this moment, the small case on the floor was more valuable to him than what his father managed for him back home. He reflected on the passenger aboard the sinking Titanic who took an apple and orange from his stateroom instead of spending time gathering his jewelry. He knew this applied to him and where he was in life. Financial security was a mental concept; security that mattered was what he needed and possessed in real time.

When the mind reached this state, the energy it produced was always reflective. For Jake, the Age of European Exploration came to mind. The box of luggage in the aisle made him feel like a fifteenth century Portuguese sailor embarking on a voyage destined to sail the west coast of Africa. When the mariners left the ports of Portugal, they carried just one small piece of luggage aboard the ship for a year's pelagic journey into the unknown. Unlike the Portuguese sailors, the contents in his box needed to last but a few hours. His journey was not into their kind of unknown world. Certain predictable results awaited him, and this was

Jake's paradoxical dilemma. He lived as an engineer with the constraints of scientific laws where everything was predictable, but the voice of adventure inside him could always be heard calling from afar. His nature had the need of unpredictable adventurous action. Jake moved closer to the open window at his seat and welcomed the cooler on-shore breeze.

Seated throughout the bus were Sierra Leoneans going on vacation, returning to their studies in England, or commuting back to Europe for business. Most on board wore their traditional colorful national dress. A couple of older men were dressed in business suits with sweat beads rolling down their faces. It was a common practice for traditional Africans of the older generation, when traveling or going out, to be dressed in suits regardless of weather conditions. They always carried an umbrella, a shield that kept them from the elements of rain and sun. The scene mirrored the changes taking place in Freetown, a unique historical place where a British cultural transplant took place in the nineteenth century. By the age of these men and the manner of their dress, Jake knew they were of the old Creole order, the settlers of the Freetown colony from the time of colonialism. They had been a proud ruling class whose educational energies strengthened the infrastructure of government during colonial and post-colonial times unequal to any other place in the British Empire. They were the doctors, lawyers, teachers, politicians, and government workers. Their educational compatibilities with the British created a climate where occasional inter-racial marriages occurred between them. The Freetown community always accepted the children of these unions. However, marriage between the Creole and non-Creole Sierra Leonean seldom occurred in former days. A Creole's birth gave status and position. It was as important to them as it was to the American Northeast Bluebloods. Now, in modern times, their world was slipping from them as they had known it in history. These older men seated alone represented a fading past. They sat together, a microcosmic symbol of a changed world. One where values, customs, even histories had fallen prey to the greater masses demanding change in the global order of events.

Three Middle East males came on board together and moved in Jake's direction. They carried nervous-looking demeanor, speaking to each other in low guttural tones. Though they spoke English and the local Krio language, they chose to use their Lebanese-accented Arabic. A multi-linguistic person, when stressed, always used his primary language among his own in a mixed group. Political correctness always exhibited itself as an art with the Lebanese here in this country. These three revealed tension when they went against the grain speaking something other than Krio or English. Their whispers in Arabic made Jake take notice. Two of the men sat across the aisle from Jake. The other sat behind him. They placed in the aisle a piece of indigenous-made luggage similar to his. With so many of these local pieces of luggage on board, Jake concluded they were a onetime-use item: inexpensive and disposable after passengers completed their journeys. Even luggage kept in the tropics carried a lingering unpleasant musky smell. He gave no further thought about these three carrying only one piece of luggage.

The Lebanese in West Africa had influenced the region over a hundred years. They were an unassimilated Middle East cultural enclave, and their presence presented forceful competition among the local ethnic groups with their small storefront businesses all the way from the capital city to the most remote interior village. They coexisted with indigenous populations by trade, learning local languages, and bribery. The country of Lebanon herself lauded her ancestral lineage all the way back to the ancient Phoenicians, who were the sea merchants throughout the Mediterranean Basin, a claim never disputed by those who had examined her descendants' entrepreneurial skills over the last century. Wherever they went they entrenched themselves into local economies with small businesses and enterprises in a remarkable way. Most people considered them open and gracious in their domestic community. If one extended the Arabic greeting, "Marhabba, keef hallak eyom," to a male member of the family, an invitation would be extended for a cup of their traditional black Turkish coffee, sweet like honey and thick as syrup. When the coffee was finished, they entertained by turning the empty cup upside down so the dregs could flow as gravity permitted. The pictures found inside the cup determined what the future held. Regardless of where these descendents of the ancient Phoenicians settled, they had one common thread: their language and national identity to the country of Lebanon. However, the skill used to enable them in business became useful for some on the dark side of human nature. This shadowy side included the infamous Siamese twins: bribery and diamond smuggling. History always showed the two living in close proximity.

A few European expatriates settled in front of the bus. Everyone now waited for the last few passengers to board. The first of the latecomers to enter was a well-dressed, older Creole who appeared troubled with a tense focus. Jake recognized the man. His leathery face and weary eyes swept across the rear of the bus. Concerned looks stared at the three Lebanese clustered around Jake, then his eyes paused momentarily on the engineer sitting next to the open window. At first, it appeared he wanted to give a physical greeting gesture, but froze and gave a slight, concealed nod, turned, and sat down. The Creole's thoughts were in turmoil. He regretted having acknowledged the man sitting next to the open window—he knew that engineer. Of all the expatriates in this country to see on this shuttle, unfortunate fate had to make it this person. He hoped the young engineer wouldn't become part of his problem.

Jake saw and felt the avoidance from the elderly man. He had been his consulting engineer on an important building project. The man carried no hand luggage, and his conversation was with another party seated alongside him.

Jake remembered his involvement with him when the Creole made a special trip upcountry to the construction site over which he was in charge. He came to his office on business.

"Are you Mr. James?"

"Yes, what can I do for you?"

"I'm Eben Coker from Freetown. I understand you're the engineer in charge of this project for the government. One of our historic Anglican churches in Freetown is in need of restoration. We want to shore up some of the weak areas, and at the same time give it a new look. We're in need of professional engineering help. If you can find time to fit it into your schedule while you're still here in the country, our church will appreciate it."

It was for Jake to find out later Mr. Coker knew everything going on in the country. He even knew the date his contract was up with the government.

"Mr. Coker, I'll be glad to look at your engineering issues when I return to Freetown."

"My, you're a young engineer. According to the government records in Freetown, you have extensive commercial building experience. Yet, you're so young. This speaks well of you."

"Thank you for the compliment. I'll let you know by phone when I'm available to meet with you in Freetown. I'll need at least four or five days to review the project and draw up the plans."

Jake remembered when he left the office that his tall stalwart frame spoke of what he was in life: a pillar for others and someone who lived with purpose.

Any historical structure was of special interest to Jake, even if it were a church. It was the Anglican missionary efforts in schools and higher education in the Freetown colony that built its standing in West Africa. Fourah Bay University, situated high in the mountains above Freetown overlooking the beautiful harbor, was the first western-style university of higher learning in this part of the continent. "Athens of Africa" was the image it carried in the old days.

Within two weeks, Mr. Coker received a call from Jake's office upcountry. They scheduled a time to meet together at the church for an inspection of the building. For five days, Jake worked with Mr. Coker in the capital city drawing up plans that would comply with structural engineering standards. Eben Coker's personal life was unknown to Jake, other than it was common knowledge he was a successful businessperson. He was involved in several businesses, the major one being the owner of an import and export company. He had earned the reputation of honesty and fair dealing. The Lebanese business community had high regard for him. After they became better acquainted, he opened up to Jake, and they became friends.

"Here in my country, Mr. James, life has been good to me. My family, including my son and daughter, believe in four principles: God, family, education and hard work. If we put God first, the others are easier to come by. My family remembers the old Jewish proverb, 'to not teach your child a trade is to teach him to steal.' My people sacrifice everything to get their children the best education possible so they'll have a trade."

"You sound like my father and grandfather, Mr. Coker. They transferred all those values down to me, but the God part didn't stick. I left the church when I was sixteen, never went through its door until we started your church restoration project."

"Well, it sounds like you're the Prodigal who will someday return home, and when that day happens, your family will be waiting for you."

"It was the university that put the death knell in me. My wild and adversarial years as a teenager changed after I went away to the university. I exchanged my rebellious energies for a disciplined academic career. It was there they cloned me into the secular model. I discovered man must respond to life within the context of his own experience; this didn't include religion. My mother and father were devout, religious people, but at some point in college I decided I could be as good as they were without the church and God part."

"My son went through the same problems, but once he went into the real world he came back to his roots of faith. That'll happen to you someday."

"What about your daughter and her experience?"

"My daughter never wavers in her faith. She's my teacher and example."

"Perhaps, there's hope for me."

"There's always hope for you. I have two children who reside in England: a married son who works with me in my business and a single daughter who is a practicing criminal defense attorney. She also serves as the family attorney in matters of legal business affairs. My daughter is religious. If you were around her, the secular forces driving you would weaken."

"That being the case, Mr. Coker, I'll run the other way."

The old man chuckled. "You do have a good sense of humor. One should always have that in life. I know all about university life too. I did my masters in London, returned here to teach and became an administrator in our Freetown school system. In the old days, I taught English Literature when the Shakespearian classics were a part of the curriculum. I did one play a year in the school auditorium for the public. Even today, when I go to London I enjoy live stage productions."

"You have an intriguing background, Mr. Coker. I'm most familiar with Shakespeare's Hamlet."

"Oh, this is interesting. What part of Hamlet stands out to you?"

"There are numerous favorite passages, but the part I like most is the one when Polonius gives advice to his son, Laertes, before he goes away:

Neither a borrower nor a lender be
For loan oft loses both itself and friend
And borrowing dulls the edge of husbandry
This above all to thine own self be true

"Excellent choice! Even I've given this advice to my son in some of my business dealings throughout the years. In fact, when my two went off to study in England, I used the same words as guiding principles for them to follow."

Those conversations between Mr. Coker and Jake happened four months ago. Now, here on the bus he sat quietly without acknowledgment of any personal encounter. Jake was aware that men in this country with his social and economic standing never took the shuttle. They always used a personal vehicle and driver. His avoidance of Jake and riding the shuttle didn't show the right picture. Conversation between the Creole and passenger seated beside him continued with quiet intensity.

The driver of the bus pulled out and joined others on the roadway with a heavy hand on the horn and a voice prepared for road rage. In Freetown, road space was the arena where gladiators performed at the wheel. They competed in battle with pedestrians, vendors selling their produce, baskets, and wares; but the biggest opponent of all was the taxi. Everything mechanical or electrical broke down here in this city except horns on taxis. In this fray of incessant noise, if conversation were required, being able to lip-Upread was an advantage. The vehicle sped up, passed the outside din. From behind, Jake felt a hand tap his shoulder with a voice attempting to penetrate the humid air, noise, and rattling of the bus.

"Are you American?" the voice said.

The question came from the left side near the open window. Jake turned around in his tight quarters straining to see over his left shoulder. Staring at him was a face that carried intense, deep-set eyes, the kind seen at poker games with high stakes on the table. He was one of the three Lebanese men who boarded the bus speaking Arabic.

Again, with a raised voice, the Lebanese asked, "Are you an American?" The forceful tone in his voice and the look on his face told Jake this person got what he wanted in life. The Lebanese, with concealed motives, found it difficult to restrain his intimidating nature.

"Why do you ask?" Jake said.

14

Jake knew dialogue required invisible fencing between the engaged for there to be mutual respect. This party had moved the fence too close by the tone of his voice and the cold direct question. Jake's nature was to think fast on his feet. His response to a question with another question would serve to readjust the fence. He continued looking at the man in his turned position, waiting for an answer. The man's eyes seemed to show calculated hesitation. By this time the bus had increased its speed, jostling everyone from side-to-side. Jake reached over with his right hand and grasped hold of the open window. While he waited for a response, someone settled in alongside him on his seat.

"I've a brother in New York City and need to get a letter to him as soon as possible. I'm looking for someone on this flight to carry a letter and mail it when he reaches the airport in New York. This will allow him to get the letter much sooner than if it's mailed in Freetown or London. After London, I'm flying on to Beirut. It'll help me a lot if you can manage this?"

Jake was an astute engineer. His analytical skill in critical thought served him well in his business. It was his job to establish weaknesses in building structures, and right now he was looking at a different kind of structure: one built out of words with attitude. It was an odd request from a total stranger. How did he know he was an American on his way to the States?

When the Lebanese saw hesitation looming over Jake, his narrow, pupil-beady eyes softened. This lessened Jake's resistance in accepting the letter.

"I'll be spending a couple of days in London before flying on to New York. This will delay your letter; however, I'm willing to post it for you."

The Lebanese pulled something from his front, shirt pocket and handed it to Jake. It was a standard-size envelope with a first-class US postage stamp. When Jake turned around, the eyes of the elderly Creole at the front of the bus were looking in his direction, then he quickly glanced away—again, refusing to acknowledge him. Now, seated next to him was the Lebanese from across the aisle. A trio of overweight Middle East men with hardened faces had invaded and occupied his private world. They sat in stone silence avoiding eye contact.

To reach the airport, the shuttle had to cross the mouth of the Sierra Leone River by ferry. When the bus arrived at the dock for the estuary crossing, passengers saw a floating transport built to carry no more than eight regular-size vehicles. The bus had priority to load first and drove to the front of the ferry. It would navigate five miles across the mouth of the river, and from that point proceed on to the airport. Most of the passengers chose to exit the bus for the thirty-minute voyage. The elderly Creole also left the bus without glancing in the area where Jake sat. Jake chose to stay on board. The man who gave Jake the letter to post in the States got off with other passengers while his two companions remained on board and continued their nervous-looking silence. The scene of the river took Jake's attention from those seated around him.

Engines groaned in labor as the ferry moved out. In slow, rhythmic motion, the water began slapping against the front of the floating carrier of men and metal. Of all the scenic views here in this land, the estuary crossing was most pleasurable. To the left was the wide-open Atlantic Ocean and to the right were the sudden-rising, velvet-covered, tropical mountains whose tops were marked with white clouds under the veil of a deep blue sky. The ferry ride carried picturesque value equal to any found on a Grecian, Mediterranean cruise. Its beauty shortened the voyage.

All the passengers began boarding the bus again once the ferry neared the disembarkation side of the estuary. Everyone returned to the bus, except the Lebanese who gave Jake the letter to mail. Passengers resettled themselves in the seats they left and the elderly Creole still avoided looking in the direction of Jake.

The ferry lowered its ramp onto the driveway that led up to the main road. The bus drove off first, and by the time it had reached the two-lane road leading to the airport, a late-model Mercedes passed alongside Jake's open window. The front of the vehicle had a Sierra Leonean driver and seated in the back were two Lebanese men, one being the man who gave Jake the letter to mail in New York. The two seated around Jake whispered in Arabic and paid special attention to the car driving by. Jake sensed something awry. He felt his shirt pocket to see if the letter were still where he had placed it. His gut feeling told him something was wrong with this scene. His profession again influenced his response. The immutable laws of math and physics had always ruled the science of engineering. However, the engineer had to factor-in variables as they related to materials used in a specific project. He perceived this case had variables; more data was required. Without sufficient answers to these unknowns, he chose to remain alert and do nothing. He knew the plane flight would soon put closure to this part of his journey.

The bus pulled into the airport parking lot. Jake forced himself into the aisle in front of the two Lebanese seated nearby. The older Creole who had avoided conversation with Jake up to this point, stood up, took several steps back toward Jake and placed in his hand a piece of folded paper containing a written message, saying softly, "There's something rotten in the State of Denmark."

It was a passage from Shakespeare's Hamlet when Marcellus spoke of the ghost of King Hamlet. The Creole knew Jake was familiar with this passage. The words he spoke sounded cryptic. Then he moved to the front of the bus, exited, got in a waiting car and drove away. Jake pushed the note inside his pocket, reached for his luggage on the floor. When his hand clasped the handle of his case, another identical piece stared him in the face. It rested in the lap of the Lebanese who sat nearby. He then remembered the three Lebanese boarding the bus with a piece of luggage like his. No further thought was made of it—other passengers had similar-looking cases.

Chapter 2

The Flight

PASSENGERS ARRIVING AT LUNGI AIRPORT had used three modes of travel to reach the site: vehicle, hovercraft, and helicopter. The helicopter service, operated by an East European group, had the reputation of poor maintenance, lacking seat belts and windows. It was the brave, desperate, and uninformed who patronized them. People were converging at the air terminal from three different directions. Jake's flight had already landed. There was no other large passenger plane at the airport, and from where he stood, it was visible on the runway. He thought it looked more like an outer space vehicle than a large jet aircraft capable of carrying 200 people. His initial impression came from living in a remote tropical region beyond the reach of technological comforts. For those few moments, his perception gripped another reality.

He moved toward the air-conditioned terminal building, pressed his way through the workaday crowds of vendors of fruit, watches, and African-made jewelry. Inside, he found the airline ticket counter bustling with eager passengers. He placed his luggage at his feet at the end of the waiting line. What he hoped for was missing—an air-conditioned terminal. The electrical power was down. Heat, with high humidity, had pulled from Jake every ounce of water he had drunk before boarding the shuttle. His clothes dripped with sweat, and with people filling the building only made conditions worse. The two Lebanese who sat near him on the bus were in line several passengers behind, their faces still frozen with the look of apprehension.

It tested one's ability to remain civil with the power down and a room filled with people waiting to be processed. It was a common practice for people who lived here in the tropics to shower at least once a day in ambient water temperature, and for many, it was a twice-a-day activity for the relief of heat, stickiness, and perspiration.

He heard the ticket agent say, "Next please." Jake, now at the front of the line, stepped up to the counter.

"May I have your passport and ticket please?"

He handed his documents to the agent noticing his moisture-ridden face. The company required its personnel to wear uniforms. The light blue jacket the agent wore had taken on dark perspiration spots under the armpits and across the back between the shoulders. The agent said nothing as if talking increased his discomfort. He handed the documents back without lifting his eyes, then, with a mechanical-sounding, unmelodious voice, said, "Next!"

Jake took his ticket, passport, and single piece of luggage to the next agent where it was weighed and tagged.

"Sir," Jake said, "my luggage piece doesn't need tagging, it's a carry-on case."

"I'm sorry, Sir, but your case is too large. It'll have to go to the baggage hold. Please take it over to the inspection table for clearance."

Luggage inspectors stood behind a long narrow table covered with open baggage. Passengers stood in front of their cases on the table and watched the inspectors paw through each one. When it came Jake's turn, he flung his case on top of the inspection table and waited. The inspector's weary, wrinkled brow dripped with sweat. He reached for a piece of cloth in his front pocket, gave his face a once-over wipe, then gazed at Jake like he was a wall, saying, "The power always goes down here when one needs it most. Nothing works nowadays. The government's corrupt, eats the money, and leaves nothing for the people."

Jake knew the comment from the agent was a statement rather than an invitation for discourse. He avoided a response, was about to open his luggage for inspection when the inspector stopped, looked over Jake's shoulder toward someone calling his name.

"Please wait a minute, Sir," the inspector said. "I'll be right back."

He walked over to a remote area of the large room and engaged in conversation with a Lebanese. It was apparent from body language they knew each other before this meeting. Though the room was full of passengers, Jake recognized the person talking to the inspector: he was the man on the bus who gave him the letter to mail in New York. A couple of minutes later the agent returned, and without opening Jake's luggage, said, "You can proceed to the waiting area, Sir."

"Thank you," Jake replied.

The airport baggage handlers took his single piece of luggage, threw it on top of other pieces going to the plane's baggage hold. To his surprise, when he entered the flight departure waiting room he found it air-conditioned with sufficient seating. This section of the airport was a different world; there was no jostling, clamor, and heat. Passengers were relaxed with cold drinks and had access to clean restrooms. Jake reflected on the presence of the Lebanese who gave him the letter to mail in New York and his association with the customs agent; it aroused his suspicions—something wasn't right.

Heightened security was everywhere. The engineer knew the tourist-type traveler, upon seeing all the open baggage inspected, would conclude safety in flight came first. However, those who lived here and followed local events and reports from the United Nations knew these efforts were to thwart anyone attempting to smuggle diamonds out of the country. Sierra Leone had gained world notoriety from her prized diamonds. The British ruled the area in 1930 when someone uncovered the first diamonds. In recent years the industry had expanded into new fields. Men with ill intent, like flies to a rotting carcass, had swarmed here for personal, political, and ideological gain. They plundered and raped the land, leaving the country and the people as the violated. Middle East people were always at the top of the list in this widespread mafia-type smuggling industry.

Smugglers here preyed upon the weakness of poverty and failed efforts of the masses to enforce change. Diamonds reaching the black market had always left the telling story of corrupted individuals with blighted souls.

The greatest weapon employed by smugglers was the use of illicit money offered as bribes to politicians, government workers, police, customs agents, and diamond miners in the mud pits. The amount of money transferred in bribery depended on the position of the person receiving the bribe. Bribery here was like nature's food chain. A person bribed at the bottom received just several hundred dollars. A feeder stationed at the top of the chain, depending on the amount of diamonds going out, would demand thousands for looking the other way. The flight today would carry two hundred potential smugglers. The number caught with diamonds, taken to a back room, threatened with jail and end up joining the rest of the passengers after paying off the right

22

people, would never be known. The big operators who engaged in illicit diamond smuggling were successful because they controlled both ends of the market, from here in Sierra Leone all the way to their European and Middle East connections. Hospitals, clinics, and schools had succumbed to a languished state; yet, the dark sides of foreign elements continued unabated with bribery and corruption, depriving the country of its natural wealth.

Jake stared at the British Airways plane from the waiting room. It rested on the runway like a giant bird ready for its flight north to a colder climate. While he pondered a northern cooler climate, a tall Nordic-looking woman moved between him and his view of the aircraft and sat next to him. She turned, looked at him with a gentle smile, saying, "What brings you here to this country?"

Her striking beauty with chiseled features and deep cerulean-colored eyes gave Jake momentary pause. He usually saw beautiful women from afar—today, it was up close. He managed a response.

"I can assure you it's not for the diamonds they have here in this country. I'm returning home after a one-year contract with the government."

She gave a relaxed sigh.

"Sir, you're fortunate to be able to stay in one place for a long period of time. My job keeps me moving about between several countries."

By her self-presentation, Jake knew she possessed magnetic public relations skills. Her physical and verbal command equaled her self-confidence. They sat side-by-side, like two strangers all alone waiting for something to happen in life, she in her articulate dress, Jake in his typical everyday work clothes.

"May I ask what business takes you to different countries?"

"Yes, you may, but allow me to introduce myself first—the name is Ingrid. A large company that buys and finishes gemstones for the wholesale market in Europe employs me. I come from a family of gemologists. We emigrated from South Africa to the UK, and I find it more profitable to travel than cut stones in a shop. I evaluate rough stones for my company at the time of purchase, and this requires me to travel a lot to gem-producing countries. Of course, Sierra Leone is a big supplier of diamonds."

"It's my pleasure to meet you, Ingrid. I'm Jake. My work here in the country was up near the diamond fields. I'm sure you never get out of the bigger cities with your job."

"I promised my folks when I took this job never to go on any dangerous assignments. I remain in capital cities and the suppliers of rough stones come to my company's office."

"Where will you go when you reach London?"

"I've a brother who operates two taxis in London. He chooses to run one around Gatwick. He'll pick me up, take me out to dinner, and then I'll catch another flight to Manchester where my mum and dad live. After we arrived in the UK, my folks bought a bed and breakfast. My mum manages the place, and my father works as a gemologist in the town. When I'm not traveling, I live in my own flat nearby."

"Perhaps, I can patronize your mother when I go there on my special mission. My folks in the States want me to get some pictures of family gravesites in Manchester. Our ancestry takes us back to this city."

Ingrid was giving cursory information about herself to a stranger. She was sophisticated and beautiful beyond the

24

level of her profession. Her language skills communicated charm and elegance. When Jake mentioned visiting Manchester, her interest reached beyond conversation. He saw her compelling blue eyes widen with interest.

"Jake, please visit Manchester! I'll show you all the interesting historical sites. I'll give you my business card with my mum's number, and when you call, please ask for me. I'll personally give you an extensive tour and even pay for your boarding there at my mum's place."

"Is it my look of dishevelment and impoverishment today that elicits your gratuitous patronage?"

Jake knew his dress never impressed the opposite gender. He always looked like the prince in the role of the pauper outside the palace walls and never attempted to prove otherwise. He was always eager to challenge tradition, and his dress was part of his rebellion.

Ingrid made a mental note that she had never met anyone as handsome as this person whose dress appeared so scruffy, tousled, and unkempt. At least his hair was combed. Judging his appearance, she almost had second thoughts about inviting him to Manchester.

"If you want to call me your patron or benefactor, I'll accept the title. One does not judge a book by its cover. Perhaps your visit to Manchester will give me the opportunity to discover the book's contents. Besides, travel around London and Manchester areas is expensive. My offer may serve to influence you to come our way."

Ingrid projected the atypical stereotype traditional woman: was assertive in a way that made her look flirtatious and bold. Her height, commanding beauty, and personality would level any playing field of the opposite gender. It was her assertive nature that surprised Jake. Ingrid handed him her card with the number of her mother's bed and breakfast.

"Ingrid, I may take you up on your offer if you can accommodate my idiosyncratic ways. Please write your brother's name and phone number on the back of your card. Perhaps I can hire him when I schedule my trip to Manchester. I usually fly, but I want to see the countryside."

"I'm delighted to do that, Jake."

Taking the card, she wrote her brother's name and phone number on it, then handed it to Jake. Her smooth and delicate hands revealed the absence of Jewelry; this made Jake take notice she wore none at all. Her appearance had survived well in the severe tropics, a natural enemy to anyone with her attractiveness. Most found themselves wrinkled and washed out. Perspiration and fatigue, the enemies of a good appearance, had lost a battle today. Ingrid looked untouched by the climate, even without the help of jewelry.

"If you'll excuse me, Jake, I want to get a bottle of water."

She walked away leaving the engineer with his thoughts on her statement of dissatisfaction of spending too much time traveling abroad. His attention fell on where he would be seated in the plane. He needed an aisle seat, and to reassure his concerns, he took from his front shirt pocket his airline ticket, noted his assigned passenger seat, replaced the ticket, and remembered his experience at the travel agency in Freetown.

"How many pieces of baggage will you carry on the flight?" asked the agent.

"Just one, the one I'm buying here today."

"I have a family taking extra luggage; they may be overweight. Do you object if I assign some of their luggage to you on this flight when they check in at the airport? If it exceeds your weight allowance, I'll pay the extra?"

"Sir, It's an airline policy for passengers to carry their own luggage. When I fly, I adhere to this rule."

Jake remembered his terse response to the agent. Though the agent appeared disappointed, he continued taking necessary information to complete the ticket transaction.

"Tomorrow, you can pick up the tickets." He remembered these words being the last ones spoken. The agent was Lebanese.

After mulling over the brief history of his conversation with the ticket agent, his mind imploded about the letter he carried on his person. He realized he had violated a cardinal rule: something was in his possession from a stranger. It wasn't a package, nevertheless. he had received it from someone he didn't know. He took the letter from his pocket, ran it through his fingers. It was smooth and flat, then, held it up to the light—it looked transparent. The overhead loudspeaker gave the announcement for boarding. All rational thoughts pondered about the letter eluded him. By this time, Ingrid had returned.

Unlike most airports, here passengers were required to walk some distance across the hot tarmac to board the aircraft. Ingrid and Jake conversed as they strode together to reach the plane. The distraction of the intercom and the effort required to reach the plane delayed any mental discourse about the letter.

No one ran or moved in a hurried manner. Each party knew there was an assigned seat. They reached the boarding area at the end of the line, shuffled toward the ramp leading up to the front door of the aircraft. Jake looked up into the group now entering the open door. Among them were the two Middle East men who sat near him on the bus. One still clutched the single piece of luggage like his. He wondered why they were able to carry theirs on board while his went to the cargo hold. Bribery had reached even people who worked with the airline.

Young flight attendants greeted Jake and Ingrid as they entered the fuselage of an already cooled-down aircraft. Most passengers had found their seats. Ingrid's seat was near the front. Jake helped place her carry-on luggage in the overhead storage compartment with careful notice that her eyes follow him like he was a rough diamond about to be processed by experienced hands. Racing through his mind were others in his history who had plied their skills in capturing his attention, but none had been as compelling as this Nordic beauty.

Passengers occupied every seat. When Jake reached his assigned seat, he saw ensconced behind him his two Lebanese stalkers. He felt like he was in a phantasmagoric nightmare with these two people fading in and around his life.

Jake had the issue of claustrophobia, one of his psychological shortcomings that forced him to seek out less confining accommodations in public transportation. When he booked flights he always requested an aisle seat in a first-class section, but on this flight out of Africa the airline provided only economy class. The plane was in the air, the "fasten your seat belt" light was off, and his mind soon drifted back into a state of remembering unfinished mental tasks. Before boarding the plane, he was reflecting on how serious this letter issue could be. He took the letter from his shirt pocket, placed it on his lap, saw that it contained no return address and lacked a zip code. By touch and appearance, the envelope contained something inside.

Because the person who gave him the letter hadn't boarded the plane, further suspicions were raised about the two seated behind him. It would served him to keep the letter out of sight. He stuffed the letter back inside his pocket, stood up, and made his way to the restroom at the rear of the plane. The two men seated behind stared as he passed their seats. The restroom was empty. He entered, locked the door and found the overhead light sufficient so that when he covered it with the letter he could tell there were pages inside—but he saw no writing. The severe tropical humidity made it easy to force the letter open. Inside, were two folded pages. His suspicions proved to be true: the pages were blank. The letter was a fraud, and the motive of him carrying it was as unclear as the blank pages staring him in the face.

The wordless pages swirled confusion inside Jake, matching the level of turbulence now in flight. He struggled to balance himself as he navigated around people who now stood waiting to use the facility. Something was awry with these two thug-looking men seated behind him. He remembered his Creole friend on the bus and the note he had given him. Did he still have it? He reached into his pocket, found the folded piece of paper, leaned forward in his seat and covered the missive—it was for his eyes alone. It read: "*It's necessary for me to shun you on this shuttle. The avoidance is not intentional. My urgent mission is to cancel the London trip of my courier who sits with me.*" Again, he quoted Shakespeare from Hamlet—this time in script, "*There's something rotten in the State of Denmark.*" Then, he added, "*Please contact my daughter in London who will give you a complete explanation.*" Her full name, phone number, and office address were written down. He now understood why the elderly Creole had avoided him on the shuttle.

Jake's assigned aisle seat served him well for his claustrophobic tendencies. Up to this point in flight, he hadn't spoken to the passenger seated next to him. She was a young, well-dressed Sierra Leonean in western clothes with a look of sophistication and poise that made her appear like a model on her way to Paris for a fashion show. Jake never went out of his way to break the ice with the opposite gender, was shy and insecure with women in social settings. Though he was successful in the business world, his track record with women was dismal.

The flight was into its third hour for a scheduled seven-hour trip. Flying north in the same longitude meant no time change. The scheduled arrival at Gatwick was four in the afternoon. His luggage contained a light jacket for the cooler weather in England, and the Hilton hotel where he had made reservations was adjacent the airport five minutes away. His stay would include shopping for a new wardrobe and a new piece of travel luggage.

The stewardess interrupted his musings. "Sir, do you have a drink preference?"

"Give me a cup of coffee, please."

"Do you wish cream in your coffee?"

"Please serve it black. Miss, can you also bring me a bottle of water?" She reached for the container of coffee but found it empty.

"I'll be right back, Sir."

After the stewardess left for the kitchen, the passenger dressed like a model who sat next to him moved into his space, asking, "Sir, is Western Pennsylvania your place of childhood?"

When a stranger initiated conversation with a question, Jake always responded with a question of his own; however, because she had pinpointed the geography of his younger years, a response question escaped him.

"Yes, and how is it you're privy to this information?"

By this time he could see she was American by her speech.

"The same way you know I'm from the States. Speech can give one away. I'm a speech therapist and linguist. I went beyond the therapy part and specialized in speech differences as it occurs over broad geographical areas of the country. Speech is a form of DNA in its syntax, spoken accents, and rhythm. You know I'm an American by what you hear in my speech. Do you remember the record in the Bible when Peter denies Jesus in the midst of his own compatriots in Jerusalem? It's when Peter speaks he reveals where he's from. They said to Peter, 'Surely you are one of them, for your accent gives you away.'

"In many cases, speech acts as a roadmap; it can trace the earlier part of one's life. This is my hobby and pastime. I practice just on Americans when I get a chance. I'm not a hundred percent accurate but good enough to create conversation as I have with you. There's a scientific basis for what I do; however, there are many variables. How I deal with these determine my accuracy. Until I heard your speech, you were someone from almost anywhere in the world, with a few exceptions, of course. I know the region of your childhood by your word enunciation, rhythm, and sentence structure. These are big footprints most people carry around. Your case is easier than most because the region you're from involves people of the same linguistic background. The greater permanence a population the easier it is to achieve a higher rate of accuracy. However, the diverse infusion of linguistic influence from other countries and the transitory nature of our modern age, language patterns change, making it more difficult for me in my game of guessing."

Jake had reservations accepting everything in her spiel. It didn't sound scientific enough. However, she was right in his case.

"What brings you to Sierra Leone?"

"I'm doing research, gathering information in West Africa for a project that will show existing speech linkage between West Africans and African Americans. We already know a lot about the Gullah African American in South Carolina whose language traces back to Sierra Leone. Speech can act like a genetic marker leaving a trail wherever it goes, but over time the trail becomes less identifiable."

Jake was a trivia junkie and used it often as his trademark; however, this conversation was going nowhere near his turf. He had the need to wedge himself into her conversation about something he knew.

"Do you ever play the game of chess?"

He could tell right off that the conversation had shifted to the other extreme: she knew nothing about chess. It was now his turn to act knowledgeable with intellectual ploy while she sat in the discomfort of ignorance.

"I'm not a chess enthusiast, and know little about the game, and even less as the years go by. Any chess activity in my life falls into my university experience."

"Are you aware," he said, "chess is a centuries-old game, it never changes? We play the game of chess today as they did a thousand years ago. Permanence is the remarkable trademark the game of chess displays in window showcases of the world. It's my game for leisure. The difference between the two games we play is yours involves people without fixed rules and boundaries. Mine uses objects with arbitrary laws. The enforcement of these laws is necessary for our games to work. Unfortunately, the masses are less adept at keeping your game alive because of impermanence and mobility. For survival, both of our games we play depend on immutability."

"Sir, you make an incisive statement on our changing world. It appears I'm playing with a losing hand of cards when it comes to permanence. Speaking of permanence, do you know what book is the oldest and most read in the world?"

"I've set myself up for a sermon, haven': I? You play a good mental form of chess yourself, even while holding a losing hand of cards."

"I won't give you a sermon, Sir, but I'll tell you this book will outlast all others."

There was a need for Jake to escape this big train coming at him. He tweaked the rails of the tracks in his favor.

"What a remarkable person you are, with so much drive, ambition, and intellect. Your accomplishments speak well of you."

"Well, when I was growing up my needs were great. My parents taught me to believe in myself. What I lacked in life just increased my drive to work hard."

Jake reflected on how interesting and stimulating this person was. It entered his mind, why did she leave the tropics so overdressed for the occasion of this flight? The flight attendant returned with his coffee and water, then looked at his neighbor.

"Do you wish anything to drink, Miss?"

"Nothing thanks." She turned toward Jake, saying, "When the plane lands, a driver will pick me up and take me to a singing engagement at a large church conference in London. I can't take the chance of spilling anything on my clothing with a beverage."

"It occurs to me, if your musical talent matches the rest of your persona, the crowd will love you."

"Sir, you're kind. My name is Ann Slovan. Yours is…?"

"Jake James, Jake's short for Jacob. I earned the abbreviated part of my name at a young age when wildness ruled my life, and that isn't to say wildness is far from me now. I think it has only taken on a different form, but in those young years I believe my parents thought my name should sound less biblical."

"Oh, I'm sure it wasn't because of that. We all have our own quirks in life, and sometimes it's a natural thing for parents to assign us a special sobriquet."

"If we all have quirks, then you must have at least one, and did you get a sobriquet from it?"

"I opened myself up for this one, didn't I? I'll say that I had more than one quirk when I was a kid, but I won't tell you what my private nickname was."

Before Jake knew it, this articulate person seated beside him knew almost everything about his life. He was always a slow warmer to new people of the opposite gender; however, Ann's disarming approach had a way of breaking through his barrier. She knew his name, why he went to Africa, his business at home, and a lot more private trivia. Jake pondered this, thought if he were a spy, he'd prove to be most ineffective for his country with a weakness toward divulging his life to graceful people, such as this person. It was as if a cloud overshadowed the two, both became quiet. Better put, Ann became quiet.

The constant loud hum inside the airship, created by forcing itself through the thin atmosphere of thirty thousand feet, occupied any space left inside Jake's mind. He pushed the seat as far back as he could for a short nap before arriving in London.

He was never a good sleeper in travel; today was no different. With eyes closed in a relaxed position, his mind picked up speed. Jake needed quiet—Ann needed to talk. He pondered the level of energy used in verbal discourse. Which activity consumed more energy, talking or listening? Today, it was listening.

The longer he meditated, the quieter the whine of the engines, but his tranquility was short-lived. Off in the distance, he heard a soft voice competing with the sleep-world he was about to enter. Someone was speaking his name close to his ear, almost like a whisper. Half-asleep, it startled him.

"I apologize for my intrusiveness—my non-stop rambling. This is not my nature, I do this when I'm nervous or afraid. Right now, I'm both of them."

Necessity, the mother of invention, had forced Ann to have confidence in this total stranger who sat next to her. Right now, she needed a friend. Though she thought him full of arrogance, underneath, she saw innocence and acceptance. She continued talking in low whispered tones. It was apparent to Jake she was under stress and needed help. He followed the level of her stress by watching her eyes dart and shift, giving punctuation to her verbal script. She was showing the other side of her nature, not the self-confident, assertive professional as before. He wondered why she had chosen him as her confidant.

"Do you know the process of getting through customs in London?" asked Ann.

"It's easy. Gatwick airport is like most airports in major cities. You show your documents, answer their questions, and declare taxable items; sometimes, they'll require luggage pieces to be opened."

"That's what I'm afraid of. I fear they'll open my luggage and find illegal contraband."

Jake was startled by her statement. He made a cold, silent retreat that registered on Ann's face; her eyes stopped darting and her face froze with a look of angst. Jake was generous with his money but wasn't warm to the idea of being charitable with his time and attention to someone involved with contraband.

A long pause followed. He avoided looking at her, thinking that she was trying to move into his circle that no one was allow to enter. Then she spoke.

"I know you're taken back by what I told you—I see it on your face, but please hear my story."

She leaned closer to Jake, spoke with a melodious whisper.

"I met a person in Freetown who asked me to take a package to his friend who lives in London. He arranged for someone to pick it up after I clear customs at Gatwick. At the time when I agreed to this, I wasn't aware of the problem of diamond smuggling. I'm naive, but I'm not dishonest."

She looked away from Jake—it was the tears forming in her eyes she didn't want him to see. Her look of despair made him remember his own times of helplessness when no one stood with him. Memories that carried hurt melted his coldness.

"Did you know this person who gave you the package?"

Still looking away, she found it difficult to respond. "I met him just once. He was a friend of an acquaintance I went to dinner with on a couple of occasions. If the package contains contraband, I've no way to prove it's not mine."

"And where is this package?"

"It's in one of my luggage cases. I'm fearful they'll open it when I go through customs."

With moistened eyes, she turned her head and looked at Jake.

"This is serious for me, isn't it?"

36

"This will present a serious difficulty for you if they inspect your luggage and find contraband. I suggest you inspect the package after you retrieve your cases before going through customs. If you find something, hand it over to the customs officer and tell them your story. There should be no problem. I'm available to help you do this."

"Oh, thank you, I appreciate it! Your suggestion is so simple—why couldn't I have thought of that—It's a splendid course of action!" With a look of relief showing on her face, she took tissue, wiped her teary eyes, saying to Jake, "You're a kind and thoughtful person. I will forever remember what you've done."

Calm settled over Ann. The two seldom spoke until the plane began its descent into Gatwick.

"I think it best, Ann, that we remain seated until the passengers exit in front of us."

"Yes, I think you're right. If there's a delay, my driver will wait."

They were the last passengers to deplane, and by the time they reached the door of the aircraft, Ingrid was there waiting.

"We meet again, Ingrid. How was your flight?"

"I fly so much it makes me loathe aircraft. I have first-class flying privileges with my company, but this flight has none."

The three walked together to the baggage terminal where they saw passengers already pulling luggage from the table as soon as the conveyer coughed them up. While they stood waiting for their luggage, Jake saw across the other side of the long moving oval-shaped baggage table his two Lebanese shadows—they seemed to follow wherever he moved. On the floor near their feet sat their single piece of luggage. He wondered why they were here at the baggage table when they had carried only one luggage piece on board the plane.

One of the two kept his eyes in the direction of Jake, the other surveyed the security police moving about. The one observing the police took something from his pocket, opened the luggage case on the floor and put it inside, closed it, then placed the luggage on the turning baggage table. No sooner had he done this, that two airport security officers approached where they stood. The luggage joined other pieces on the table.

One of the police officers demanded to see their passports, the other officer was on his mobile phone. Together, the security police took them to an area where additional officers met them. They all entered through the door that read on the outside: "Security Only."

Jake resumed the task of helping the two women with their luggage. Ingrid took hers, saying with a warm smile, "I hope to see you in Manchester, Jake." She saw Ann required his assistance, so she moved on to clear customs. Ann brought over a cart where Jake stood by her luggage cases.

"In which luggage piece did you pack the article?"

"It's the smaller one on top."

"Let's move it over to a quiet area and open it."

Ann pushed the cart over to a corner of the large open room. Her facial composure froze in her state of anxiety. Her eyes began darting again. The look on her face reminded Jake of the time he made his first skydiving jump. Looking out the open door at five thousand feet made him freeze too.

"With hands shaking nervously, she turned to Jake, saying, "I'm too nervous, please take my keys and open the luggage."

Using her keys, Jake unlocked the case. She quickly pushed it open, turning everything over inside, but found nothing.

"I know this is the one I placed it in. The person who asked me to carry the item wanted it packed in a carry-on piece, but when I checked in they said it was too large to be taken on board and had to be included with the rest of the baggage."

"Is there a reason for them to request you to keep the item in your carry-on luggage?"

"I'm inexperienced in the real world outside academia. Sorry it involves you. At the time when I agreed to carry this, I understood the transfer of the item was easier if carried in an accessible smaller case."

Ann's self-deprecation, innocence, and vulnerability gave Jake a tinge of guilt after having given an initial cold response to her ordeal. He did his best to make it up to her.

"Ann, these things happen in life, and you're not at fault. Unfortunately, pilferage at airports is a common occurrence. I hope everything of yours is still here."

"Let's move on, Mr. James, there are important events in life awaiting us."

They pushed their way through the swirling crowds toward customs. After the formalities of giving the agent the paperwork and showing their passports, the customs agent waved them on; neither opened any case. Ann's concerns now were with the party picking up the package she started out with.

"I hope the party meeting me here doesn't show. This is a big embarrassment for me."

Ann's anxiety over the matter soon became reality. A woman approached her.

"Miss Slovan, I believe you're carrying a package from a friend of mine in Freetown. I hope it's with you."

"The package given to me by your friend was taken from my case at the airport in Freetown after I checked my baggage. I'm terribly sorry."

Great expectations across her face now melted into despair. Friendliness turned to anger.

Jake took special notice of the verbal interaction between them. Someone in Freetown had taken advantage of an innocent and trusting person. What the package contained meant a great deal to this individual, and it was clear she didn't believe Ann was telling the truth.

"Miss Sloven, if you give me the package I'll see to it that you are paid well for your trouble."

"Madam, please understand the package wasn't with me when I arrived here at Gatwick. I opened and examined the case at the luggage table when I picked it up here before going through customs. Someone at the Freetown airport took the package from my case, and I had no control over what happened. I did this in good faith and regret the misfortune of your loss."

Jake's opinion of Ann's lack of street smarts changed when he saw her confrontation with the pickup woman. When called upon, she demonstrated a reserve of confidence and strength.

"If you'll excuse us, we'll be on our way. Let's move on, Mr. James."

Their roles had now changed. She walked in command of herself down the long wide corridor pushing her luggage cart. Jake had become the follower. The emotional strain made her eyes teary causing Jake to respond in a way that was not part of his nature: he placed his hand on her shoulder, saying, "You impressed me, Ann, you demonstrated a lot of strength and courage back there."

Adversity had served a purpose: two different worlds had come together. When they reached the area where vehicles picked up passengers, they exchanged business cards and phone numbers. He assisted with her baggage and waved goodbye as she drove away.

Jake turned to go to his nearby hotel, felt a hand touch his arm—it was Ingrid.

"I know I sound repetitious, Jake, but I hope to see you in Manchester."

Someone took her luggage, placed it in a taxi near the curb and drove off. The driver was tall and handsome with sandy hair. He was Ingrid's brother.

In his hotel room, Jake still sat on the bed with the lights turned off. He had retraced his steps reviewing every part of his journey from Freetown to Gatwick. He now saw the bigger picture of how everything came together with him ending up with a case full of contraband that didn't belong to him. He stood to his feet, turned on the lights in his darkened hotel room. Glaring at him was the picture of the open luggage case showing the sacks of contraband diamonds he'd carried through customs. The hand-written note given him by the old Creole man aboard the shuttle troubled him. His ominous, cryptic words were still in his pocket. Were they a harbinger for what awaited him? He knew there was something rotten somewhere, and it wasn't in Denmark.

Chapter 3

Wimbledon

AFTER THE MENTAL AND EMOTIONAL intrigue of the contraband discovery had settled, Jake's concerns turned to his own baggage. He had on his person all necessary documents for travel; however, inside his own case that was lost in travel were photos and items important to his personal life. It was urgent that his case be retrieved at the British Airways before they closed. If he hurried, he could be there in ten minutes. But first the contraband must be secured.

Using the chair by the desk as a stepladder and his universal luggage key as a flathead screwdriver, Jake removed an overhead air vent cover into which he placed the six bags of contraband diamonds, After storing the luggage piece that held the snakeskin and two ebony-head carvings in the room closet, he gave a last-minute look, For now, the luggage would remain in the hotel room until he returned from the airline office.

Anxiety pulsated through Jake. The urgency of his mission to reclaim his lost luggage gave flashback scenes of Ann going through customs under the fear she might be carrying hidden contraband. The depth of her stress was measured by the tremors in her hands and the fear in her eyes. The irony of it all was that he was the carrier of contraband and was now showing his fellow traveler's nervous tension.

Jake's case was different: personal property was taken and it may contain a paper trail of his activities here in London. Diamond smuggling was a mean business with those who made a living at it, and violence was sometimes its consequence.

Driven by quest of the unknown and swiftness of gait, Jake reached the airline ticket counter with the need for a brief respite. After heavy breathing normalized, he stepped up to the counter.

"I wish to talk to the person who handles lost baggage."

A small balding man with round, beady eyes and a long workday appearance came from a back room. Jake's height caused the short man to keep his distance; he carried the small-man syndrome, and standing too close was intimidating. When he spoke, he looked right at Jake's chest and avoided eye contact.

"Follow me please," he said.

Segregated according to size, the baggage rested next to the wall in a side room. Jake looked over all the cases, turned to the man, saying, "My luggage piece isn't here. Is there more baggage elsewhere?"

"No," he said. "However, there's a piece in my office someone just brought in."

He followed the agent to his office through an open door. Inside, he saw what looked like his luggage on the floor by his desk. He grabbed the luggage handle, turned it so he could read the underside. His name appeared in bold print.

"This is my luggage! The handle shows my name written on it."

"You'll have to produce some kind of proof that you're the owner."

Jake showed the gentleman his airline ticket, saying, "You can see my name is on the handle of the luggage piece, and inside the case are documents showing my name." "The proof of your ticket is enough, but you'll have to fill out a form and go to customs for final clearance."

Jake placed the case on its side, opened it with the universal key he'd used earlier. Everything inside belonged to him. Underneath the clothing was the miniature chess set he and his late grandfather had played games on. Until now, he'd never realized how old things from another time could bring such comfort, a time when things were better. After clearing customs, he returned to his room at the Hilton.

After putting his personal effects away, a blanket of calm and confidence return to Jake. He was about to close his case when his attention was drawn to something shiny. Lifting it from the case, he saw that it was a key that carried a stamped, imprinted name: Wimbledon Storage Company. A small tag on it read, locker 132. Vivid scenes moved in front Jake's fresh memory, scenes of the airport luggage table coughing up baggage pieces for waiting passengers with two men holding a case like his, who before being taken away by the airport police, discarded the case by placing it on the moving baggage table but before doing so, it was opened and something put inside.

What Jake now held in his hand was something important to what was going down in a nefarious operation here in London, and he was in the middle of it with the contraband and the key he held in his hand.

Retrieving his own luggage case that held a key placed there by smugglers, were brush-strokes on the canvas of a developing picture. Jake did not go down to the dining room for dinner. Sleep evaded him for most of the night. By two o'clock in the morning, everything had fallen into place.

He knew there was just one point in his travels that provided an opportunity for his luggage to exchange hands without his knowledge. It was an orchestrated event. The three Lebanese seated around him on the bus operated as an organized trio to take his luggage and switch it with another identical piece. It happened when he turned around to talk to the person who handed him the letter to mail in New York. After they had switched their piece of contraband luggage with his, he then carried theirs through the airline check-in counter at Lungi where they tagged it as his. This was why the luggage he carried went uninspected—the smugglers had paid off the inspector.

The exchange guaranteed a non-suspicious American going through customs at Gatwick undetected. It was at the airport in Freetown where their agents in the baggage department made the transfer. They took a few personal effects from his case, packed them in the contraband piece, so if opened, it would appear to be his. The Lebanese who distracted him with the letter scheme, and who later arranged for the case not to be inspected, was the lead man in planting the contraband. The two who shadowed him were to stay at his side until Gatwick.

Had events gone as planned, they would have approached him after clearing customs requesting the luggage in his possession. They would prove the case he carried was theirs by opening his that was in their possession—the exchange would have made everything simple and easy.

The tide changed at the wrong time for the smugglers. They lost control of their operation by the police taking them away for questioning at a critical time. Someone had informed the police of something going down. Now, he stood holding the bag. However, in his case it was smuggled contraband diamonds. *Something told him this operation reached all the way back to the Lebanese travel agent who had sold him his tickets, as well as his luggage piece.*

Jake returned to a level of calm. His normal assertive nature settled in and took control. The key placed in his luggage had the name of the storage company stamped on the front with a locker number. It had to be connected with the contraband he stored overhead in the air vent. Jake's energy always flowed in the direction where excitement gave an invitation. He was never a person to avoid conflict or challenge. With a readied pen, he called information to secure the phone number of the Wimbledon Storage Company. When dialed, a recorded message gave him the address and office hours. Mystery with Intrigue, awaited him at the locker site—it pushed his cutting-edge curiosity to the point of no return. He wouldn't rest until he knew what was in the locker at Wimbledon.

When the police detained the two agents, it created a failed smuggling operation. It also slowed down its news reaching the parties involved in it. Information of the bungled operation would soon be common knowledge among the smugglers. Jake needed to arrive at the storage facility by eight o'clock in the morning when it opened. He remembered that Ingrid's brother owned and operated a taxi here at Gatwick. At six o'clock, her brother received a call requesting a pickup at seven.

Jake closed the door of his hotel room carrying his own empty luggage case, leaving the other identical case containing the snakeskin and two curios locked inside. The "Do not disturb" sign was clicked on to prevent cleaning people from entering. He placed a small piece of folded paper between the door and doorjamb. It would carry a message when he returned. Outside the hotel were several taxis waiting to accommodate travelers into London. A tall, thin driver standing alongside a taxi waved him over.

"Good morning, I'm Ingrid's brother, Eric."

"Good morning, Mr. Spense. My name is Jake James. I want a roundtrip to Wimbledon."

Eric Spence was a tall, young, lanky-looking Scandinavian with typical blond hair and light skin. He was as handsome looking as his sister was beautiful.

"Where do you wish to go in Wimbledon," asked the driver.

Jake got in the taxi, reached over, gave him the address.

"This is an easy one. I pass this way all the time."

"What's the driving time to Wimbledon from here?"

"Sir, it'll take us about forty-five minutes with the traffic we have today."

Forty-five minutes was an eternity for Jake when all he could see were metropolis scenes replicating themselves over and over. They made him feel like a tourist visiting an ancient land with a guide repeating the same words at each ruin. After the second ruin, they all looked alike. To fill in his boredom, he decided to use the ancient relic of communication with the driver. He hoped the conversation wouldn't be jejune.

"How long have you driven a taxi here in London?"

"Sir, ever since I bought my first taxi four years ago. Are you from the States, you sound American?"

"Yes, I'm American on my way home after working in Africa for the past year."

"Must be difficult living away from your family and all."

"Well, it wasn't all that bad. I have a business I go home to check on every two or three months. From what you said, you have more than one taxi in operation."

"Yes, Sir, I have two taxis, and I do very well."

"Your sister tells me you're from Manchester."

"Yes, I'm from Manchester. My family still resides there, but my wife and I live and work here in London. We have an interest in vacationing in the States sometime. We want to see Yosemite Park and other major attractions."

"Just avoid the large cities and you'll enjoy your time there. I'm planning a tour up in your area of Manchester while here in England. Are you interested in driving me?"

"Yes, Sir, I'll enjoy going to my old place."

Jake reached over, handed him his business card. They continued talking most of the trip, and when they neared the storage site he turned within himself with contemplations of what awaited him at the locker. By this time Jake had built a rapport with Eric, a result of his friendliness and knowing his sister, Ingrid.

Jake looked at his watch, determined that their arrival time at the storage site would be around seven fifty-five. Different thoughts voiced themselves over what to expect at the locker. Would he find someone watching the box for activity? It was his impulsive choice to move on this—others would soon find out the diamonds didn't reach the agents.

They pulled up in front of the storage site. The large gate of the chain-link fence surrounding the complex was already open, and someone was entering the front door.

"Mr. Spense, wait for me until I return. I'll be right back!"

Jake left the taxi for the front door carrying his empty luggage case. Special attention was paid to the parking lot. Eric's taxi stood alone.

Inside, he asked the attendant, "Where are your storage lockers?"

"I'm just the custodian here filling in for the regular desk employee for a few minutes until he arrives. I'm not too informed about the procedures, but I think you must sign in with identification."

Jake pulled the locker key from his pocket and held it twelve inches from the attendant's face. With a look of persuasive authority, he demanded, "I want to pick up a package in box 132."

The man gave the look of a blank stare. This wasn't his job. He'd never done this before. His eyes went to Jake, then back to the key. He leaned to one side to see around Jake hoping the counter person had arrived. Jake knew human nature, and the man must not have time to be overly rational.

"Please, I'm in a hurry and my taxi is waiting for me!"

The man looked once more at the front door before blurting out, "The locker is behind the door to my left about halfway down on the right side."

Jake took hold of the door handle commending himself in getting the response from the man behind the counter. Balance, he thought, did the trick. He applied pressure, but not to the extent of pushing him into a corner. When he released the door, it closed with the sound of a swish and a click.

He was alone walking down the long narrow room filled with lockers on both sides. Security cameras overhead provided surveillance from a central office. Jake's impulsivity often made him do battle with his conscience. Today was no different. The thought of violating the law by unlocking this door almost swayed him to turn around. He wavered, but reason overruled: he had the smuggled diamonds, and this key was part of the illicit operation. Inside Jake lurked the cool breezes of challenge, the hidden part wanting to experience the energy of quest and excitement. In doing battle with his conscience, reason was his best defense. Some people yielded to the temptation of the senses, the comfort and gratification of things, others fell into the paradigm of adventure, the drug of exhilaration, the challenge of gambling against the odds. He was of the latter. However, it was the nobility of the act that enhanced the intensity and gave relief to his pulsating conscience: *he was hurting smugglers and terrorists*. The thought of hurting people who brought pain on innocent victims through terrorism emboldened him.

Jake looked around once more to see if anyone were nearby. The story he had heard as a child about Moses came to mind. Moses looked both ways before killing the Egyptian and burying him in the sand. He pushed from his mind the thought of banishment to a desert. His act was different but his motive the same: justice for the unjust. The key held in his hand was forced into the lock. Before pulling the door open, he looked once more up and down the long hall filled with lockers. Inside were three packages wrapped in plain brown paper, each the size of a ream of paper. He quickly placed the contents inside the luggage case, closed the door, and removed the key.

Confidence filled his stride as he walked out of the building toward the waiting taxi. Stepping in, he said to the driver, "Let's get back to the hotel!"

While waiting to pull out onto the busy roadway, Jake saw a fast moving vehicle turn into the parking lot. Someone got out of the vehicle, went inside, and returned to the car running. It was then he knew someone had checked the locker. Jake turned to the driver.

"Can you force yourself into the traffic and speed up? I'll make it worth your while."

"Are you in difficulty, Sir?"

The driver pushed his way into the traffic, Jake continued to watch the scene from the rear window. The vehicle in the parking lot was now on the public roadway and moving at full speed in his direction. He turned to the driver.

"Yes, I believe I'm in great difficulty. Behind is a car following us. We need to lose it."

"Sir, leave it to me. This taxi driver knows Wimbledon!"

The driver left the main highway into side streets and back alleys. He seemed to know the streets like he was from the neighborhood. He turned on a quiet street and stopped. They waited five minutes.

"I think we've lost them, Sir."

The driver pulled out from the parked position into the roadway, and out of nowhere appeared a fast-moving vehicle. It was the one they were trying to elude and it was heading straight toward them with no crossroad for them to turn on. The driver of the taxi, who up to this point was a polite and helpful English driver, suddenly turned into a different person.

"Hang on," he said. "We're going to do the chicken split."

Jake thought he was in a racecar the way Eric drove. He refused to slow down and turn around. Instead, he accelerated his taxi forcing it to give everything it could down the middle of the road. It appeared at this point it was the old game of highway chicken, and Eric seemed to know what he was doing. Jake's adrenalin forced his past experiences to a conscious level. At this stage of his reformed life, he watched at what was going on in front of him from underneath a veil of remorse. He remembered those times when he endangered the lives of others, and himself, with this exhilarating experience. Eric's driving revisited Jake's history. This was de je vu for both of them, except for embellished terminology. He hoped the split came at the right time.

Jake identified with Eric. Below the surface of their present danger, the wilder years of youth had returned, and the event was fusing them together in verbal silence. Both vehicles moved at top speed heading toward each other. It was the game of chicken. When they came closer, a hand holding a gun appeared outside the window on the driver's side. Just before impact, Eric pulled the split with both sides of the vehicles scraping on the drivers' sides. The taxi moved on. Jake turned and looked back. In the middle of the road was a gun. The vehicle had lost control and hit a parked car. Both men managed to free themselves, one clutched an injured hand hit by the scrape of the two vehicles, the other ran to pick up the dropped weapon. Both fled the scene of the accident.

"Are you all right, Sir?"

"I'm fine! You did some bang-up driving back there. My flow of adrenalin was as great as a high bungee jump at an amusement park, and we didn't have to wait in line or pay for the experience, but you did get some scratches on the side of your taxi."

"Sir, in the States you used to call this the game of chicken. Here, wild young people call it the chicken split."

"I like the word split, if it happens at the right time, like today."

"If you ever meet my wife or family, I hope you won't tell them of this event."

52

"We can keep this between us as friends. You need not worry about the cost of repairs on the vehicle. Before we leave for Manchester, I'll have a check for the repair."

Conversation faded into silence. Alongside Jake in the seat was his luggage case holding something of illegal value that was pulled from the jaws of evil. Eighteen hours earlier, he was on his way to the States to reconnect with what he had left a year ago in his business. But now he was embroiled in a new dangerous world for himself—it was the possession of the key to the locker that untapped his latent hunting spirit—this was what pulled him over the precipice. The urge to see the contents taken from the locker went unabated. He lifted the case cover enough to slide his hand inside, peeled back the cover of the top bundle. It showed British pound notes. He had arrived three minutes ahead of Middle East agents by acting on instinct and aggressive boldness. With the voice of the driver coming from the front, his private world of thought ended.

"Sir, your card shows you're an engineer. My brother's an engineer with an oil company in North Africa. There are three siblings in our family: my brother, a successful sister and fine artist. Then, there's the taxi driver."

Jake thought he implied he didn't measure up to where his siblings had arrived in life.

"What you did today gave me a picture of what kind of a person you are. You're like me—not afraid of risks. This is why you own two taxis at your age. If you keep this spirited nature, you'll end up on top."

It was clear to Jake that both of them had certain common interests and similar natures. He welcomed this. He needed someone to depend on in his new dangerous world.

"I'll be calling you in a few days for the trip up north."

"My wife works most of the day, but if for any reason you can't reach me on my cell, just leave a message at my home and I'll get back to you."

"Today, you helped me out a great deal. I won't forget it."

The taxi stopped in front of the hotel.

"I need to find a bank where I can rent a safe deposit box to store some items I have. Can you recommend one?"

"I sure can. My wife works at a Barclays in downtown London and will help you do this if you like."

"I'll appreciate her help. Are you available to pick me up at one o'clock to drive me there?"

"I'll be here at one sharp."

Jake paid Eric the registered fare with a bonus of a hundred pounds. He carried his case through the lobby to the elevator. His world had now picked up speed. He thought survival under these extremes without falling over the edge would be a test of what and who he was. The elevator seemed to take forever to reach the lobby. When he reached his hotel room, the door looked normal. The "do not disturb" sign was still showing and the small piece of paper wedged in the door was still in its fixed position. Upon entering the room, everything looked in place. He shut the door, heard the sound of the click of the safety lock. Jake held in his hand the reward of prey that he had taken from the wild, then began to ruminate. He was now safe inside his lair. The hunt was over. The excitement had peaked and was now ebbing with throbbing euphoria. He stared at the luggage case like a lion looking at what he brought to others in his pride, but there was none to view or take their fill. He thought of two kinds of predators: those that ate their capture on the spot and those that brought it back to the den. Everyone carried a weakness, and given the opportunity, it could slip to the surface. What he just accomplished was a conscious act of personal challenge of living on the edge to feed his wilder hidden part. His state of euphoria submitted to his conscience, the higher law, a law always in competition with his vanity. It allowed guilt to do its bidding. It served its purpose. Jake felt guilt, not because of the actions he had taken against the smugglers but because of the pleasure derived from doing it.

Jake was out of the tropics, but clammy hands had returned. He opened the case containing British notes. Three packages wrapped in heavy-duty paper came into view. All three bundles were in uniform size. Attached to the middle package was an envelope containing the message: *"The three packages are for the payment of your last shipment of excellent diamonds. We wait for your next shipment."*

Later, Jake would learn that English was the language used in the physical part of diamond smuggling operations because some of the agents were not literate in the Arabic language. Information outside smuggling activity coming from the leadership moved about in written Arabic. They used one language for moving diamonds, the other for information. He placed the letter back inside the envelope. Upon careful examination of all three packages, the estimate of the pickup was five hundred thousand pounds. This was money going to smugglers in Freetown as a payoff for an earlier delivery of diamonds.

Jake came to understand after reflecting on this amount of money going to someone for the illicit transfer of diamonds, that it was only part of the cash flow. Contraband diamonds brought into London and Europe tripled in value over the cash payouts to the mules bringing them in. While schools and hospitals were languishing in the country for funds, criminals reveled in their inordinate lust for diamonds.

Jake placed the British notes alongside the diamonds behind the air vent cover.

With Jake's hotel room in need of cleaning, and not wanting the luggage associated with the room, he took both cases with him downstairs to the hotel's restaurant. He chose a table in an area with a full view of the hotel lobby. Halfway into his meal, two Middle-East-looking men left the elevator walking toward the front exit of the lobby. They carried nothing in their arms but looked tense. Jake rose from the booth in the restaurant and followed them. Outside, a vehicle waited with a driver. When they drove away, Jake made a note of its description and tag number. He returned to the restaurant, paid the bill, picked up the two cases, and went to his room expecting the worst.

Upon entering his room, anger ripped through him. His room was upside down: opened drawers and personal effects strewn across the floor. Somehow, they had found his trail in their search of the contraband. Jake closed the door and locked it. After removing the front cover of the air vent, he found everything as he had left it. He set in motion an urgent plan to make the diamonds and British currency secure elsewhere. Both were placed in the case with the false bottom; his own case would carry the two curios, snakeskin, and personal effects. He removed the belt from the trousers he wore, wrapped it around the luggage piece containing diamonds and British notes, then called his taxi driver.

"This is Jake James. Can you come right back to the hotel and come up to my room? I want to go to the bank right away!"

"Sure, I'll be there in a few minutes."

With two cases packed, Jake was ready to leave. A last minute look served to assure him nothing remained. The office received his call informing them of the break-in. They sent someone right up. When the management saw the ransacked room, they quickly made an effort to bring closure to the problem at hand. Publicity was something they wanted to avoid.

"We're sorry this has happened. Have they taken anything of value?"

"Nothing of value," he said. When Eric arrived, he found the door open, leaned inside, and when Jake saw him, he addressed the office person.

"My driver is here. I must leave so please check me out downstairs."

Jake carried the two pieces of unsightly luggage as they both walked down the hallway toward the elevator. His finer sensibilities surfaced and told him that he looked like an immigrant getting off a ship onto Ellis Island in the early nineteen hundreds. The two moved to the front door after Jake checked out of the hotel, politely refusing the offer of the hotel porter to carry the baggage. They found the taxi where Eric had parked it.

"Eric, take me to Barclay's bank. Also, call your wife and ask her to prepare the paperwork for two safe deposit boxes."

Eric discussed the request with his wife, looked at Jake in his rearview mirror, saying, "She can handle your request, but we need to get there soon. The Bank closes in two hours."

Chapter 4

Incognito

ON HIS WAY TO THE BANK, Jake forced himself to reflect on why he allowed himself to fall into this net. The same energy that drove him to success at home was in full play here in London. For him, it was an addiction, not to drugs or alcohol, but to the lure of adventure and excitement. Fulfilling this need came in different ways. At home, it was the need for big projects out in front, going after something beyond reach. Here, it was diamonds at Gatwick and the locker at Wimbledon. They had opened a different kind of door that satiated the addiction in a different way.

Jake was coming to realize his efforts in keeping these diamonds and British notes out of the hands of smugglers and terrorists must be justified by a worthy cause. He remembered his grandfather's photos of his hospital in Africa, the people he'd helped. Because of the civil war, it lay in ruins today. He'd visited the site only a few months before leaving the country. Now, something was giving birth inside Jake to reclaim what had been lost: he would return the diamonds and British notes to the country to restore what had been destroyed. The weight of this responsibility now moved him to consider concealment, for himself and the contraband. The bank was his first step in this journey.

By the time the taxi driver delivered Jake to the bank, a certain destiny loomed over his life. He had gone too far to turn around. He carried through the front door of the bank the belt-strapped case of five hundred thousand pounds of British notes and six sacks of uncut diamonds. At the bank, Eric introduced his wife to Jake. She had everything ready to process the opening of an account and signing for two safe-deposit boxes. After completing the paperwork, he followed a bank attendant inside the vault, took two safe-deposit boxes and his luggage case to a private inspection booth with a locking door.

Using a bank safe-deposit box was a common practice for Jake in the States. Here in London, it would serve to safeguard several million dollars of uncut diamonds and British currency. The cramped quarters inside the booth made it difficult to lay everything out in an organized manner. He placed in one box all the British currency taken from the locker at Wimbledon. Before closing the cover, he removed two thousand pounds from the currency stack to cover the cost of Eric's vehicle damage. The second box received the six sacks of rough diamonds. It was in this cubicle with diamonds, currency, and two safe-deposit boxes Jake found closure to the contraband: it was secure and destined for a hospital. In the court of public opinion, his closing argument for his defense in keeping the contraband would come from the masses who would receive treatment at the hospital. He already felt more secure. The two boxes found their way back into the vault where the attendant closed and locked both doors. When he heard the doors shut, saw the keys withdrawn, it brought finality to the saga of the contraband's safety. His burden, delivered intact, was now secure from the hands of people who excelled in theft, bribery, and violence.

Warm feelings of justification bathed his conscience in his finished transaction. It was his innocence he needed to declare to the world, but he knew the world in its ordered system had no ears. Like the dove sent from Noah's ark, his voice would find no dry land to rest on, and the echo of his cry of innocence would return with an altered response: that he had complicated his life and changed it forever.

The small, green chameleon found in the African tropics kept coming to mind. It had the talent of disguising itself by changing colors from light green to a dark black. They were not always green, though they were always slow. Their strange-looking eyes could each turn in a circular motion independent of each other, like tiny telescopes, poised, ready to see anything anywhere. They were a fascinating creation, a slight organism, sluggish, but made with tools to survive. Man came less equipped for survival in the wild. He had to use his bigger brain to compensate for what the animal kingdom possessed in natural talent. There was a compulsion to cover, to change and adapt to his created jungle. The first step in this journey was to rid himself of the old luggage. He needed eyes to see and camouflage for concealment. Eric, his taxi driver, was waiting.

"Eric, can you store my two pieces of luggage until I have need of them?"

"I'd be glad to keep them for you. We can store them in the boot for now."

"Eric, let's go to a luggage shop."

Selected was a piece of lightweight, handsome-looking luggage along with a locking leather briefcase; both gave hope in his pursuit of disguise. Now, the task was to find a hotel with limited activity. Camouflage required adjusting to circumstances at hand. Turning to Eric, Jake said, "I need to find a hotel near Victoria Square."

On two previous visits to London Jake had stayed in the area where a cluster of small hotels was situated side-by-side. It was within walking distance to important sites of

60

interest. Tourism would help him blend in. Finding a room presented a challenge, not having made a prior reservation. There were two things going for him: reduced travel from the States because of the weakness of the dollar, and it was not the time for heavy tourism.

When they arrived in the area, Jake asked the driver, "What do you think of this section of town for hotel accommodations?"

"Sir, this is tourist town. You'll be safe here."

Most of the hotels in this area were owner-operated by an immigrant population. The rooms were not spacious, but they all served a complimentary breakfast. If staying inside was important, this was a benefit to the patron. It was at the second stop where Jake found success. He secured two rooms for three nights, one for himself, and one for a Mr. Smith. He would sleep in Mr. Smith's room, a room that faced the main street with a large bay window looking out at everything going on down below.

Eric was pleased his sister, Ingrid, had become acquainted with Jake. It was good business to run one party around in his taxi than fifteen or twenty different people. However, he thought it strange for his sister to invite a guest to Manchester, especially on such short notice. She had never done this before. Anyway, he liked Jake.

When Jake returned to the taxi, he handed Eric an envelope containing two thousand pounds.

"Eric, this envelope contains enough money for your vehicle to be painted a different color. It's in our interest your taxi carries a new look. Find a shop that will do a rush job. If it requires more money, I'll cover the cost. In a few days, you'll hear from me about the Manchester trip. Please call Ingrid, your sister. Tell her I'll see her in Manchester, and also, convey my thanks for the invitation."

Before the driver left, Jake placed inside his new luggage all the contents of the old cases, including the two curios and snakeskin. Eric agreed to store both old cases at his place. After he drove off, Jake made his way to the hotel room registered in his own name, placed his luggage on the bed and took from it several pieces of clothing, hung them in the closet, then ruffled the bed covers to make them appear slept-in, locked the door and proceeded to the room registered in Mr. Smith's name. Upon entering the room, he sat on the bed, removed his shoes and reclined fully clothed, thinking how pleasurable it was to have reclaimed his world of privacy and anonymity. His mind stopped turning, and the new world he had entered became dark and still in the tunnel of sleep.

Sometime later Jake was startled with rays of light coming through the window shades from outside street lighting. Where was he? His thoughts were blurred. Everything shot at him in fragmented erratic waves. He struggled to crawl out of the tunnel of deep sleep. His sense of time and place were lost. He waited for his real world to come together. The human body had a way of lending assistance when under stress by allowing deep sleep to act as a sedative. His chamber of darkness was temporary therapeutic anesthesia. With thoughts now balanced, he discovered he was dressed, except for his shoes. He looked at his watch using a crack of light coming through the window; it told him it was three o'clock in the morning. Thirty-five hours ago he had arrived in London—it felt like a year. When in a position of fleeing, a person's universe became dichotomous: on one hand time sped up, on the other, it slowed down. The longer Jake stayed awake, the more he put himself together. He turned on the light, looked about the room. It was small, sparsely supplied and carried a well-used appearance with the unpleasant scent of Indian Curry. He hated curry.

Knowing there was a complete change of fresh clothes in the luggage case, he proceeded to undress for a shower. Everything found in his pockets went on the nightstand by the bed. There in plain view, along with all the rest of his personal effects, was the note written by Mr. Coker. With everything coming down as it did here in London, his request to contact his daughter had slipped his mind. Before getting into the shower, the words on the paper passed Jake's eyes twice. By the time he finished bathing, his day's activities had fallen into place.

It was four o'clock in the morning, and business activities for the day were in full play. First, Jake called his father and checked with him regarding the family and his business. Then, he wrote a summary of the events as they had happened up to this point.

The case holding the rolled-up python snakeskin was open on a table at the foot of his bed. From where he sat he could see the snakeskin—it seemed to have eyes staring at him. He walked over, lifted from the case the rolled-up python skin that had a width of twelve inches. A python snake in the wild was subtle, quiet, and a formidable predator when in search of its prey. One of the ways they captured large python snakes in Africa was to drive long stakes into the ground forming a circle. The distance between each stake determined the size of snake they wanted to capture. Inside the circle of stakes, they placed an animal too large to escape through the openings. The snake entered the trap through the space between the posts, and once it swallowed the animal it was unable to slither back through the trap with its engorged belly. The snake was then table meat for the evening and its skin a commodity as a curio.

Jake took the rolled-up snakeskin, unfurled it across the floor. From head to tail the skin showed the length of fifteen feet. His attention was drawn to an envelope taped on the skin that read: *Freetown Curio Shop.* It was in the wrong place on the skin to identify a business shop for the public. Inside the envelope, he found a sheet of paper and a key. The paper contained Arabic writing.

Mystery shrouded the snakeskin scene. Everything came to a pause inside Jake. The skin of the crawling creature was taking on a life of its own having arrived in the contraband case with a key and a message written in Arabic. Jake felt energy pulling him into a darker, self-created jungle.

The vivid picture of the snake trap hung over Jake. In the throes of the tangled web he had created, he was forced to look at the trap he had built for himself by keeping the contraband, the British notes, and now the snakeskin with another key.

It was seven o'clock and breakfast time downstairs. The paper and key found in the snakeskin, along with other written records, were stored in the briefcase. After returning from breakfast, Jake read once more the note from Mr. Coker. It requested him to call his daughter upon arrival in London. He was given two telephone numbers: her office and a private number. Jake called her office.

"May I speak with Miss Siana Coker, please?"

The receptionist replied, "Miss Coker is not in. May I ask who is calling?"

"I'm Jake James. My call is on behalf of her father, Mr. Coker."

"Sir, Miss Coker instructed me to give you a personal message that she'd be in court this morning until eleven o'clock. She's anxious to talk with you away from her office as soon as possible. She recommends you call her at eleven-fifteen."

The receptionist gave Jake her cell number. It was the same number her father had written on his note. After he hung up, his phone rang. It was Eric Spence.

"Mr. James, this is Eric. I'm free this morning if you need me."

"Pick me up as soon as you can, I have a busy day."

"I'll be there in ten minutes."

It was a relief for Jake to board Eric's taxi with just a briefcase instead of two pieces of luggage. Locked inside the briefcase was his story. Keeping it secure for the record's sake was high priority. At the bank, he made a copy of the snakeskin letter and placed it with his written record of events in his safe-deposit box.

"Eric, let's find a clothing store."

"Sir, do you want upscale, downscale, or something in between?"

"Upscale is fine."

Chapter 5

The Barrister

ERIC PARKED HIS TAXI, went with Jake to shop for clothing to replace his tropical, musky-ridden wardrobe. Jake solicited Eric's advice for purchases knowing his wife had educated him well on what was in vogue and suitable for this time of the year in London. It was strange bonding with Eric. He never had friends at home, those he associated with in the States were his employees, and were always distant. The bonding here in London came about from the risk-taking experience of eluding smugglers who were attempting to retrieve their lost shipment of British notes. A memory came to Jake, the kind of memory that creeps in when events momentarily remove an unconscious barrier. When younger at home, he had heard sermons about Providence intervening in the affairs of men. In those days, homilies sounded like annoying whispers. However, after the event in Eric's taxi in Wimbledon, if those sermons passed his hearing again, he would turn up the volume. This was a new strange world for Jake. Danger had created a level playing field: Eric had become someone more than his taxi driver—he'd become a friend.

Back at his hotel, Jake entered the room he registered in the name of a Mr. Smith, the room he would occupy. After unpacking his newly purchased clothes, he lifted the new leather briefcase to his face, inhaled the fragrance of fresh leather, leather that had never visited the damp, humid tropics. He felt like a new person.

After opening the door to the hotel room registered in his name, he ruffled-up the bed, making it appear occupied. Adding to the lived-in look were his old tropical clothes that went to the closet and drawers.

At eleven-thirty, a call was placed to Mr. Coker's daughter. She answered the phone.

"Hello, this is Siana Coker."

The voice sounded British and professional.

"This is Jake James. Your father requested I call you about some unexplained events he wasn't able to discuss with me before I left Freetown."

"Yes, I know. I was expecting your call. It's important we meet together at a convenient time away from my office."

"What's best for you?"

"Meeting today for lunch works well in my schedule. If this is all right, I'll send a car with a driver to pick you up."

Jake gave her his address and phone number, then added, "The driver will find me waiting outside the hotel."

The barrister's driver arrived in a late-model, upscale vehicle, polished and looking like it just came off the assembly line. Jake hopped in, and right away the driver became chatty.

"Miss Coker says You're Mr. James. My name is Samuel. I've worked for the Cokers for many years. They're wonderful people. Miss Coker owns several taxis and when I'm not driving her, I drive one myself. The vehicle we're in today belongs to her."

The accent of the driver told Jake he was Sierra Leonean, seemed to know a lot about the Coker family and appeared to be a trusted, reliable employee and called upon when it involved private family matters.

Jake knew the barrister's mother was English, that she met her father at the University they attended together, married, and lived their lives together between Freetown and London until she passed away two years ago. The lawyer was the younger of two children.

The driver pulled in front of a restaurant whose clientele was the upper-income business-type people, got out, went around the car and opened the door for his passenger.

When He entered the lobby of the restaurant, he found it quite full of people, either waiting for the host to seat them, or preparing to leave. A woman came up to Jake.

"Are you Mr. James?"

He recognized her voice as the person he had heard on the phone.

"Yes—and you're Miss Coker?"

She extended her hand for a formal handshake greeting, saying, "Yes, I'm Siana Coker, and you're the gentleman my father speaks well of."

"How did you recognize me among all these people?"

"Oh, you look American, and also, my father gave me your description. I've reserved a special private area for our luncheon where we can talk without being overheard. Please follow me."

The woman who met Jake was not dressed like a lawyer who had just arrived from court. Her fashionable attire embellished her outlay of diamonds, and it was apparent the gold holding the stones in place wasn't pinchbeck. She looked more like a celebrated fashion model than a barrister. He followed her to their booth noting her mannerisms and air of self-confidence. It all made her a commanding impression in any court scene. She had strong blue eyes, was tall, willowy, and possessed the beauty of

Nefrariti, the Queen of ancient Egypt, whose bust was on display in the Cairo Museum. Her exquisite-looking jewelry, some might consider over the top, highlighted her attractiveness. She was a member of the barrister club. In England, there were two classes of lawyers: the solicitor and barrister. The difference between them was like comparing a medical doctor in general practice to a specialist in open-heart surgery. In the past, the solicitor referred cases to the barrister for court judicial action; however, in modern times this was somewhat breaking down. The thought did enter Jake's mind how she would look wearing one of those traditional wigs in court.

The barrister sat across from Jake, eyes fastened to his, and for a moment the two were in silence. The lawyer found it difficult making the mental adjustment from client to someone who was a friend of her father.

Right off, Jake could see she was used to being in control or attempted to act in such a way to make others feel she was. It was clear she was on a mission for her father and proceeded as if someone had hired her for a case. Without small talk, she commenced.

"My father wants me to give you the bigger picture of his avoidance of you on the shuttle bus. He has high regard for you and appreciates your engineering skills, especially your contribution to the restoration of the church in Freetown. His purpose of being there on that shuttle was to cancel the flight of his courier. His nemesis in Freetown had bribed certain customs people to plant illegal contraband in his courier's baggage, and the London customs officials had already been informed and were waiting for the arrival of his flight. Had the courier left on that flight, my father's reputation would be in ruins. Included with the planted contraband would have been forged documents incriminating him. If a court found my father guilty, his import and export licenses with the governments of the UK and Sierra Leone would be in jeopardy.

"This was all coming against my father by a competing disreputable company owned by a certain Lebanese involved with diamond smuggling operations— also a big player in moving diamonds to aid extremists in Europe and the Middle East. Some of his agents were with you on the shuttle. Their operation moves them between Freetown, London, Paris, and Belgium delivering smuggled-out goods to parties who act as legitimate businesspersons. They sell the illicit diamonds for cash, launder the money which then is used to fund terrorism. Smuggling diamonds through the contiguous country of Liberia is more difficult since the political climate in both countries is better; therefore the airport in Freetown is their major pathway to move the contraband out of the country.

"Mr. James," she continued, "my father is a successful business person. What he is most successful at is honesty. He has friends within the Lebanese community he partners with outside his own family-run business. My father was on the bus with you because one of these Lebanese business associates gave information on what was going down at the last minute with his courier. The bus carrying the courier and his luggage required interception before he got on the plane. My father didn't acknowledge you on the shuttle because of the agents who sat next to you. It was not in his best interest to bring attention to himself on the shuttle."

About the time Jake thought there was a cessation of recurring nightmares, the barrister had given another shaker. The picture lacking detail changed with one brush sweep from the messenger. It had all the right shapes and colors to fill in unanswered questions.

Relief seemed to come over the lawyer with a suppressed sigh, an expression of a completed task assigned by her father. Like a lawyer, she rested her case, different in presentation, nevertheless the same objective.

With cold, rigid formality, the attorney had everything down to precision. She had informed the headwaiter they were not to be disturbed, a way of discussing confidential matters without interruption. Jake thought her to be a person with the need to be in charge. People with this need had few friends, and those who did have friends had proximity restrictions. Jake was correct. The lawyer had a record of building walls around people like him, the result of subtle negative experiences over her mixed race when she attended the university. Jake was one of those university students.

He soon found her modish dress matched her elegance of intellect. She was good in her role of bluestocking by demonstrating scholastic aptitude and trivia. She could use those qualities at will if it served as a source to hide behind. He detected her defense mechanisms because he used the same ones, but for a different reason. The waiter arrived at her signal. They submitted their orders.

In an act of courtesy, or because of genuine interest, the lawyer moved from just giving information to an exchange of dialogue. She was a barrister and could frame questions well to achieve maximum return in answers. She posed her first question so open-ended Jake didn't know where to start.

"Mr. James, Why did you go to Sierra Leone?"

"Do you want the long or short version of it?"

"Whatever version tells your story."

Jake was never a person who went out of his way to give details of his life to others; his resume held these matters. He felt there was a fencing challenge lurking somewhere in the discourse. Perhaps it came from being a lawyer, a single one—the type that had difficulty turning off the profession when not engaged in work.

"I'll give you the long version of why I went to Sierra Leone. When I was a junior in college, all the portion of my grandfather's estate going to me went into undesirable blighted property. I was a young risk-taking gambler. I gambled on the city changing the zoning map to include what I bought as part of the industrial zone. In two years, I sold the property with a net gain of one million dollars. With a Master's degree in engineering at the age of twenty-three, I gambled the profits from my initial investment in the construction of a shopping center and subdivision. This catapulted me into land speculation and subdivision development. By the time I was twenty-nine, I was bored and wanted to do something with greater satisfaction than just making money. Contributing to my adventurous, dissatisfied life was the memory of my late grandfather who had served with a mission in Sierra Leone as a medical doctor. It was his life that impacted me as a child and influenced me to see the place he always talked about."

"What was your grandfather's name?"

"His name was Baron, Dr. J. Baron."

Jake saw the barrister's face shift from a cold stance of professional gameplay to a look of void, like two worlds were about to collide.

"Oh my...I remember my father speaking of him."

The human brain never receives its full credit for its cerebral powers in organizational skills. It allows memory to store facts, feelings, and history below the conscious level. In a moment's time, the brain can throw all these together in an organized and synthesized picture, like a chain linking together rational thought. Sometimes, it's a hair-trigger thought, a scent, or the sight of a face; *today, it was the name, Coker.*

Flashing before Jake's mind was a scene when he was ten-years-old visiting his grandfather at his home. He had asked his grandfather to tell him a story about Africa. He was always a good storyteller. Like the time when the pet mongoose ran a black cobra snake into the hospital office, killed it in front of the excited nurses. Then, there was the time when a large cobra got into the chicken house, swallowed an egg, went through the chicken wire to another section and stopped because the egg inside the snake was larger than the mesh of the wire fence. With half its body on one side of the fence, the other half on the other side, it swallowed another egg. The poor snake was trapped, unable to escape frontward or backward with the wire mesh between the two eggs it had gulped down. His grandfather told him, "I didn't need a mongoose to kill the snake." On this occasion, Gramps told a different kind of African story; it left the memory of him being a teacher who used tactile principles.

He said, "Jacob bring the metal box from over there in the closet, and I'll tell you about Africa."

He opened a creaky closet door. On the floor rested an old, rusty, grey, metal box with a handle on its top. Expecting it to be heavy, he lifted it up from the floor. It was quite light.

Gramps said, "Set it in front of me on the floor."

He expected a treasure, something of monetary value, or something exciting.

"Open it up," he said.

He opened it, and what he saw was disappointing. All it contained was a bunch of old letters in their envelopes.

"Jacob, take ten of those letters out of the box, read the names and country of the sender."

This letterbox to him was not Africa. Nevertheless, he took ten letters and began reading the names of each one with the country associated with the name. Some of the countries were Sierra Leone, England, Ghana, Canada, and Israel. Later, he was to learn half the box held letters from Sierra Leone.

"All these letters came to me in America after I left Africa. They came from people I helped. Always remember, Jacob, bread is the only thing you can throw upon the water and have it come back to you later in life. You don't know this principle now, but someday you will.

"Jacob, you're an avid stamp collector. If you will take this box of letters and give me a list of the names and addresses of the senders, you can have the stamps for your collection."

His ten-year-old spirit was elated. It was a treasure box. He removed all the stamps from the letters, copied down the return addresses and gave them to gramps. Three of the letters were from a Mr. Lewis Coker. His grandfather had a special drawer where he kept his stamp collection, right alongside the chess set they often used.

When Jake gathered his inner composure of the flashback, he said nothing to the lawyer about the name of a Lewis Coker he had found on three of the letters.

"Mr. James, You're an interesting person—a successful one too. Where do you get all your energy and ambition?"

"In my case, I was born on wheels, made for excitement, and never shrank from the opportunity to gamble big. Along with this came intuition about coming changes in an expanding community—I gambled on it. Miss Coker, do you believe gambling in this form to be energy and drive?"

"The legal view of this is yes, but only if you're playing with your own money."

Humor was used by both to fill in time. Everything reached a point when Jake asked, "How do you spend your leisure hours, Miss Coker?"

"Now you're getting personal. Do you try to get non-professional with all your opposite-gendered lawyers?"

"Just the lawyers whose fathers I'm acquainted with. Besides, you aren't my lawyer—yet."

"Well, this does place you in a special category, doesn't it, and my father tells me you're an honorable person. Since I never get to talk about myself, I'll divulge to you that my spare time is spent at my church and reading a lot. If there's time left over, I practice a leisure pursuit of designing and making jewelry. In fact, several shops have bought some of my designs."

"Are these pieces you're wearing some of those designs?"

"They're not just my designs, but my workmanship. I did everything but cut and polish the gems."

"My, you are talented! And may I say, a delightful person too. I'm sorry your law practice is not in Freetown. Had it been there, perhaps our meeting would be under better circumstances."

The lawyer's eyes looked downward like she was embarrassed or apprehensive about a conversation centered on her personal life. She thought well of this person seated across from her because of her father; but he ruffled her comfort zone with his direct, fast-moving manner. Besides, he could never understand or fit into her world. Half-smiling, she came back with direct eye contact to redraw her boundary. Jake had crossed over into her fortress.

"Freetown has many special memories. I have relatives in Freetown with my father's family and relatives here in England on my mother's side. I'm a person of two worlds."

Jake understood her statement: she was uncomfortable in his singular world. She was telling him their two worlds were far apart—they came from two different backgrounds. She turned inward and more professional.

"My father asked me to assist you with anything you may need. Please feel free to contact me at any time on my private number."

Her closure was abrupt. Jake followed in kind, saying, "Thank you for your time." They stood up together. The last words spoken to Jake before leaving were, "I appreciate you helping with my father's engineering project in Freetown. If you have legal matters here London, or if there's something I can help you with, please feel free to contact me."

Jake chose to secure his own taxi for the return trip to his hotel. After boarding the vehicle, he evaluated his meeting: the lawyer was professional, articulate, and suspicious. He would leave it for history to define her suspicion—he was sure it was about him. When he checked his voice mail, there was one message. It was from Ann, his passenger friend on the flight into Gatwick. She sounded upset.

"Oh, Mr. James, something awful happened. I went out to lunch, and when I returned to my hotel room at one o'clock, I found my room ransacked. My luggage cases were open, the mattress and bedding turned over and my clothes strewn out on the floor."

Jake called Ann. She answered with frightened emotion in her voice. Not wanting to heighten her state of almost hysteria, he avoided relating his own unpleasant hotel experience. Both had innocently fallen into issues of diamond smuggling, and at this point were unable to control events. It would seem best if Ann removed herself from the danger at hand.

"Ann, when are you leaving for the states?"

"I have tickets to fly out in two days."

"I suggest you either get another hotel or see if you can change your flight to an earlier time."

"After finding my room devastated, I was so upset I canceled everything on my calendar."

"When do you want to return to the States?"

"Right now, if I could get a flight."

"Ann, Get on the phone, see if you can find a flight that works with your schedule, and give me a call after it's confirmed. I'll come by your hotel, pick you up, and take you to the airport for your flight."

"Thank you, Mr. James, I'll do my best and get right back to you."

In the shadows of Jake's mind, he always had suspicions the package Ann carried on board the plane was illicit. He had come to believe the woman who showed up at the airport to pick up the package was part of a smuggling ring. They believed Ann knew what was in the package, that she intended to keep it, and that it was still in her possession. Hence, her room was broken into in their search for the contraband.

Jake was in a crucible of high-pressured events that served to polish his inner self-mirror. They brought clarity to his audacious nature. It was now his guilt time. The intrigue of Ann's drama had untapped his adventurous nature again. Something inside made him enjoy this elevated danger, even Ann's crisis was paradoxical: he didn't wish this unpleasant experience upon her, but part of him was challenged by it. He wondered if this were what he searched for when he went camping in the wild all alone, or the time when he put his entire grandfather's inheritance on the wheel of property speculation. Could this driving force also be something destructive when the excitement of adventure overruled reason?

The taxi dropped Jake off at his hotel while the driver waited for his quick return. Thoughts moved to Ann's situation and state of mind. After entering Mr. Smith's room, the one he slept in, he packed a raincoat inside his leather briefcase. Everything seemed as he had left it. He looked into the room registered in own name—it appeared as he left it. After closing the door, he locked it and left for Ann's hotel in the waiting taxi.

Upon entering the hotel lobby, Jake placed a call to Ann. She was excited to hear from him.

"I was just going to call and tell you I was able to get a booking at a decent hour. We have about three hours to get to Heathrow to check in."

By the time he reached her room, she had all her luggage packed and was ready to go. While she was doing a last-minute check through her disheveled room for anything missed, it occurred to Jake he had reserved and paid for just three days at his hotel. He needed to book further dates to guarantee a continued stay—he dialed the hotel. The hotel manager sounded distraught.

"Mr. James, you should come right over because someone broke into your room!"

He stood speechless. Jake knew the predators had widened their circle. His attempt to hide had come up short. Mr. Smith's room, the one he had slept in, now awaited his inspection. Jake avoided telling Ann about his hotel room. He remained somber and silent as he carried her bags out to board a taxi. There was just one way for the smugglers to find his hotel: it was his meeting with the lawyer at the restaurant. Jake figured if the lawyer were not part of this, then they followed her to learn of his movements. He persuaded himself to wager on the side of Mr. Coker's reputation and his daughter who offered assistance.

After entering the taxi, he said, "Ann, did they take anything from your luggage?"

"No, there's nothing missing. However, when I first arrived and unpacked, I found something loose in one of my cases. It was a curio of large indigenous shells made in the form of a necklace sold to tourists. I threw them in my briefcase to keep them apart from my personal effects and have forgotten them until now. I don't want to take it with me. Please, can you take the necklace and do whatever with it?"

She opened her briefcase, handed Jake the string of shells. The news of what happened at his hotel room occupied his thoughts, but he managed enough focus to place them inside his own briefcase.

"Ann, I need to stop at my hotel to pick up my luggage on the way to the airport. It's not out of the way. We can still get there in good time."

The taxi stopped in front of his hotel.

"Ann, I'll not take long."

She waited in the taxi while he ran in, went to Mr. Smith's room and unlocked the door expecting the worst. It was found undisturbed; everything in the room appeared intact. He then went to the room registered in his own name. The lock was broken. Everything looked like Ann's torn-up room, then, returned to Mr. Smith's room and packed his personal effects along with the two ebony heads. Upon leaving, Jake asked the manager, "Did anyone see who broke into the room registered in my name?"

"Sir, we have a lot of people moving about here, but one of the housekeepers did say, 'about the time the incident happened, she saw some men talking Arabic leaving the area of the room.'"

Jake congratulated himself by keeping a step ahead of the smugglers; renting the two rooms served its purpose. He checked himself out and left with his luggage. Like helpless chicks out in the open with hungry hawks overhead, the taxi sped along with Ann's thoughts on her flight, Jake's on matters of survival. He knew he needed the help of the barrister. Her number was in his phone and when he dialed, she answered knowing it was Jake.

"Hello, Mr. James."

"I appreciate you answering my call at this inopportune time. I have an urgent matter I must talk with you about; however, I can't discuss the specifics where I am. Can we arrange a meeting together? Wherever we meet, no one should see us together or know the place of our meeting. I'm being followed."

"What are you doing now?"

"I'm taking a friend to the airport for a flight to the States. It'll take about two hours."

"I'll call you back," she said, then hung up.

The taxi arrived at the airport in good time. Both labored with their luggage and refused the aid of baggage handlers. Ann carried her briefcase with a smaller piece of carry-on strapped over her shoulder pulling another behind. Jake struggled with two large luggage pieces along with his briefcase; one of the cases belonged to Ann. After finding her airline, they waited in line. Ann was nervous, but underneath Jake could see some of her strength radiating self-confidence. She handed her tickets to the agent for processing her changed schedule. Jake saw the outside jacket; it held her old tickets and carried a stamp with the name of the same travel agency he had used in Freetown. This was another piece of the puzzle falling into place. Both had been pawns, used in a conspiracy by an organized team of people to carry contraband through customs. Their guardian dark angels were those two who sat behind them in flight.

"Mr. James, Let's give God the opportunity to work everything out in our lives. He can help us if we allow Him."

For her, he had confidence; however, his matter was a great deal more serious than hers. For a few moments, he forced himself to lean away from reason; he wished her statement were fatidic.

The agent weighed and tagged her luggage. Her tall frame that had before carried the appearance of strength now looked weathered, her face showing stress. Their eyes followed the luggage moving down the conveyer belt for the flight to New York, then walked together as far as permitted.

"Please write me when you get home, Ann."

"Oh, I will. I want to thank you for doing so much for me. Whenever I play chess, I'll remember you."

"Sometimes, Ann, life throws us curves, but in my case, what came your way allowed me to meet a wonderful person. I wish you the best."

Jake watched her walk down the wide corridor toward her gate knowing her experience here in London had made her a better and stronger person—if she had any more room in herself for improvement. Now, he carried his luggage alone, felt he was on a deserted island that had welcomed him with wide-open arms, but alone, marooned, and without a compass. He had fled two hotels because of diamonds and British notes. Temptation was hanging over him to get on the plane with Ann and fly out to a safe haven, but something inside caused his scrapping nature to surge forward to struggle with the odds before him. He knew he liked adventure, but right now he wasn't sure about the long haul. He sat for fifteen minutes pondering the world he had created for himself before the barrister returned his call.

"Hello, this is Jake."

"Mr. James, I had to rearrange my schedule before I could get back to you. I'm free to meet with you under your conditions. There's a parking garage about four miles from the airport—we can meet there. My driver will pick you up in front at the loading zone. You're to go out only after you get a call from him. He'll then take you to this garage where we'll discuss your matter inside my vehicle while the driver stands guard."

Jake hung up, waited twenty minutes before his phone rang. It was the driver. "This is Samuel, Miss Coker's driver. I'm pulling up near the front, please come now."

Jake slid into the vehicle, and they were off with a speed that questioned safety. Outside, darkness was looming overhead with an enlarged, radiant, red sun settling in for the night. Inside, the driver kept patronizing the rearview mirror for any following cars and kept changing directions of travel. It was four miles to the garage. He drove twelve before arriving, pulled in, and drove to the third floor where flashing lights were visible from another car. The driver drove toward the lights, parked several spaces away, jumped out, grabbed Jake's case, and led him over to a car with darkened rear windows. He opened the door, saying, "Please get in." He placed the luggage at Jake's feet on the floor. It was dark inside the vehicle, and seated beside Jake in the back seat was someone with the outline of the barrister. Outside, Jake saw his driver join the lawyer's driver. Both moved to an inconspicuous area and stood watch over the broad scene like loyal praetorian guards responsible for Caesar's welfare.

"I'll start at the beginning, Miss Coker. When I arrived at Gatwick, I took from the baggage table the piece of luggage I checked in at Lungi airport. Upon opening my luggage in my room at the Hilton, I found diamonds hidden in a concealed compartment. Without my knowledge, someone on the shuttle switched my luggage for another piece like mine. While waiting for my case at the baggage table at Gatwick, the police took away the two agents your father spoke of. They were there to take back their contraband case after I cleared customs. They would have approached me, saying, 'There has been a mistake with our luggage pieces. We have your luggage in our possession and you have ours.' They would have shown me the contents of my luggage, and I would have welcomed the exchange. Had the police not detained them, they would be in possession of their contraband case and I would have my own. Also, enclosed in the contraband case was a rolled-up snakeskin with an attached piece of paper with Arabic writing and a key taped to the paper."

"Who knows about this," asked the lawyer, "and where are the diamonds now?"

The lawyer forged a somber tone in her voice. He didn't tell the barrister about the money found at Wimbledon.

"The diamonds are in a safe deposit box. Just you and I know of this matter.''

"Mr. James, you did two things right: you safeguarded the diamonds and told no one about them. This still does not help in your personal safety. You've stumbled into the violent, criminal underworld system of diamond smuggling. It robs the country they came from and provides millions of pounds for the terrorists. There's a lot of blood on illicit diamonds leaving the country, not to mention the loss of revenue for hospitals and schools."

The barrister continued: "If I'm to be your legal counsel, I must give you the choices you have. First, you can turn the diamonds over to the British Customs Agency. They'll take action to return them to the country of origin, but I assure you they will never reach the country they came from. On the other hand, you could act on philanthropic idealism and return the value of the diamonds to the people in the form of a school or hospital, but I must advise you that what is in your possession is contraband, and as such, you are an accessory to a crime if you show intent to conceal it from the authorities. You mentioned earlier that you are a gambler, Mr. James. Circumstances before you now could be the greatest gamble of your life.

Brief silence punctuated their meeting. Jake knew performance was part of every professional role, and detection came easy for him when he was cast in the character of a villain. He had further insight by reading *between the lines of what the lawyer said. The tone of her voice said it all and had there been sufficient light inside the darkened vehicle, her eyes would have shown even a clearer message: that she had pleasure dangling him over a cliff forcing him into a predictable outcome of twitching, tightfisted, sweaty hands. The irony of it all was that he and her father were professional friends.*

84

Jake's hands were sweaty and tightfisted but not from the lawyer's judicial cliff-hanging verbiage. His stress came from the burden of his decision to return the contraband to the land of its origin. The slumbering voice of Jake's conscience was awakened to the need of moral clarity. Seated in an upscale darkened vehicle in a downscale parking garage, he was ready to do battle against prevailing odds. His conscience, now alive and alert, would join him in the throes of competing against the odds, the strong opponent being written law.

Subtle pathways had been created by the lawyer showing preference to none. It was left for Jake to choose. Pathways existed for two reasons: scenic value and something used to go somewhere. If he chose to keep the diamonds for a worthy project in the country they came from, it would be a path fraught with legal jeopardy while others would embrace the comfort of its natural beauty.

Jake came to believe that because he had done pro bono work for the lawyer's father, she felt obligated to help him. The lawyer had successfully concealed her natural interest about a person who was successful, yet had eccentric traits that didn't match the image of success. She was uncomfortable with his openness about himself and his life and he pushed too hard to get into hers. He was like a mirror forcing her to see her own hidden feelings about others who lived in a world she didn't belong. At this stage, they were two gladiators meeting in the middle of an empty coliseum sizing each other up before serious conflict, and with no crowd to entertain, fencing bouts would continue.

Snapping words came from the lawyer, "Now, let's look at the piece of paper and the key in your possession."

Jake took from his money-belt a copy of the snakeskin paper and the key that came attached to it. In the darkened car, he handed her the key and paper. She switched on the overhead light and examined the paper with Arabic writing. After inspecting the key, she organized her thoughts and switched off the light.

"Mr. James, you have a piece of paper here containing valuable information. I can't interpret this verbatim, but I understand enough to say it's a message with an important signature attached to it. This other item is a key to a post office box. When I was a child, I sometimes played with Arabic-speaking children and learned some of their spoken language, but none of the written. I'm going to give you the name of an honorable and loyal person. He's a close friend to my family and will get you the complete translation and provide any other assistance. I'll take the paper, give it to him tonight and he'll get back to you. His name is Sydney, a patriotic Sierra Leonean and silent activist for his country. He has friends here in London and carries a lot of influence in his country of origin."

Jake placed the key back inside his money belt. The lawyer continued.

"The action taken at the airport by the police caused the agents to lose the contraband. They believed my family was involved in creating the police matter. This was why I was under surveillance and the reason you were followed to your hotel. The moment you bought your airline tickets and luggage in Freetown you became a selected target to be a carrier for moving diamonds through customs at Gatwick.

"From this point on, you and I must not meet in public view. You can call me anytime. If I can't answer, leave a message and I'll get back to you. Sydney will reach you in twenty-four hours."

Jake considered the lawyer a good facilitator for his welfare. At this point, he allowed himself to believe she was willing to be a silent, innocent accomplice—both with the same goals: return the value of the diamonds to the country of origin. The thought of informing the police faded as a plausible choice. With business concluded, Jake was preparing to leave when she spoke.

"It'll be best if you find a place to live near Sidney's neighborhood. It'll provide a greater level of security. If you like good West African food, you'll enjoy his neighborhood. I took the liberty when you first called to check with Sydney to see what was available in his area as a suitable place for you to stay. There are no hotels in the immediate vicinity; however, one can rent rooms and small studio apartments on a weekly or monthly basis. Your experience in Africa will make you feel right at home there. If you want to go with my advice, I'll call Sydney and see what he's found."

Jake was never short on answers. "Yes, I can handle this." Opinions were forming in Jake's mind. The barrister was struggling to fulfill her father's expectations with a stranger from another world knocking on her door. Was she a person who lived and walked among people of learning with idealism ending outside the classroom? Could it be that she was testing him to see if he moved with the same crowd? On the surface she was treating him as a client, the result of her father's request, however, there were signs of undercurrents. Perhaps she had the need to have him defined and would use others to aid in that process. Everything about the lady showed dichotomous personhood: she was thoroughly British but was proud of her geographical and cultural past.

Responding to Jake's answer, she called Sydney.

"Hello, Sydney. Regarding a room for Mr. James, have you found anything yet?"

There was a pause.

"The price for the unit is fine with him. His main concern is that people in the area know who he is, and be on alert for strangers showing up. It's in his interest no one calls on him from outside the neighborhood. I have a personal request and will discuss the matter when I see you."

The driver who picked Jake up at the airport got in his vehicle and drove away. She instructed her driver to take them to Sydney's neighborhood.

There was no talking in the car until she asked, "Where're you from in the States, Mr. James?"

"I'm from just outside Pittsburgh."

"Was you grandfather from this area?"

"Yes, his practice was in my hometown."

"How many children did your grandfather have?"

This questioning continued until Jake said, "Why is my grandfather the subject of our conversation?" What was constant chatter in the form of questions became veiled silence.

She parsed her response in a sullen way. "I'll answer that question at a later time." He understood by her reply that this question was out of bounds and was going out of her way in refusing to tell him something she knew about his venerated grandfather. This deepened the mystery about her personal life.

The driver turned down narrow side streets leading to a neighborhood where there were shops with West African goods and food products. Inside the shops were food dishes Jake had come to enjoy in West Africa. The pungent aromas acted like stimulants that forced his synapses to reach for memories of gourmet delights of the past. The smell of palm oil, hot pepper mixed with joloof rice and groundnut stew, brought to memory the friends he had dined with in Africa.

The scenery changed when the lawyer's driver entered a residential area and came to a stop in front of a home with three floors. Out of the three-story residence came a tall thin man dressed in typical casual clothing. He was graying, appeared to be about fifty years of age. When he reached the car, the lawyer lowered her window and spoke to him in deep Krio, the language of the more urbanized Sierra Leoneans. Then, she turned to Jake.

"Mr. James, this is Sydney I've spoken about."

Sidney got in the car on the front passenger side. The driver stepped out, stood at the front of the vehicle while they discussed the paper. The lawyer took the paper with Arabic writing, handed it to Sydney while both continued speaking Krio. Jake understood a few of the words. Sydney gave it scrutiny.

"I'll go back to my office and make some contacts. I think I can get a translation of this within the hour."

They were now using English so Jake could understand. Sydney continued. "The place Mr. James will be staying is at the address I've written down." He handed the barrister a small card with an address and key.

"I suggest the driver take the gentleman there to see the place, bring him back here in about thirty minutes, and by then I'll have the translation ready for you."

On their way to the apartment, the lawyer looked at Jake, saying, "No one but you and I know about your deposit box. Let's keep it that way. Sidney will keep the translation in confidence, and his translator will never make an association with its meaning. How far do you want Sydney involved in this matter of the paper and the key?"

"He can go as far as he wishes if his loyalty never comes into question. Whatever develops, and wherever I go with this, I'll keep you informed."

"Sidney and my father go back quite a few years. He used to work in my family's business before my father helped set him up here in London. He's done well with several small stores and properties. Sydney also has many contacts that can do almost anything you want. All I told Sydney was that someone exchanged your suitcase for one like yours, and when you opened it, you found the snakeskin, letter, and key. I didn't tell him about the diamonds, although, he probably thinks there's more to the event than what he's been told."

When they arrived at the site where Sydney arranged for Jake to stay, he was surprised the barrister got out of the car and went in with him to look at the one-room studio apartment. It was a two-story building with the apartment located on the bottom floor, was clean and well furnished.

"The place is humble but suitable," Jake said. "I appreciate your help. It appears I've become dependent on someone besides myself, something that rarely happens."

Jake saw her eyes look down, leaving the message that she didn't want that responsibility.

"Mr. James, your success in the States with your business must allow you to own a large beautiful home with all kinds of help around. Now, you're staying at a site where unemployed laborers stay. Are you sure you can handle this?"

Unknown to Jake, the lawyer had a purpose in convincing him to stay here. She was throwing one stone for two birds: she would help secure his safety and at the same time probe who he was. It would be a controlled environment, living in and among those below his standard.

"Miss Coker, in answer to your question about my affluence, I'll have to say, I don't own a single home, just shopping centers, commercial buildings, and open tracks of land. I don't even have help, as you call it. I do have employees. Where I live is in a four-room cabin on my mother and father's five-acre farm. I'm never home much—always away at job sites or seeking excitement around the world—like going to Africa."

The barrister found it difficult to believe Jake didn't own the home he lived in.

"You're something else, Mr. James, some piece of work, I must say."

Chapter 6

The Snakeskin

WHEN JAKE AND THE BARRISTER arrived back at Sydney's, they saw him coming in their direction. The lawyer opened her window and Sydney handed her two pieces of paper: one was from the snakeskin with Arabic writing, the other its translation. Sydney got in the car and they drove back to the apartment where Jake would stay. The lawyer sat on the sofa with Sydney. Jake chose an old wooden kitchen chair, took a pen from his pocket and copied the written translation on another piece of paper in his own writing. None spoke. The translation of the Arabic script read: *Attached is a key for the new post office box 222 Trafalgra Square. When emptied of contents, return key to Freetown with next payment.* It was signed, Samir. Below Samir's signature were four names listed without explanation. They stood as nondescript pillars in support of a building that housed corruption and violence.

The event of the contraband luggage case that Jake carried through customs at Gatwick was bringing together three people whose interest was beyond the case itself: Sydney, a latecomer to the group, a patriot and activist for what was best for his country, a barrister, who wanted justice for her father, and Jake, the innocent man who kept the contraband for the greater good. Each would become dependent on the other in events that would unfold.

It was clear Sydney arrived where he was by the way life had formed him. Jake understood why the barrister chose this person. Sydney saw the big picture, was intuitive, decisive, and wanted the best for his land. He read in Jake's eyes the script of his intent.

Up to this point, the lawyer had been doing a favor in helping Jake, her father's friend who had fallen prey to violent smugglers. It was a perfunctory task without feeling and intensity. However, after reading the translation signed with the name Samir, both Jake and Sydney noticed her eyes and body tensing. Samir was the man who attempted to plant contraband in the luggage of her father's courier in an attempt to destroy him. The barrister's thoughts were now entertaining the exchange of services in a quid pro quo with her client: she would help him if he reciprocated in bringing down Samir. She had defended and worked with clients on the wrong side of life enough to know that Jake, who had kept the diamonds, might be a candidate she could use for this purpose. He took chances, was bold, daring, and eccentric—qualities needed to get results. She didn't want avengement, but justice, and she knew sometimes justice walked the tightrope of covert action. Perhaps her client would succeed in walking the rope. It was worth a try.

The snakeskin letter and the Wimbledon locker showed Jake that information and payoffs were by deposits and pickups. Everything indicated lockers and post office boxes moved from site-to-site to prevent detection and suspicion: one for cash pickups, the other for moving confidential information on their operations. Europe controlled the money lockers, and Samir was the operative in Freetown who ran the smuggling system and moved information to and from London. Samir was a committed terrorist ideologue but always made his creed subject to self-interest. He had broadened his power base by aligning himself with European operatives in the terror network. This connection gave him greater control by imposing fear on those inside his organization. Samir kept himself insulated by using trusted agents, men related to him from his consanguineous clan. This guaranteed loyalty and protection. Jake knew time was important if they were to make use of the key in their possession.

"Sidney, we need to pick up the contents inside the box. Once we get the contents, we must copy everything and replace the originals as they were. What we're doing here is a big step toward filling in the broader picture. When this is over, the police will have what is necessary to bring down some of them. It's imperative everything operates on a high level of secrecy and trust. No one must know our plans."

"Yes I know," Sydney said. "Siana has given me clear instructions."

Jake could see Sidney was helping out of loyalty and commitment to the Coker family. There existed a mutual principle: create a better homeland by disrupting foreign malevolent forces who were raping the country.

"Sydney, I have the vehicle license number of a car driven by these agents. If you can trace the ownership and address of this party, we'll put in motion our own operation."

"I'll have people getting on this right away," said Sidney. "Once we find where they're staying, we'll keep surveillance on their movements."

"Sydney, how do you motivate your people to be loyal and helpful?"

"It all has to do with our roots, the country of our birth."

The evening moved on, the discussions ended and everyone left, leaving Jake to experience his first night in his studio apartment. He unpacked his luggage, hung his clothes in the closet and pushed the two ebony heads that came with the contraband under the bed. He was dropping off to sleep when his telephone rang.

"Is this Mr. James?"

"Yes, this is Jake in living darkness."

"This is Siana Coker. I apologize for waking you. I just wanted to see if you're settled and everything is all right."

After his brain waves were more at his command, he felt equal to the caller. He responded, "Sidney and I are going to make a hit on the box tomorrow. We need help getting copied any papers we pick up there. Can you find the closest place to the post office where we can make copies? After the copying, I'll return the originals to the box."

"My concern is for the safety of you and Sidney, so please take care. I'll call tomorrow morning and let you know if I've found a convenient place for this to be done."

"Thank you, counselor."

Jake hung up and lay still and quiet. The voice he just heard penetrating the darkened room carried the marks of subtle change. Before he slipped into his night's undisturbed sleep, he pondered why the counselor had a streak of concern about him. Unknown to Jake, the barrister had motives beyond a client-counselor relationship: it was justice for Samir.

Jake awoke the next morning from a loud pounding at his front door. Someone was calling his name. "Jake, are you awake? I have some information for us to look at."

He struggled to wake up. Stress had taken its toll. His watch indicated it was nine-fifteen. He had overslept.

"Just a minute, Sydney."

When he opened the door, Sydney stood poised ready to enter with a folder in his hand; it contained something he thought important to their issue.

"Good morning Sydney."

"Cusha, how de body."

Jake thought he was in Sydney's country when he spoke using a typical Krio greeting. He spoke impeccable English, yet chose to address him in his cultural language with personal warmth, revealing a certain degree of trust. He felt honored.

"Jake, I just returned from the post office making a rough sketch of the floor plan. I want us to make a study of it before we take action."

Sydney placed on the table what he had prepared for this meeting. It appeared quite complete with floor dimensions and the location of the box itself. Also, indicated were street configurations and adjacent buildings.

"Sydney, if you can get me some latex gloves, I'll do the pickup. After you sweep the building and give me the clearance, I'll move in and take the contents. I'm waiting for a call from Miss Coker for information where private self-copying can be done near the post office. When I hear from her, I'll let you know."

Sidney left for the small errand of latex gloves. The lawyer called soon after he had left.

"Mr. James, I located a place to make copies as you requested. It's a short distance from the post office. I'll meet you there at twelve-thirty. Samuel, my driver, will pick you up at your place, drop you off at the post office, then take you to the copying site where I'll meet you."

"Aren't you crossing the line in what you're doing?"

"In answer to your question, I'll say yes! Your gambling nature is contagious."

What the lawyer didn't tell Jake was her ulterior motive: she wanted to use him as a bridge to get to Samir. She knew if the post office box yielded the right information, it could bring his downfall.

"I'll arrive there at twelve-thirty. If you can bring something to steam the envelopes, it'll help expedite the copying."

He hung up, Sydney returned with gloves. Jake needed his briefcase for this operation. Everything inside the case went into his nightstand, except the curio necklace of shells Ann had given him; they joined the two ebony heads stored under the bed. He placed the key to the box inside his coat pocket, and the two of them left the apartment. Sydney would coordinate everything by standing watch in and around the post office—phones would keep everyone in touch. Jake stopped at the front of the driveway waiting for Samuel—Sydney drove away in his car. When Samuel arrived, they went together to Trafalgar Square to wait for Sydney's call when everything was clear for the pickup.

Sydney knew nothing about the six sacks of diamonds that came with him through customs. Jake and his lawyer had agreed to this. She also kept this information from her father. Jake and the barrister had few common interests, but both had ulterior motives: he wanted her help in building a hospital in her country, and she wanted to use him to get to Samir. Though she was with him on a philosophical level, Jake had come to believe she had problems crossing the line that might jeopardize her standing in the legal community. Samuel drove around the block several times before Sydney called.

"Jake, this is Sydney, everything is clear here at the post office."

"Thanks, we'll start moving in. I'll let you know how it goes."

Samuel dropped Jake off in front of the post office, he slipped his hand inside his rumpled coat pocket to reassure himself the key and gloves were there for quick use. The driver proceeded to go around the block; Jake braved his way to the building and moved inside. With Sydney's description of the box location, he had no difficulty finding it. Today, few people moved about. He placed the briefcase on the floor below the box, forced his clammy hands into the latex gloves. When the key entered the lock, two voices began struggling inside: reason and conscience. The human conscience was sometimes a tricky irritant when it competed with reason. Reason told him what he was doing, though it was against the law, it served the greater good. However, from within came another louder competing message: he could get into serious trouble with the law if caught. Jake was adversarial, impulsive, and his conscience always a silent sleeper until forced onto the often-visited battlefield called choice. Too many times his conscience was a step behind his actions. Today was one of those moments. It was a roll of the dice. He opened the box, took out the contents and placed them inside his briefcase, withdrew the key and shut the door. The need to find Samuel was urgent. He stood, walked to the door, and from inside looked for his driver. When spotted, he quickly moved to the vehicle where it had stopped.

"Let's be on our way, Samuel!"

When the driver determined no one was following, he went straight to the site where the copying would take place. The office complex belonged to the barrister's law-school friend and when entering the outer office, the lawyer met him.

"This is the office of a friend of mine. She's allowing you to use her equipment because of owing me a favor. She'll be back in a couple of hours, so if you hurry, you can finish this before she arrives."

Both went into the copying room and shut the door. Jake slip on a new pair of latex gloves, removed the articles taken from the box and commenced the process of copying. Everything was in envelopes, each containing a voided postal stamp. He stacked them in the order they came out of the box—they were to be returned in the same manner. The small electric water steamer the lawyer brought along was doing its job. The barrister watched as if she were assigning a letter grade for his performance. When Jake saw her intensity, he stopped and looked at her.

"Miss Barrister, am I doing this right?"

"I'm not aware I'm here to give my approval. However, you appear to be doing well."

"Then why are you so tense? You keep looking at the door with your eyes, and then back at me. It's like you're at a tennis match."

"If you were in my place, you would be tense too watching someone engaged in a rogue act?"

"You're calling me a rogue! Some think I was born a rogue with modest civility. Are you joining that crowd?"

Jake saw the lawyer take a step outside her protective zone, saying, "Wouldn't you agree that you and I are made to be adversarial to each other?"

"Conflict can sometimes make life interesting and challenging. And for some, it can act as a drug creating a state of euphoria."

"I prefer solace, Mr. James."

The lawyer continued watching Jake take each letter, hold it over the steamer, remove the contents and copy it.

After she saw everything was going well, she said to Jake, "You're doing a good job. I must leave for my office and am leaving a key you must use to lock the door when you finish. You can give the key to me later."

Jake turned, looked at her through his mischievous, darting eyes, saying with intended friendly sarcasm, "Enjoy your solace."

She gave no response, closed the door and left avoiding direct contact with his eyes.

Everything written on the pages taken from the envelopes was in Arabic. He made two copies each of the envelopes and contents inside. Some of the dates on the envelopes indicated postings as far back as six weeks. This led Jake to believe posted envelopes to this box arrived on a regular basis with blank paper inside, then taken from the box and returned when they needed to move information. This made the contents from the other side of the box where the postal employees worked look normal with canceled postage marks. When the project was finished, Jake placed the envelopes with their contents back inside his briefcase.

Half the mission was completed. The next phase was returning the originals to the box. It was important to make everything appear undisturbed, leaving the message of normality to those who would visit the box. Jake knew that the key he had in his possession was only one among several, and a box pickup could be imminent. He also knew there was a high probability that if they found the right information in these envelopes, it would raise their operation to a higher level.

The copying room underwent scrutiny before leaving. With everything in order, Jake went to find Samuel outside to finish the task. It took a short time to reach the post office and replace the envelopes as they were before. Back in the car with Samuel, he breathed a sigh of relief, called Eric Spence, the taxi driver who had helped him when he was in trouble earlier.

"Hello, is this Eric?"

"Yes, is this Eric"

"This is Jake. Eric, I need the two luggage cases I gave you to keep. Can you bring them to me at the bank within the hour?"

"Yes, I'll be at the bank in forty-five minutes. The luggage pieces are still in the boot of my taxi."

"Great, I'll see you there."

Sydney was his next call. The information of success with the post office documents gave him relief. Jake congratulated him for his work, then requested that he bring an interpreter to his place tonight at nine o'clock for the translations of the copied documents. Turning to Samuel, he said, "Please take me to my bank."

Before arriving at the bank, Jake placed a call to the lawyer. She answered and sounded disturbed—he had called Sydney before reaching her.

"Did I have to receive your news first from Sydney? Anyway, I'm glad everything went well."

Underneath the barrister's strong-sounding resolute veneer, she could be fragile in close encounters when conflict was in play. At this point, she wanted Jake to be dependent on her. Samir was her target, and by him calling and leaning on Sydney threatened that dependency.

"Miss Lawyer, I know you think I go out of the way just to antagonize you, but it was an oversight. I'm trying to get a meeting tonight in my apartment at nine o'clock to hear the translations of these documents we just picked up. Sydney will bring his translator, and if you can manage, I'd like to meet with you earlier to go over some plans I have."

"It's not in my character to be alone in a man's room like you're suggesting."

"Miss Coker, I respect your position on these scruples, but what we review tonight must be in absolute secrecy. Do you know of a place of privacy suitable to you?"

Jake, being on the phone, could not see her look up and roll her eyes with a show of exasperation. "What time do you want me there?"

"Seven o'clock is fine."

The barrister's response about being alone with Jake opened his mind to the small world she lived in. Was her reservation from religious scruples, or was it something about him?

Eric arrived at the bank on time. Samuel drove away and returned to his duties. After placing the six sacks of rough diamonds in his briefcase, he was ready to meet with the lawyer.

On the way to his studio apartment, Eric was asked, "How big is your place where you and your wife live?"

"We have two bedrooms with a garage parking space, but moving to a bigger place is on our agenda."

The conversation continued while they drove to Jake's humble one-room, studio apartment.

"What's the duration of your marriage?"

"Two years, Sir. Are you married?"

Eric knew Jake would be visiting Manchester at his sister's invitation, and to know his marital status was important to him at this point. He was concerned about his sister's aggressive style and didn't want her to get hurt.

"No, never been married, not even close to it. Not to say, of course, I haven't thought of it. My frenetic world is too restrictive to have a competitor by my side. The energy that drives me would make another person unhappy."

"Mr. James, your outlook will change when you meet the right person."

"Yes, that's what my mother and father say. It hasn't happened yet."

"How long will you be in the UK?"

Jake pondered his question, then answered as if he were talking to himself.

"Eric, right now I live in a world of extremes. Tomorrow, my fate could be the dungeon at the Tower or ensconced as an icon for justice. It's for time alone to do its bidding with my fortune here in London. To answer your question—I don't know."

When they pulled into the driveway, he said to Eric, "I want you to see where I live. Come on inside."

Jake never lived in an ostentatious way and never needed a lifestyle to match his portfolio. He carried his briefcase packed full of illegal contraband and copied Arabic documents. Eric carried the two cases from Africa, and upon entering, he looked with dismay at the apartment he had chosen to stay in.

"Sir, pardon me for saying so, but it's apparent you're a person of means, so why are you living here in this place?"

Jake paused to answer. He didn't want Eric to know his story after arriving in London and knew that the best way to obscure truth was to tell the truth. He would obfuscate the real reason why he chose to live here by using certain known traits about his life.

"Eric, I maintain a simple modified stoic lifestyle. There are two ancient philosophies still in practice today, Stoicism and Epicureanism. The former held the belief that what is best in life comes from self-denial. The latter believed the opposite: that pleasure without restrictions gives man his greatest utopia. My pleasure in life is adventure and challenge rather than what comes from physical comforts. Thus, I have my humble dwelling."

"You're over my head, Mr. James. You need to talk to my sister, she's the brainy one."

"You have just as many cells up there as your sister, the difference being that yours fire in a different pattern and are used in a different way. Someday, I'm sure you'll understand this."

He paid Eric well. Before he left, Jake reminded him of the trip to Manchester.

Chapter 7

Law and Conscience

JAKE HAD SCHEDULED A MEETING at his one-room, studio apartment for eight-thirty and would include Siana, Sydney, and his Arabic-translator friend. Siana agreed to arrive at seven as requested by Jake. It was his intent that she be informed of all his activities since arriving in London in view that she was now his lawyer and had gone out of her way to arrange secure housing. Action taken in their combined efforts to secure the terrorists' papers made this meeting necessary.

It was four o'clock when Jake reclined on the sofa for a short nap and soon found himself awakened by a knock on the door. Glancing at his watch, he realized the alarm failed and the lawyer was five minutes early for their meeting. He made himself presentable, slipped on his shoes and opened the door. Staring at Jake was a frozen, stone image showing displeasure of having agreed to meet under these the circumstances. Jake was first to speak.

"Good evening, Miss Coker, May I take your case?"

The lawyer was now showing a tetchy, half-forced smile.

"Good evening. You already know this is not a comfortable time of my life coming here with just the two of us present. I want you to understand it's because you have a connection with my father this meeting is happening."

"Miss Barrister, you're something else. How does a person like you who is so erudite become so religious you can't be in the same room with a reputable opposite-gendered party on business?"

"Mr. James, you have a way of being frank. Will you please get on with the purpose of my being here?"

"Right…well, we do have a lot to go over before Sydney arrives, so let's start. I'm glad you're here because I want you to know my whole story since arriving at Gatwick. The reason for closing the shades is because a lot of contraband is on the table."

The lawyer's face glared with apprehension. Her deep blue eyes scanned the room like she was reading the body language of a defendant under interview, or a prosecuting attorney poised to establish an argument in court.

"Already knowing part of your story doesn't augur for a good night."

"Miss Barrister, what I tell you tonight is confidential. After I discovered the diamonds in the case inside my hotel room, I went to the lost baggage department of the airline searching for my own luggage. Upon its retrieval, I returned to my room and found inside the case a key to a locker in Wimbledon. Since the key was part of this bungled smuggling operation, I drove to Wimbledon, and using the key I found in my luggage, I took from a storage locker three packages totaling five hundred thousand pounds in British currency. This was a payment intended for smuggled diamonds. All of it is stored in my deposit box at the bank. I have with me here tonight the diamonds for examination, and this is the rest of my story."

The lawyer, on an innocent level, wanted to use Jake to get to Samir, her father's nemesis, and Jake's motive in his show-and-tell was to give the big picture of what he intended to do with the contraband hoping to get her on board with the project. Everything was going well with the lawyer's plans, until now. Jake keeping the diamonds was over the top, but he didn't go out of the way to acquire them, but stolen currency was another matter she didn't bargain for. This news of the currency tweaked her plan too much in the wrong direction.

She interrupted Jake with a burst of emotion.

"Mr. James, you're like a thunderous cloud raining on me the floods of your dangerous world! First, it was the diamonds, now it's money from a locker belonging to terrorists, and you're attempting to put me in the middle of it. You're bad news for me right now. You sure know how to stir things up, don't you? I'm a member of the legal community in this country and will not jeopardize my position by becoming a party to your wealth from these terrorists, even if it is a Robin Hood scheme to benefit others. I already crossed the line when I helped you copy those documents from the post office."

Deep serious strain covered her face. Heavy silence like the stillness of night enclosed both of them. Piercing the cold blanket of hush were unexpected conciliatory words from Jake.

I apologize for pushing my agenda without considering your feelings in these legal matters. I tend to see only what energizes me. I'm not a lawyer, but there is such a thing as the spirit of the law. I find myself looking at the spirit of the law leaning in my favor. In my case, it seizes the higher ground by taking a more noble position than the austere, cold letter of the law. I will let the letter of the law judge me after I carry out the spirit of the law, and when my peers judge me, I will call as my witnesses those who have received help, who otherwise have no help."

The barrister was impressed with Jake's analytical skills outside his formal training in science and engineering.

"Sir, your eloquence expresses in all practical terms true justice in your case; however, the law doesn't allow individuals to determine or interpret the spirit of the letter. The law itself leaves this for those who adjudicate at the bench."

"Miss Coker, since you belong to the esteemed legal community, are there times when breaking the law justifies its violation when doing so saves the lives of others?"

The lawyer suddenly found herself in conflict. She was a person who saw most issues as arbitrarily black or white—her religious faith demanded it. Now, someone with intellectual prowess was putting into argumentation the centerpiece of her faith—that she was called to help the downtrodden.

"Mr. James, You're too philosophical and idealistic. Those who engage in such actions must respond to their own moral conscience within the context of a singular issue. Law is for the governance of the whole of society—one size fits all. The bottom line is, for society to function, everyone must come under the rule of one standard set of laws without any exceptions."

Any reservation the lawyer had about coming to Jake's apartment, had now evaporated. Jake saw her as a force to be reckoned with in a court of law. She was articulate and could think fast on her feet.

"Miss Coker, if I'm too philosophical and idealistic, then your expectations of the legal system are too optimistic, and perhaps even too simplistic. Though there is one law for everyone, not everyone receives equal treatment under our system, the inequality being the lack of skill in legal counsel and the amount of money going toward the defense. There's no parity of justice between wealthy and poor defendants. The poor suffer from the ignominious inconsistency of justice in our Western legal system."

"Mr. James, you must respond to your own conscience. I'm not here to defend the inequities of the legal system, but to tell you what the law says."

"Madam, the jurors are the ones who decide the guilt or innocence of the person standing in the dock. Their verdict is the highest final voice in the court and most permanent in the system of Western Jurisprudence; however, there is a higher court. This is the one most supreme that gives the final lasting impact on society in the adjudication of guilt and innocence: it is the verdict history gives from the jurors of the masses.

"I'll leave it for history to render my vindication in keeping the contraband for the greater good because in the end, this is the only verdict that matters. I'm willing to come under the charges of legal indiscretions and suffer the pains of guilt, if posthumously, the voices of the masses record for history the verdict of my innocence.

"Counselor, by waxing eloquent I sound like a Nathan Hale. But you don't know him in history, do you?"

"Oh, but I do know him as a figure of history, and I'm afraid you're going to end up at the end of a rope as he did."

"Miss Coker, Nathan Hale was a citizen of a colony ruled by England. He chose to violate English law to benefit the greater good. He considered his acts innocent and noble. A British military court judged him guilty. Counselor let the record speak for itself. The verdict of history is what makes his gallant acts of guilt nobler than the King's law. The innocence of guilt is for history to decide. Time alone is the arbitrator of final justice and is still the friend of ultimate truth. The double-edged sword in the hand of the blindfolded woman of justice cuts both ways: one side cuts for the judicial system in a speedy trial; the other side makes its swath later in history to correct the wrongs of the first verdict. The second swing of the sword of justice takes longer than the first because it's a verdict from the masses."

Jake could see deep conflict settling over the barrister. Her argument was from a legal perspective, his a moral one in that keeping the diamonds was for the greater good. Both were on opposite tracks. Jake was defending the hill where she should be standing, speaking and acting on behalf of the needy, the less fortunate.

"Mr. James, you make plausible arguments for history, but our concerns here are for today."

"Jake stared into the deep blue eyes of the skilled barrister, saying, "I operate on a high level of intuition about unspoken motives and positions of thought. However, I'm wrong about you. I'd hoped for a commitment from you to a cause of justice and retribution for your country."

She was quick to respond.

"I can support you for a cause of retribution. This is something I already did by crossing over the line in providing a place for copying the terrorists' documents. However, the cause of justice, as you frame it, by exchanging contraband diamonds for a hospital is your burden alone."

Jake's arguments in defense of his position of keeping the diamonds out of the hands of smugglers impressed the barrister. In the fray of polemics, two voices were knocking at the door of her conscience: guilt over participation in printing the documents taken from the post office and her use of Jake to bring down Samir. Beneath the legs of her conscience, she could feel the movement of her feet stepping onto a tightrope.

"Miss Coker, though we disagree, I respect you as a lawyer of high admirable principles; however, I think it's best we put closure to our meeting for the time being. I bid you good night. Again, thank you for arranging my sleeping quarters in this secure area."

A sudden cold blanket was cast over the lawyer. Reluctant to come to Jake's place, she now didn't want to leave. For the first time, she saw this man in a different light and understood why her father befriended him. She admired his resourceful, quick-witted intellect; however, being a barrister and trained to read body language of judges, clients, and witnesses in court, she failed to see her own: she was succumbing to his innocent prowess of persuasion. *In the flash of a moment, as if she had been in a daze, she gripped herself with the thought, why am I vacillating with this person?*

It was evident to Jake she was not ready to end the conversation; she enjoyed the polemics of challenge in her special field. Nevertheless, she moved with the flow of the momentum he had created and prepared to leave.

"Please call Sydney and tell him to cancel our meeting tonight."

He expected her to refuse his request but she didn't. The lawyer moved to the front door, turned and looked at Jake. Her face now carried a friendlier, softer tone, one with a message of loneliness. Then, she spoke her last words of the evening.

"Mr. James, you missed your calling. Your adversarial nature and mental acumen equip you to be a brilliant lawyer, especially in court."

With his emotional energy depleted, Jake welcomed his darkened room. *Tomorrow, he thought, a new person will arise when his feet touch the floor.*

Chapter 8

The Ebony Curio

AT SEVEN THE FOLLOWING MORNING, Jake's phone rang. He gave a slow, deep-voice response to the caller.

"Hello."

"Good morning, Mr. James."

The voice of the lawyer he heard was a doused blanket of ice water snapping him out of his stupor. The full force of electrical synapses rushed to his aid. He registered astonishment.

"My...this is a surprise, what can I do for you?" Jake's interest was heightened with the caller's lingering pause. He waited while the one whose voice he heard gained courage to continue. "Perhaps, we can continue where we left off last night, provided the contraband and money from the locker at Wimbledon are not in my possession or control. Otherwise, I'm available to help."

Jake thought negotiations were in the air. Now acting as a client, she wanted to plea her case down to a lesser offense.

"This being the case," he said, "let's reschedule for tonight and complete the agenda of translating the documents with Sydney and his translator friend."

"I'll see if Sydney can arrange this. I'll be there at seven, and Sydney can arrive with his friend at nine o'clock."

After hanging up, he knew the lawyer had done two things after serious thought: moved closer to a gray line with the law, and exposed herself to a dangerous involvement with smugglers.

Awkwardness was on display from the start when the lawyer arrived. For Jake, it was important she knew everything in the event her interest reached the point of becoming involved with the hospital project in Africa.

"Miss Coker, you don't have to handle anything here in the form of contraband. These are here tonight just to show you the potential they have in doing something good in your country"

He took one of the bags of uncut diamonds from the briefcase and placed it on the table. By the time he finished emptying the sack of diamonds on the table surface, her tense expression showed a state of conflict over right and wrong. Wrong was being in same room with smuggled diamonds, right was the knowledge that contraband diamonds could help the people of her father's land.

"Miss Coker, it's my intent to return the value of these diamonds back to your country in the form of a hospital in the honor of my grandfather."

She sat peering at the wall, then turned and faced Jake. "These diamonds are a part of a system supporting terrorism. I'm fearful for my country and the potential there is for the expansion of this evil through these kinds of people who will stop at nothing to impose and sponsor their violent cause."

She stopped speaking, stared at the diamonds once more to get courage to say what would follow. "Money can buy people if it comes in the right amount. There are a lot of diamonds and money with you here in London. All you have to do is take it and walk away. Sydney and I can do nothing to stop you. Does it tempt you, Mr. James? Does it move you to the threshold of keeping it just to show you're smarter than others? How do you feel inside with your human frailty and the temptation to keep the contraband? Do you feel good about having the power this money gives you?"

For the first time, the lawyer saw anger in the eyes of the engineer. Up to this point, he had shown nothing but a thick skin of impervious steel with her barbs and nuanced sarcasm.

"Miss Coker, your predisposition toward me is egregious. It's apparent something about me confuses you. You're no longer acting on behalf of your father. Now, it's all about you. You have come here tonight to disprove your father's report of me. Apparently, people in your past have left emotional scars on you, and now you tag me as one of them. The court you put me in doesn't allow rebuttal because you're the judge and jury. Are you now ready to pronounce my guilt? Your bias toward me is quite glaring. Is your involvement with me here in London because of your father or a design to get the kind of reinforcement you want or need? It's in your interest I flee with the contraband and money so I can fulfill your expectations. Only then, you'll gain freedom from your state of indecision of who I am. Miss Coker, I gamble in the real world of high finance in land development at home, but your stakes are higher than mine because you gamble with what's inside you, the soul of what you are. You are gambling on what you want me to become. Miss Coker, your gamble in my taking everything and running is a game you can't win. You fail to see the picture of my grandfather's history in your country and my financial worth at home. Please do what you do best: be analytical. Separate me from your prejudices, and become someone who'll help your country."

After venting, Jake now appeared approachable.

114

"You're right, I'm in a state of confusion about you. I can no longer be your legal counsel, just an interested party. I'll admit temptation is with me to step over the line and commit myself to an overriding moral principle for a just cause in your plan to build a hospital with the contraband. However, I'll not yield to this, but will try to keep my personal history from interfering with what you do to help others."

Jake could see by her body language that she wanted to talk about herself.

"Mr. James, there's some truth in what you say about my prejudice. I think the picture you paint is unfair. I want to tell you about myself. My father is a Creole, as you already know. He comes from a proud lineage whose ancestry reaches all the way back to the time of the settlers from Nova Scotia. It was the period of history when the British intercepted slave ships on the high seas and resettled them in the Freetown colony. The colony became the beacon of Western education with the efforts of the Anglican Mission. Some became as British in culture and education as the British themselves. They were the doctors, lawyers, and teachers of the colony. After my father graduated from Fourah Bay University, he did his post-graduate work in England earning his master's degree. He met my mother in England, they later married and went to live in Freetown. My father was in the educational system until he joined my grandfather's import-export business and became one of the most successful businessmen in the country. My mother and father spent their time together between London and Freetown.

"My older brother was their only child until I came along. My mother gave birth to me at the age of forty in a London hospital. I was the child of a British citizen; this made me a member of two countries and two cultures. Two years ago, my devoted mother passed away. So you see, I'm a person of two worlds: half Creole and half English. I find myself trying to live in these two worlds at the same time. Both histories of me have common religious and educational backgrounds. My father's religious side comes from the Anglican Christian faith, my mother's, also the Church of England. The churches throughout the borders of the old colony reflect the more simple times of those early colonial years. History books must never exclude this proud past of my people. The British should consider their transplanted Western influence in Freetown with the Creole community as one of their greatest successes. In addition, the Anglican Mission must be recognized and credited for its expansion of faith and education.

"You are already familiar with the other part of me, my mother's side. This is your world. Your world is simpler; it has less conflict than mine because it's so singular. Freetown accepted me as one of their own. In England, the universities I attended I competed with the best and brightest. I performed as well and better than most academically; yet, full acceptance into their esoteric inner circle eluded me. I heard their classroom idealism, but it never matched on-the-street fulfillment.

"This is why I have such hesitation about you. When I see you, I see someone who accepts half of what I am—your half."

Her emotional treatise in defense of her reservations about Jake had created a quiet, solemn, suspended atmosphere. Then he spoke.

"When I lived among the people of your country I never saw in them your attitude about my being white. Now, when I meet someone who is half of my world, using your

116

description, we have conflict over my whiteness. Miss Coker, do you know what being white is?"

A flash of anger stiffened the face of the lawyer.

"Sir, please don't patronize me on whiteness. If you were black using the term black instead of white, I would be just as upset as you see me now. I know what white is. A loving and devoted white woman gave birth to me. For twenty-six years, she was my life. Today, I'm a walking stealth white person with enough color inside me to catch people off guard in the way they act and respond."

"Miss Coker, the world is an ocean. If one uses the right bait, they can catch any kind of fish they want to find. The problem is you want to catch a certain type of fish to reinforce how you want to think; therefore you use the kind of bait those fish feed on. Right now, you're fishing in my waters trying to find my weakness, but the big fish isn't taking your bait, is he? Are you successful in finding me off guard, Miss Coker?"

This was the first time the lawyer had ever spoken her feelings in this way to someone outside her comfort zone. It was also the first time anyone ever addressed her in such a sharp and direct accusatory manner. She didn't know what to say. She felt good about releasing her bottled-up feelings, yet she was offended by the truth of what he said.

"To answer your question, I've not been successful in finding you off guard—not yet."

"But you expect to when I'm not looking?"

"My experience and training tell me I must prepare myself to expect anything from people I don't know."

"You allow color alone to define what you are, and by your own definition, you don't belong anywhere. Instead of defining yourself by what is on the inside, you permit your perception of what others believe to be your reality."

117

Jake detected she was struggling to deal with her religious scruples that were in conflict with her resentments of the past. Her compartmentalized life functioned well by living in her bubble, but his invasion of her space forced her to look in the mirror she had kept covered.

"I'm in an unfair position in this debate because my response is from an emotional history, and yours is from the argumentation of reason."

After she said this, Jake felt he had pushed himself too near her inner emotional fortress and should retreat to neutral ground.

"Tonight may be my evening to use logic because you've come with nothing more than a strong will to lift the cover from suppressed hurt. This is commendable; I await my defeat from you on a different topic at a later time."

"Sometimes, in my quiet inner self, I look objectively where I am and wonder if I've become guilty of the same prejudices directed toward me in earlier years. I'm a religious person, and for me to cope with inner conflicts of my past, I find people of faith better performers in meeting my expectations. The difference between the Church and State is the State attempts to establish equality by written law, and the Church uses the higher standard of the law of love. The Church teaches a transcendent idealism that comes from the heart and works in real life. It's the highest model that Blacks and Whites can live under, especially, people like me. Because my world is so macrocosmic, I need the church to see the details. The details of life make life worth living, Mr. James."

When she said the word details, a quickening happened inside Jake. *This was where they were different, he thought. She looked for details in life; he searched for the landscape, the distant dream. Things up close made her happy; what could not be touched, but seen from afar, gave him purpose.*

Siana stopped talking, stared off into space as if a strong sedative just took effect. Her energy now drained, she sat silent and alone within herself. This was the first time she ever made a torturous, emotional journey with such incisive, articulated discovery in verbal form. She had described in her own words the inner struggles of her past in front of an active listener outside her emotional fortress: someone who was white and not in her church. This placed validation on the credibility of her statements. She had forced herself through the constraints of mental and emotional surgery. At this point, Jake became fond of her name, Siana. It carried the outside aura of her internal goodness.

It was a time to talk while they waited for Sydney to arrive. They were two people with baggage and hurt from two different worlds. Jake's came from negative reinforcement of behaviors derived from being a hyperactive, impulsive child and teenager; hers came from being exposed to racial hypocrisy in academia. His experience drove him from the Church; her experience made her dependent on her faith.

Jake took a step into memory that he rarely visited.

"The details I remember in my life about religion are hard pews and the monotone voice of the preacher invading my inner world of dreaming while waiting for the benediction. I was a good dreamer. Sometimes I acted on my dreams, like the time when I was a twelve-year-old doing a home science project for extra credit in my science class. The objective of my project was to hatch fertilized chicken eggs with a self-designed incubator that created a constant temperature required for egg hatching. I devised a box with a warming system using light bulbs. Temperature control came from ventilation. At the end of the incubation period, the hatching chicks inside the eggs chirped as they broke the shells from inside with their beaks.

"Life never moved fast enough for me, and I always pushed anything along at a faster pace. At the age of twelve, I thought it was unnecessary for these hatching chicks to struggle. I took two of the hatching eggs with beaks poking through the shells and placed them apart from the others. I peeled the shell barrier from around these two struggling chicks. The released chicks stopped moving and chirping. They died, and those I left to struggle by themselves, lived. I looked at the dead chicks and learned a big lesson: the chirping heard from inside the shells of the hatching eggs was not a call for outside intervention; it was a signal life was on its way.

"To help somebody who is struggling to come into life, we must know the difference between the call for help and the announcement of life. Miss Coker, I'm in your path to cause you to struggle, and I choose not to help release you like the hatching chicks by running away or changing from what I am. You alone must break the shell standing between you and life in the bigger world. The chirping I hear from inside you is a sound announcing that life wants to come out."

Looking wounded and subdue, she came back at Jake more as a client than a barrister. "You offer a big challenge for me. You're a person of many talents. Tonight, you've combined with your adversarial nature the roles of psychologist and preacher."

"I'm far from being the latter." Jake placed the sack of diamonds on the table back inside his briefcase.

Sydney arrived with his translator at nine o'clock and introduced his Arabic-interpreter friend. Each of them took a pair of vinyl gloves. Sydney's young friend, who was a student at the university, was like a member of his own family. He appeared to be fluid and capable of his assigned task. The top of the table contained all the copies of the terrorists' documents. They would soon learn their efforts in securing these documents by breaking the law were justified.

Every page showed Arabic writing. Each sat listening to the verbal translations with fixed eyes staring into space. Jake had a tape recorder for the record, so if review were necessary at a later point he could access the translation. The translations of the documents were tedious. Everyone took notes. They were full of names of individuals in Freetown and London who gave money to support terrorism. The documents also cited on-going cell activities in different places in Europe. Samir, Mr. Coker's nemesis, was the leader in Freetown. Catatonic stillness filled the room.

The language was structured in such a way that the average person would miss its real meaning, a form of steganography—only those looking for hidden meaning would understand it. This required the translator to re-read the difficult passages.

Sydney was first to speak. "If the two of you will excuse me, I'll take my friend home. I'll be back soon." Each expressed appreciation to the translator for his work.

After Sydney left, the barrister regained her role as legal counsel. "The police must be given these documents as soon as possible. This is an unbelievable cache of evidence; it needs to be in their hands. It will serve to thwart their operations on a broad scale."

"You're right, but we first must take action in a way that will indict those in smuggling operations and divert suspicions away from me as the person in possession of the contraband."

The lawyer wanted closure on the whole affair fearing that time was essential in processing what was found at the post office. Jake saw the need to capitalize on what they had found to bring havoc on the inner workings of loyalties within the network.

The lone piece of paper from the snakeskin was upside down on the table. It read *Freetown Curio Store*. The paper had been in plain view throughout the ordeal of listening to the translations of the documents that described the terrorists' activities. Each time Jake's eyes scanned the tabletop for another page for the translator to read, the words had distracted him. It was like a pinprick irritation. After Sydney and his friend left the apartment, the image kept passing in front of him, like an old broken phonograph record.

Jake still sat at the table, and like a magnet, his eyes focused on the word, *curio*. A door unlocked with a cold rushing wind sweeping through his mind; all he could do was utter a whisper, "The curios."

The two curios that came with the contraband luggage were under his bed where he had put them.

"Miss Coker," he said, "I want us to examine a curio that came in the smugglers' luggage case."

He left her sitting at the table, went to the bedside and pulled from underneath one of the carvings. He looked over at the lawyer whose eyes had followed him.

"The deviant mind thinks more clearly and deeply in his act of deceit than most other people. To beat him you must think as he thinks. Doesn't your Bible say, 'They are wise in their own craftiness?'"

"Mr. James," she retorted in a facetious manner, "since you know the criminal mind so well, I can use you to help me decipher truth from fiction with some of my clients."

"Miss Coker, I'd planned a career in the legal profession at one time. I was always a cogent polemist. I could think fast on my feet, but the more thought I gave it the more I realized it could never fulfill my expectations. I would be required to work in a legal system set up like a city on the edge of a desert with just one gas station in that part of town. The station would serve only those who were required to make a certain journey across the barren region. If the driver failed to get a full tank of gas at that station, he never reached the other side. This was the only station in town where they rarely filled the gas tank all the way, and those who did receive a full tank were people who had a lot of money to pay for more than one gas server. The people who pumped the gas were the ones who discouraged me about that end of town. Sometimes, I wondered if certain gas servers should switch with the drivers doing the desert trip, but giving them what others got: just half a tank for the journey. I never wanted to work in that part of town; a lifetime of pumping legal gas was too confining and menial for me. However, I always gave the lawyers credit for performing the role of a necessary evil. There were exceptions, of course, but for me, I wanted to work at the other end of town where there was plenty of fuel and a lot of life."

"You know how to make a lawyer feel good about herself, don't you?"

"Well, my adversarial nature potentiates my outspokenness, and some say this is my trademark."

"You live up to your trademark—that's for sure. There's a difference between outspokenness and inappropriate rudeness."

"I did say there were exceptions, didn't I?"

"To continue your metaphor, let me say that the honorable thing is to know who deserves the ride all the way across the desert so the pump server can work hard enough to get a full tank of gas for the trip. While we're on this analogy, Mr. James, when this is over, and if you happen to end up in the driver's seat for the desert run, and I'm the person pumping the gas for you, I'm not quite sure you'll get a full tank from me."

"Miss Coker, you've come to life here tonight."

"Your unabashed rudeness brings me to anger. Do you treat others like this?"

"Just those I like."

These words were Jake's peace offering. They seemed to work. She became silent.

"Miss Coker, let's settle our differences on this subject by doing a wager on this piece of wood. I'll give you two hundred pounds if there's no contraband inside this curio."

The lawyer looked up at Jake with a blank stare, as if what he said was out of place.

"Now, how much will you give me if there is something inside this curio besides wood?"

"Have we come here to gamble? I can't believe this creation of drama for your benefit at my expense."

"Miss Coker, the only expense you're out is what you may lose in the wager, and besides, is there a difference between our games, the one here on the table, and the other one going on in real life? It's all a gamble—isn't it?"

"There's a big difference. The one here tonight requires money—the other requires my life and future. I prefer not to gamble with either."

"Miss Barrister, you must offer something to make our life here at my place interesting. Come on, what do you wager?"

"I'll participate in your vanity, and if I lose, I'll bring over from my kitchen a complete West African dinner, but I think you have an ace up your sleeve."

"I'll accept your offer, but I prefer one at your residence." *Something cold and awkward was in the atmosphere—this engineer was pushing himself too far into her domain*

"Mr. James, you're beyond protocol and overreaching."

"Miss Coker, people who know me say I'm an iconoclast and have a longer reach than others."

At this point, Jake could tell she was uneasy with their dialogue with Sydney returning soon.

"Please roll your dice so we can see who wins this gamble."

The ebony curio was a beautiful piece of work. The carving came from the tree prized in tropical Africa for cabinetry and carvings. The inner heart of the tree was the section that produced the darker wood. The ebony head was jet black, standing about nine inches in height with a soft felt material covering the pedestal end of the carving. A knife served to peel back the felt; underneath, it revealed a smooth wooden plug hardly noticeable.

"Miss Coker, please bring me a large cutting knife from the kitchen."

With the curio upside down in his lap, he used his shoe as a hammer with a large knife to dislodge the wooden plug. When it came loose, the plug broke in pieces. Chipped-wood fragments fell into his hand after turning it over. Inside, was a packed cotton substance. A smaller knife served to loosen the packing. He took the carving with both hands and allowed the inside contents of rough uncut diamonds to pour from the hollowed-out cavity onto the tabletop. The smugglers had performed a skillful job in boring out the internal section of the dense, heavy wood to house a large quantity of contraband. The lawyer, frozen in hush, looked at the intercepted diamonds on the table, saw Jake place the ebony head, the snakeskin letter, and the key that opened the locker at Wimbledon inside the case with the false bottom that he had carried through customs. A plan had been born. The luggage piece given to Jake to carry through customs would be returned with the compliments of a different kind of justice. He went over and stood alongside the lawyer at the table.

Jake played his hand with the drama that presented itself. The lawyer was mesmerized at what she saw, and Jake seized the opportunity to move her closer to his objective of enlisting her help in building a hospital in her father's land.

''Miss Coker, please select for me fifteen of the smaller diamonds and we'll make them a part of the plant operation.''

She remained fixed in a state of awe. Her fingers lifted, one-by-one, fifteen of the smaller diamonds from the tabletop. From her hand she poured them into Jake's, saying, "Mr. James, your greatest pleasure here tonight is in tempting me to fall into your crazy deviant world."

She watched him place the diamonds inside the contraband case alongside the other items. Later, he would complete the package of the sting operation by adding two thousand pounds of British notes taken from the locker at Wimbledon. The plans for justice on his terms were in motion.

The lawyer saw the big picture Jake was painting. Her reticent nature was becoming emboldened to flirt with the dangerous world he was creating. The chances of bringing down Samir were looking better.

"Miss Coker, I'll add these diamonds from the curio here on the table to those in my safe deposit box at the bank. Their value will go back to your country to build the hospital.

"Now, Miss Barrister, when will you pay up on your gambling loss?"

"How can you be so cavalier after finding these diamonds? The scene of diamonds pouring from the ebony carving leaves me gasping for air, and you ask me to cover my loss? How can your emotions vacillate like this, unless this is the ace up your sleeve by planting the contraband just for your entertainment?"

"Miss Coker, you're much too serious and have too many suspicions about me. You're dealing with me as if I'm one of your criminal clients."

"You're not far from being one, and you won't even know that until the law nicks you."

Chapter 9

The Sting

WHEN SYDNEY RETURNED, the diamonds were still on the table in plain view. After hearing Jake's account of finding the diamonds in the ebony curio, Sydney walked over to the table, took a fistful of rough diamonds in his hand, and with laser-focused eyes watched them pour back onto the tabletop. Then, looking at Jake, he asked, "What are you going to do with these?"

The Lawyer and Sydney stood silent showing body language like they were passing a verdict of guilt. Penetrating eyes shot darts of suspicion. What Jake saw in physical gestures spoke louder than Sydney's question. The room had taken on an atmosphere lacking oxygen.

The lawyer had already been told how the diamonds would be used. Now she had fled to Sydney's corner, aligning herself with his look of suspicion. But this was the barrister's calculated move. She needed the support of both men to achieve her objective. Jake was incisive and knew what she was about—Sydney had to stay on board, or he might lose interest in helping in the project at hand. What Jake didn't realize was her intent to use both of them to get at Samir, and was walking a high wire to do it.

This was theater for the three of them. Each had an interest in what was going down: Sydney, a patriot fighting corruption in his country from London; the barrister, interested in taking down Samir, her father's nemesis; and

Jake, whose idealism was pushing him on the wheels of adventure and excitement. Each had self interest for a designed result, and because each could achieve what they wanted by working together, they sought common ground with each other.

"Sydney, these diamonds will be stored in my bank and returned to the land of their origin where they'll help establish a hospital."

Upon hearing this, Jake saw Sydney softening, saying, "That will be a noble act, a much-needed service in my country." Jake was insightful enough to know he should avoid telling Sydney that the barrister already knew his intentions with the diamonds. When Sydney glanced away momentarily, the lawyer gave a gentle nod showing approval of his discretion.

In normal fashion, Jake took charge. "Our job isn't finished just because of what we have found in the documents from the post office. We need to extend a far-reaching arm that hurts those connected to the luggage piece I carried through customs. Sydney, we need your people to plant the luggage case holding evidence. It will incriminate and expose the whole operation of smuggling here in London and Freetown. We want this to go down showing a picture of the Middle East agents themselves taking the contraband case and blaming others for their actions. The best path to follow is to plant the luggage in the boot of one of the cars the agents drive, then apprise the police in a way that will not lead them to us as the informants. The police must arrive soon after the plant or our scheme will fail."

Jake continued. "If the police can find this luggage case with part of the contraband inside the boot of their car, it'll serve to break up this cell and do damage to what is going on in Freetown."

At this point, the lawyer became a vocal contributor.

"Mr. James, as smart as you are in planning this operation, it makes me wonder if you have a former life in these activities. Your plan to frame these men with this plant is a stretch beyond the law of mathematical probability, and to be upfront with you, I must say you are pushing yourself into a corner if it fails. However, as much as I hate to say it, I will admit it's a brilliant response, and if successful, it could destroy their cell network. But I hope you do know that the agents are as good as dead if you pull this off."

"Miss Coker, you sound like a defense attorney you are. Remember, if this is the case, they'll lose interest in you and your family."

When Jake cited the safety of her family being the result of a successful operation, she never again spoke of violent outcomes.

Sydney responded: "As a result of the information you've given, we already know where two of them are staying and the vehicle they drive. When I leave here tonight, I'll pick up a couple of people and check out their neighborhood. We need to know the area well before we act on a plan."

Sydney left for his project of casing the smugglers' neighborhood leaving the lawyer and Jake alone. The barrister had a dog in this fight—it was Samir. He was her target and she was getting in deeper as events rolled on.

"Mr. James, I've already gone on record that I'll have nothing to do with the contraband you have in your possession. This is your project alone. However, you will need someone to deliver those copies taken from the post office to the police at the appropriate time, and I'll volunteer for this. In spite of my being a defense attorney, I have some credibility with several ranking officers. When this is all over, I hope I'll still have some left."

She took the copied terrorists' documents, placed them inside her briefcase. Jake carried her case as the two of them walked out together where her driver waited.

"Mr. James, I left an envelope on your table in your kitchen. It's for you to keep. It may or may not be important to you."

He gave his goodnight farewell, went back inside to welcome the wonderful world of darkness, the kind one slept under. He laid himself down on a welcomed bed in a darkened room while his rushing world came to a stop; everything became calm and silent. Then, he remembered the other curio carving under his bed. Getting half-dressed, he reached underneath the bed fumbling for the carving. His hand came across something sharp, pulled it out, and found it to be the unattractive shell necklace Ann had found unwrapped in her luggage; he remembered placing it under the bed earlier. It came to him that these shells may be more than just a cheap necklace. He carried the necklace and ebony carving over to the kitchen table, broke one of the shells using his shoe as a hammer. His suspicions proved true: the shells contained rough diamonds. He proceeded to break each shell and pick from the crushed pieces the rough diamonds. When he had finished, there were two mounds: worthless shards of shells and diamonds in the rough. Each individual shell had contained diamonds sealed with a substance the same color as the inner part of the shell. Revealed again was the extent of the smugglers' clever ingenuity. Ann did carry onboard a package in her luggage, and when the pilferer found the shells, he thought them worthless and left them unwrapped in her case. Now, the picture of everything became clearer. Because of the need for contraband carriers who could make it through customs without detection, he and Ann had become candidates when they dealt with the same travel agent. The agent used the company, not to fly people about the world, but to move the commodity of illicit diamonds. This was why they were assigned seats together and had agents from his office right behind them. The second ebony carving was a repeat performance of the first without the attendance of the lawyer as a spectator. He put the diamonds in bags, placed them in his briefcase and stored everything underneath the sofa. In his possession were diamonds worth millions, yet they could not buy him a roadmap on how to get them back to Africa for his hospital project.

He turned off the lights, crawled under sheets and welcome the darkened room, reflecting on the events of the day. He had pulled into his world a bright and lonely person. Had he unduly influenced her to be part of his world? Could it be that the needs of two people were acting like magnets? *Was there something pulling them together to make decisions that lacked objective rational thought?*

It was seven o'clock in the morning when Jake got out of bed, dressed, and took his walk to a coffee shop three blocks from his apartment. The community was ethnically mixed and friendly. On a nearby corner was a church with an attached pre-school to serve the area. Traffic was beginning to move the masses to their job sites and businesses. This looked like his place at home, except the cars were on the wrong side of the street. It was what his eyes saw here that drove him to Africa to do something new and different.

Jake became introspective. What he had going on inside himself was an addiction. The more action and stimulation he experienced, the more he needed to keep going. It had become a vicious cycle. Like last night, he went out of his way to be adversarial with Siana, then the gambling thing. Everything funneled to conflict and challenge for the adventure of it. What he had read in books and literature told him he had the propensity to addictive behaviors of alcohol and drugs. He considered his home and grandfather to be his inoculations against those impairments. His grandfather, who spent a lot of time with him, raised his self-esteem by teaching him to play chess at the age of four. At six, he could beat most experienced adult players. When he enrolled in college, most of his family never thought he would complete the first year because of his impulsive erratic behaviors. They expected him to become a college dropout, a constant job changer. He was also sure some of his family even prayed he wouldn't become a bindlestiff. However, his grandfather believed in him. He remembered his grandfather telling him, "*Jacob, with your gifted intelligence and energy, you can be whatever you choose. You just have to want it enough to reach for it.*" The weight of his grandfather's shadow had given Jake an acceptable burden because it kept him from the pitfalls people like him stumbled into. Looking back, the weight of this burden had given him life.

Jake started walking back to his apartment knowing he had just gone through one of his special times of lows after an exhilarating high the day before. He had never learned to deal with this and abhorred the thought of medication. He learned this from his old-fashioned grandfather who was a doctor. Certain professionals had suggested he take medication for hyperactivity, impulsivity, and inattention. His grandfather always countered, saying, "All he needed was structure and one-on-one attention with limited television." He believed stimulation from electronics exacerbated his condition. Jake saw himself always calm and focused when around his grandfather.

133

He reached his apartment. The first thing his eyes came upon was the large envelope the lawyer had left the night before. He opened the envelope, took the contents out. It contained old, faded, black-and-white photos. He recognized his grandfather in each of the pictures. They were from the time when he was in Africa when he was about his age. The barrister knew something about his grandfather she was keeping from him. He placed the photos back inside the envelope. It was his decision to leave it with her to talk about when she was ready.

It was nine o'clock when someone came knocking at Jake's door. Upon opening it, a familiar greeting came from Miss Coker's driver, Samuel. "Cusha Pa." He held in his hands a large coffee and a package of buttered English muffins.

"These are compliments of Mommy Coker," he said.

"Where's your coffee?" Jake asked, knowing he had already eaten a couple of hours prior.

"Thank you, but I've already eaten," he replied.

Jake reflected on the culture of Sierra Leoneans. When a Sierra Leonean addressed a non-African with the usage of "Pa" for a man, and "Mommy" for a woman, it was a term rendered to give honor and respect. These terms of respect for the Africans extended just to the elderly, or people of significant position.

"Miss Coker asked me to give you this letter"

"Thank you, Samuel."

Inside the envelope, there was a short note in the lawyer's own handwriting, *"The coffee and muffin delivered by Samuel is a small peace offering for last night. After reading about people who display your characteristics, I find I'm the farmer type and you're the hunter, and knowing you,*

I'm sure you can guess what types of literature I reference. Siana."

Jake was more interested in her first-name signature than he was in what she said. He knew it was her way of taking the first step in his direction without conditions attached to it. Then he considered the substance of what she had written. He closed the note thinking to himself, yes, those kinds of books were in his library at home, books written to help people understand the issues of Attention Deficit Hyperactivity Disorder.

"Samuel, can you take me to the bank?"

At the bank, he placed all the diamonds in one of the safe deposit boxes. From the other box, he withdrew five-thousand pounds taken from the locker in Wimbledon for pending operations. Upon his return, he went inside his apartment, found a book to read, took off his shoes, and after reading a couple of hours, fell asleep.

Awakened with a loud knock, Jake looked at his watch, struggled to get to his feet, saying to the party at the door, "Just a minute!" He was barefoot with scruffy-looking clothes and uncombed hair as he hobbled over to open the door. Standing in front of him were Miss Coker and Sydney. They were trim and proper, and when they saw him, they stood speechless. The lawyer spoke first.

"Shall we come back at a later time?"

He knew she was just being polite. In spite of the way he looked and felt, he said what he thought she wanted to hear, so with the act of graciousness, he opened the door wider.

"Oh, come on in, please. Be seated while I freshen up a bit."

The cold water across his sleep-drawn face gave life, but when he raised his face into the mirror, he knew he was in need of something more than water. A few strokes over the hair with a brush helped. What he needed was confidence and some feet under his cranium. When he came out, he tried to be at his best.

"You'll have to pardon my shortcomings, this always happens to me when I take a nap in the afternoon."

He could see the lawyer was enjoying the scene. Jake thought he saw a slight twinkle of a smile in her eyes through his blurry ones. He sat on the bed with his bare feet being a prominent part of what he was, felt like he was a patient sitting on the cold table in the doctor's examination room with just enough hospital gown to cover himself while waiting for some kind of verdict from the doctor. Because they were reluctant to jump into conversation to give him a diagnosis, he thought his condition must be serious. The patient took the initiative.

"Did you bring me bad or good news? Something must be going down since both of you are here."

"Jake, I called you, but you didn't answer your phone, so I called Siana. She came right over and picked me up so we could talk with you about planting the case. My people found the location of the agents who drove the car with the license number you gave me. They have the street under surveillance. My opinion is the sooner we act, the greater the chance to bring everything off."

"Sydney, can you plant this piece of luggage in the boot of the car?"

"Yes, planting the luggage is the easy part; doing it without anyone seeing us is the problem."

"What about one o'clock in the morning?"

"If we do this, one in the morning is the best hour. I can get any good locksmith to open the boot in three minutes, but in these circumstances, everything has to be right for there to be success."

"What can we do to optimize our project of planting this luggage?"

Sydney paused in quiet thought. With wrinkled brow, he looked at Jake.

"Last night, the vehicle bearing the license number you gave me was parked on the opposite side of the street of their residence. If the car is on the same side of the street tonight, we can bring in a large commercial truck or van, and double-park alongside their car for what looks like roadside service. The large commercial truck will obstruct the view of their car from their vantage point across the street. If we have three minutes, we can open the boot and plant the luggage. After the boot is closed, and if no one sees us, we'll be home free. However, it could be bad for us if we're discovered, but this is the chance we have to take."

"Sidney, I like the way you are willing to live dangerously, and if you agree, I think you should be the person planting the case with gloves. When you finish with the plant, let Miss Coker know so she can contact the police with the evidence taken from the box. Then call me to confirm its completion. This is a plan we can work with, and with you in charge, it'll succeed. What about you, Miss Coker?"

"As I said before, I'm committed to just one thing: contact the police after the plant. Everything else is between the two of you."

The lawyer was true to her word. She would do the service of a courier by taking the copies of the contents of the post office box to the police, and in doing so would jeopardize her legal standing and reputation. Her focus was on a legal outcome, and Samir was in her sights.

137

Sydney excused himself, saying, "I need to make my contacts and arrangements for tonight. If their car is on the right side of the street, we can act on it. Get the luggage case ready to go!"

Jake slipped on latex gloves. Siana watched him wipe down the luggage case and the contents inside: fifteen small diamonds, two empty curios, snakeskin with its letter, and the key that opened the locker at Wimbledon. When she was not looking, he placed inside two thousand pounds taken from the locker. With the luggage case closed, a plastic bag served for its storage to prevent any fingerprints from touching it. Sydney would use gloves in the transfer. The project was no sooner finished when there was a knock on the door. It was Sydney returning.

"Everything's ready to go tonight at one o'clock in the morning. If the car is parked on the right side of the street for the operation, we'll go for it,"

The lawyer and Jake gave a sigh of relief—the operation was in motion. She already had in her possession the copied documents from the post office. Now, she was poised to deliver the final stroke at the police station.

"Remember Sydney, you and anyone who touches the case, or vehicle, must use gloves. We don't want your signature on the car or luggage."

Both left Jake's place showing serious purpose in their strides. He walked with them to the driveway, returned to his room to look at maps of the streets of London to study the area where the action would take place. He called a taxi to pick him up at midnight, set his alarm for eleven o'clock and went to bed for several hours of sleep.

The taxi arrived, he donned an overcoat and hat. Not shaving for several days gave further concealment. At this late hour of the evening, traffic was light on the roadway.

When the taxi turned down the street where Sydney said the car was located, the driver slowed. In the middle of the block, Jake saw the vehicle that drove away from the hotel the morning when the terrorists tore up his hotel room. It was on the side of the street that would move the operation forward. Twenty minutes remained until Sydney's crew would arrive. Jake gave the driver directions to pull around the block and let him out. The vehicle faded into distant darkness. Cold, damp blackness concealed him as a friend. He avoided streetlights, walked back to the corner of the block he just came from in the taxi. Near the corner, Jake moved into a shadowed recessed area to prevent detection from overhead lighting. It was a storefront corner building with an ad in the front window for take-out food. Part of the writing was in Arabic.

The quiet, deserted streets allowed Jake to hear the sound of a barking dog in the distance. An occasional car drove by. The neighborhood was a working-class section of town with a high number of immigrants from the Middle East. This was apparent with Arabic writing in the windows advertising different products. The pungent aromatic smells of spices used in cooking permeated the moist-laden air.

Darkness not used to sleep under was a friend to thieves. While it provided quietness and slumber for most, it brought to life different forms of nocturnal evil. Jake and Sydney's night operation intended to reverse the order: darkness would be a friend they would use to take those who lived in it into the light of day. Tonight, the dark underworld would receive their own special kind of justice, not from the blindfolded woman who holds the scales of balance, but from their own peers inside their violent world.

In Africa, Jake had lived in a real tropical jungle. Tonight, a different kind of forest enclosed him—one of greater danger and peril. Nighttime shadows along the street provided him a cloak of hidden mystery, something he was in need of. The unsavory people on this street were bottom feeders from the top of the food chain. Needed, was more wit and less brawn. While darkness clothed him, the unknown kept others in silence.

A vehicle indicating a right turn was coming in the distance, the driver dimmed his headlights, turned, moved down the street and stopped near the smugglers' car. Several people were inside. The shadows kept Jake covered as he edged himself to the corner to peer across the roadway where the sting was about to play out. Three figures of men were getting out; one was using a cell phone. At night, without the noises of the day, the power of the mind can display elevated prowess. Jake heard no voices, but could see their movements. His eyes had adjusted to the darkness maximizing visual perception. He saw the figures from where he was as if he were standing alongside them. Within five minutes, another set of headlights came down the same roadway giving a right turn signal; this time it was a large tow truck.

Tension inside Jake was pulsating. It was not enough to be in the audience, he wanted to be on stage. In this climate of high drama, the mind of his soul created its own world of fantasy. Everything Jake's eyes saw appeared suspended in slow motion. The time it took the truck to move from the corner to the disabled, parked car seemed like an eternity. The tow truck stopped alongside the plant vehicle just behind the disabled car. He could tell Sydney was a passenger with the driver of the truck. This left one of the three in the stalled car to be the locksmith.

From where Jake stood he could see five men milling about the scene. The driver of the truck lifted the bonnet of the stalled car and gave the appearance of looking under the hood. Sydney was standing between the truck and the plant car, another knelt at the back of the same vehicle attempting to unlock the boot. Jake's intense focus on Sydney made him lose visual of the whole scene. A pedestrian was walking down the roadway on the same side of the street the truck was on. His fast-moving, London stride brought heightened tension. The pedestrian would reach the section of the block where he could view the whole operation in a matter of seconds. Sydney said he needed three minutes to do the transfer. Just as Jake was about to launch into a quick stride to take action to distract the pedestrian, he saw Sydney sliding the case under an opened boot door and someone closing it, and like clockwork, everyone moved to their vehicles. The truck and stalled car pulled out together and left the scene while the pedestrian kept walking down the street in his swift gait.

Jake stepped back into the shadows hoping the second part of the operation at the police station would go well. The story of success hung in the balance. He began walking in the opposite direction waiting for Sidney's call. It was important no one hear a telephone ring or anyone talking.

Thirty minutes later, Jake's phone rang.

"Hello, Jake, this is Sydney. Everything went well. I just got off the phone with Siana. She's at the police station now giving them the translated copies, along with the post office documents, the apartment address, and description of the plant vehicle. Siana told me that 'Because this is connected with terrorism, it has high priority, and we should get action right away.' She'll inform the police someone had delivered the packet of documents to her, and because of client-lawyer confidentiality, the person will remain anonymous. We'll get back to you later, Jake."

Sidney hung up. Jake thought he would be on the streets the whole night waiting for a response from the police. Within the hour, unmarked cars appeared from both ends of the street creating roadblocks. They surrounded the car containing the luggage case while another detachment of officers went to the flat. A number of officers entered after breaking through the door. They led the two men who had ransacked Jake's hotel room at the Hilton over to their vehicle. After opening the boot, they found the smuggled luggage case containing the planted contents. Certain cell members were now marked men. Poetic justice was destined to go full circle for some of their own.

After Siana's confidant at the police station called her with a report of what the police found, she then dialed Jake. He was still walking the streets around the neighborhood when his phone rang. He slid back into the shadows.

"Hello, Miss barrister. You're up late tonight, aren't you?"

To create good conversation, Jake attempted to pretend he knew nothing.

"How'd it go?"

"Mr. James, I join you tonight by crawling out on the limb of excitement. Do you live on the dark side of life to gain expertise for operations as tonight, or is it you're just lucky in pulling off clandestine projects? If I didn't know better, I'd believe you're with the CIA."

"Miss Coker, you should save your rhapsodizing for Sydney and his team. Tonight, they deserve all the credit."

"The three of us should go out and celebrate," said the lawyer, "They found extensive evidence inside the home that revealed connections to a larger European terrorist network. This will put closure with you and the terrorists. They'll no longer believe you still have the contraband. With what the police found, the agents will have no credibility. Their own people will see them as betrayers who stole the diamonds and five hundred thousand pounds at the Wimbledon locker. Of course, this will place all of them in great peril. Two of the agents were arrested tonight; the others are in hiding, not from the police, but from their own network."

"Miss Barrister, for once, I'm glad to hear you talking more like a prosecution attorney than the kind that pumps legal fuel at that special service station near the desert."

"There you go again—you are very trying! You know how and when to throw cold water on something to have its greatest effect, don't you?"

"Miss Coker, I'm impulsive, please forgive me. It's late and time for a truce between us. I'll give you enough British notes to pay for Sydney's time and expense for this operation—let me know what's fair in payment."

"Three thousand pounds is a fair payment for him and his team."

"Good, then I'll let you make the arrangements for payment. Send Samuel by my place about twelve-thirty tomorrow and I'll leave it with him."

Jake hung up and commenced his long walk to find a cab out on the streets at four-thirty in the morning. He found one and made his way home in good time.

His bed was ready to welcome him for a short night's sleep, but first, he allowed his thoughts to be turned on the evening's action-packed event, reflecting on the hand-written note from the lawyer, signed with her first name, Siana. He liked the sound of her name.

Chapter 10

Manchester

IT WAS A STRUGGLE to get out of bed at noon when Jake awoke. Lacking his full cerebral powers, he turned on the television for the noon news. What went down last night was the lead story. Every channel covered the event, *"Last night, the police responded to information of a terrorist smuggling operation and raided a home connected with terrorist cells here in the UK. It is believed that the group has links reaching all the way to West Africa in diamond smuggling that helps finance terrorism in Europe and the Middle East. A large quantity of money, contraband, and documents were found in the police search....*

Jake was on the phone dialing the lawyer about the news.

"This is Jake, have you seen the news today? I just turned on the TV. It's on every channel."

"Yes, I know. I've been waiting for you to call me."

"Have you heard any news from Freetown yet?"

"Yes, my father just called and said the authorities are coming down hard after the British got together with them. They arrested several, and some fled the country through Liberia and Guinea. Samir is on the run after slipping through the net. The controlling block of influence around Samir has melted away. Most Lebanese in the country are pleased with what's happened."

"This should bring relief to your father with Samir being a fugitive. Its justice well served."

"Justice will be served when he's caught and punished."

Jake noticed a change in the lawyer's attitude in recent conversations. Today was no different—she had softened and warmed. What had brought this about? Was it from his attitude adjustment, her dependence on him in pursuit of Samir, or just a deepening friendship?

"Mr. James, I want to thank you for what you've done. Your work in this matter of Samir has brought great relief to me. My father is elderly, and his ordeal with Samir has been hard on him."

The lawyer took a deep breath, pushed courage into her voice; it was a step outside her protective wall.

"You've made no reference to the hand-written note I sent by Samuel. I tried to tell you without saying it: I want you to call me by my given name, Siana."

"I will if you call me Jake."

"I need acceptance more than you. You're stronger than I am. I'll address you by your given name when the time is right. Besides, I like the sound of Mr. James."

Jake found his world spinning. When it came to emotional issues with the opposite gender, even on a superficial level, it paralyzed his normal assertive effervescent nature. He was a bold, outspoken engineer type. He dealt with certain fixed laws that never changed. Everything came packaged in definable terms. However, emotional confrontation about feelings left him insecure—he lacked the skills to tie together loose strings to make things fit.

"As you prefer, Miss Siana. I'll practice saying your name at night before I go to sleep so I can pronounce it right in the daytime. Even when I go to the States in few days, I'll keep in practice. And speaking of going somewhere, tomorrow I'm leaving on a tour up north for a couple of days before leaving for the States."

"You don't let grass grow under your feet, do you? Where were you last night when I called and gave you the results of the police action? Were you in the area where everything went down? Haven't all the recent events energized you enough for a deserved break?"

"I'm a prisoner locked inside my hunting spirit. I've accepted this as my fate. Planning and busyness are some of my therapeutic responses in dealing with depression. Being busy with new stimulating plans in a big way is the only thing that calms the boiling caldron of my dissatisfaction. Perhaps you already know that creating conflict is part of my disorder."

"In the short time of our knowing each other, your conflict has been very apparent. With your issues, I can understand why a person of your background and success has never been married."

"How is it you know my background?"

"I'm sorry, perhaps I spoke out-of-turn. Let me explain."

"There's not much to explain, is there? It's all about my being white, not fitting into your ideal world. What kind of a background check did you run on me?"

"I wish you wouldn't say those things about being white—It's about me and who I am inside, and you must understand my being part of your schemes led into deep waters. You're persuasive and can move people with your energy. I had to make sure who you were before I stepped near the grey line in my profession. Because of Samir, I was willing to step over that line providing your record backed

146

you up. Mr. James, in my position I know how to secure anyone's personal history. I can say I'm sorry, but it's too late now."

"Siana, the only time you spoke out-of-turn was when you gave an opinion on why I'm not married. Would you enjoy my commentary on why I think you're not married?"

"Please don't try, I've dug myself too deep by thinking out loud, further exhaustion of this subject will only make matters worse. Can we just leave it as it is and remain friends?"

Jake hesitated.

"I have thick skin. I see no problem in our friendship continuing."

"I appreciate what you said. Please have a pleasant and safe trip up north."

Samuel arrived at Jake's front door right on schedule. They visited briefly, then he drove away with a sealed envelope of three thousand pounds of British notes for the payment of Sydney's work. Siana would handle the transaction. He called Eric Spence to pick him up for the Manchester trip.

"Eric, please call your sister, Ingrid, tell her I'm taking her up on her offer to give me a tour of Manchester, and if her mother has a vacancy for two nights to book me. Also, tell her I look forward to seeing her again."

He wondered why Jake didn't call her himself, they seemed to have hit it off well, but he didn't know Jake was still in a mental state of processing his confrontation with Siana; he didn't want an interruption by talking with another woman.

By the time Jake showered and packed for the trip, Eric was at the door. He was surprised to see Eric's taxi had already been painted. It looked like a new vehicle.

147

"Eric, Is your wife all right by herself while you're away for a couple of days?"

"Yes, Sir, her unmarried sister comes over to stay with her on occasions like this. Besides, we have good neighbors."

"Are your parents retired?"

"My father still works as a gemologist. This trade seems to run in the family. My sister and I both trained and worked as gemologists when we were young. However, we now have other ways of earning a living. Ingrid has already told you about my mother who runs a small enterprising bed and breakfast. They have four bedrooms upstairs they rent out and serve a large breakfast every morning to the people who stay overnight."

Jake took in the beautiful English rolling hills covered with sheep and cattle. The English countryside, with the scattered quaint buildings from yesteryears, gave rise to the memories of a historic people, a people who created the biggest empire ever to rule the world. His reflections came to a sudden stop when Eric handed him his phone, saying, "Sir, my sister wants to talk to you."

"Hello Jake, this is Ingrid. You know who I am, don't you? I'm the person who asked you to call me if you came to Manchester. I'm disappointed you didn't call me first. Do all men like you avoid assertive women like me?"

"Ingrid, you're the one who should know men and their reactions to you. Do you always get your way with men by laying guilt on them?

"When they're important to me, I do. Please don't make plans with the guy driving you, I have my own car with your tour all arranged. Anything with me is adjustable to your schedule. Of course, you can bring your driver along if

148

you like, but I'll do the driving. I like being the person in control."

"Ingrid, I believe you're flaunting your gender and professional role, something you're good at, but underneath, there's a shrinking violet."

There was short silence. Then, with a subdued tone, she responded.

"Jake, you're intuitive about human nature, aren't you?"

"When it's to my advantage, I try to be, Miss Spense."

"Jake, I can see you're going to be a challenge for me.

"Miss Spence, I've been a challenge to a lot of people in life."

"The time you're with me, Jake, I'll work overtime to be your equal, and still be your friend. May I talk to your driver?"

He handed the phone to Eric. It was clear why a large company employed this kind of person to do what she does. She thought fast on her feet, had a forceful persona, exuded self-confidence, and knew her trade.

When Eric pulled in front of his parents' home, it showed symmetry with the rest of the neighborhood. Everything looked pristine. The building reminded Jake of some of the older dwellings in his own town back home. The house appeared to have a basement with two stories.

They walked toward the front door, it swung open. Standing in front of Jake was Ingrid, the tall figure of carved beauty in the dress of a housekeeper. The last time she saw him he was dressed quite tawdry; now, it appeared they were both on equal footing, but he had suspicions there was method in her madness. She was outside her palace walls

149

playing the role of the pauper in disguise for his benefit. She embraced Eric in family tradition, turned toward Jake with eyes that flashed with an intended message. His wall of formality prevented a full embrace. They had visited at an airport in Africa for thirty minutes, now he was a long-lost friend.

"Jake, it seems you and I have met somewhere before."

Women like Ingrid carried all the natural beauty and talents to move at will into the space of an interesting party. It appeared Jake was the object of her intrigue and was trying to occupy part of his space with a performance for his benefit. The clothes she wore were the kind used when doing chores around the house. She lacked makeup with her hair arranged in a long blond curly ponytail. Her tall svelte features captured the typical image of her Scandinavian ancestors that pillaged parts of Europe. Now, she stood gentle and kind with a look of rustic beauty, prepared to capture the attention of any interested suitor. Standing side-by-side, anyone could tell Eric and Ingrid were siblings and close. Jake noticed a distinct contrast between the two: Ingrid possessed strong dominant piercing eyes telling of self-confidence and purpose—her brother blended with the crowd.

Eric had spoken well of his sister. Her education included university training in microbiology, and in her spare time enjoyed painting. Before she closed the front door, she looked out and saw Eric's taxi.

"Oh Eric, I see you have a new taxi."

"No, it's not new. It's just new paint with a different color." The eyes of Jake and Eric fastened on each other, each knowing the reason for the new paint.

Jake took notice that Eric showed discretion when responding to his sister about the new paint. He obliged Jake by carrying his luggage upstairs to the room where he would sleep.

"Mr. James, I'll drive you out to dinner somewhere if you wish?"

"Eric, I'd appreciate it."

His sister, with a flash of sparkle in her face, responded.

"Eric, Jake came here at my invitation and I promised him I'd be in charge of his activities while he's here. I'll attend to this if you don't mind. I'm going to my flat and will return in an hour to pick you up, Jake."

After a short rest in his room, Jake heard a soft knock at his door. When he opened it, Ingrid was there standing taller than ever. She was dressed in gorgeous attire for an evening out. Her natural beauty complemented everything she wore: a necklace, bracelet, and two rings, all diamond-laden with large stones. It was difficult to grasp this was the same person who earlier wore cleaning clothes. He saw she was comfortable in who she was. Her change of dress from what she earlier wore enhanced the intensity of the message of her eyes.

They walked downstairs to Ingrid's waiting vehicle. He opened the door for her on the driver's side, walked around on the other side sat and next to her on the passenger side. "Where would you like to eat, Jake?"

"At the nicest place in town, I have something to celebrate tonight."

"Is it about someone, an event, or both?"

True to form, Ingrid cut through the chase and didn't use small talk to reach the question.

"All of the above and more," he answered.

151

Jake was good at conversation. Since she broke the ice, he continued.

"Your brother told me you're a smart sister. Did you come packaged with these smarts, or did you work to earn them?"

"Some of both. I studied and learned gem cutting when I was sixteen-years-old. This was my paternal grandfather's trade, and he passed it on to other family members. By professional training, I'm a microbiologist, and painting is my hobby.

"Since you're a microbiologist, and British, I'll ask you a question in your field. Are the British still in a tiff about the American, James Watson, receiving more notoriety in the States than British born Francis Crick for their research together in the discovery of the spiral DNA double-helix?''

Her response was rapid.

"Jake, that's before my time. There's still discussion in the science community over that matter. There's always competition between shirttail cousins, isn't there? You're either well read, have a good memory of your genetic studies or do work in biological science to reference this subject. What do you do?"

"I'm a civil engineer."

"Oh, you don't look like an engineer. You're too young and nice looking to be one of those."

"What does an engineer look like?"

"I guess I got myself in trouble, didn't I."

"Sometimes, trouble is in the eye of the beholder."

Still on Jake's mind was the story on the news today about the smugglers. His impulsive nature drove the matter into a conversation.

"I'm sure the terrorists are beholding a lot of trouble today."

Then, realizing his statement was misplaced, he attempted to get back on his mental feet.

"Are you following current news about the diamond-smuggling, terrorist cell that was broken up?"

"I follow anything in the news about diamonds. They have a history of bringing out the dark side of people with ill intent. What the news media has covered today is common knowledge among people in the diamond industry. It's just that someone has given them the proof to change rumor to fact."

She continued to demonstrate mental adroitness on this subject until she pulled into the restaurant driveway.

"Jake, this is one of our finest places to eat. I called earlier and made reservations. England's not known for good eating-places, you know, but this one makes up for all the bad reviews She gets. When I asked if you had a preferred place to dine, I wanted to give you the feeling you were part of the decision-making. That's my style!"

"Miss Spence, you like your hands on the controls, don't you? At least, there's something going for you—you're upfront about it."

When they entered the restaurant, it looked quite upscale. Jake knew Ingrid wanted to impress him as an in-charge person; he allowed her to lead the way. His experience here with her was quite atypical of any previous engagements with women. This was the first time a woman had taken him on a date and been so aggressive about it. He always thought himself adventurous by choosing to be different, living on the edge and taking chances with new experiences, but this person, in her own way, matched his eccentric ways any day. Ingrid refused to allow him to pick up the tab, even after his strong insistence. He yielded to her exercise of power—he allowed her to pay the tab.

153

When she dropped Jake off before going to her flat a few blocks away, she said, "Good night Jake. Breakfast will be ready downstairs at seven-thirty tomorrow morning."

The next day, Jake got up early enough to shower before going down for the complimentary breakfast. He found the small side room with tables and chairs where they served overnight guests. At the other end of the room, he saw Eric and Ingrid. True to form, Ingrid was the spokesperson for the two of them. Today, she was dressed in a smart casual manner.

"Jake, we wanted to keep you company at breakfast."

He sat down. "It will delight me to have breakfast with you."

"We'll have our breakfast in the other room. Mum is preparing it for us there. Today, we've brought in extra help to assist our guests with breakfast so we can be together."

Ingrid was in beautiful contrast to what she was last evening. Last night she displayed her glamorous beauty—today it was her natural beauty. In her family's home, she was the little girl and would always be so. The senior Spences came out, and Ingrid introduced them. They all sat down together at the family table. This was a special occasion for Jake to be the guest of his benefactor at her family breakfast table—all arranged by Ingrid.

Ingrid's father took charge. "Mr. James, we welcome you with us at our humble breakfast table. It's our custom before each meal in our home to say grace."

Everyone seated at the table bowed their heads. In conformity, Jake also bowed his, although a bit tardy. This gave the impression he was less than devout. Being table correct, he followed in conversation and led in etiquette. He reminded himself to speak when spoken to, and avoid asking questions.

The head of the table spoke first. "Mr. James, what is it you do?"

One had to be a total stranger at the breakfast table of a close-knit family governed by discipline, tradition, and loyalty to grasp the meaning of the age-old adage, "Your home is your castle." Here, Jake saw the king at his table with his royal subjects around him allowing an outsider to participate in conversation. This scene was a duplicate picture of the home he came up under, but he saw it at home from the inside circle as a member of the royal household. Being a stranger here showed the palace with a different view. He looked across the royal breakfast table as a subject and did his respectful polite bow.

"I'm a civil engineer, Mr. Spence, just returned from Africa on my way to the States."

Then, he broke his cardinal rule by asking a question.

"What do you work at Mr. Spence?"

"I'm a gemologist, Mr. James. I cut precious stones for the wealthy and affluent. I've been doing this for many years and am approaching retirement. The shop I manage wants to sell and I'm not sure how things will go down if another company comes in. They may bring in their own people and replace the ones we have there now."

Every king who has sat on a throne had detractors beyond the palace walls. When the ruler of the castle discussed with a stranger and commoner at breakfast the rumblings going on outside the walls, it showed insecurity.

"Is it on the market at this time?" Jake asked.

"I believe they just put it on the market,"

The conversation moved to general subjects. When they finished with breakfast, Ingrid reminded Jake they should soon leave for the planned tour of the city.

When they drove out of the driveway, Jake noticed the mother and father peering with interest at them through the curtains. The parents didn't want them to know they were watching, but they had high interest in this stranger their daughter had invited into her life and into their home. They knew well her flamboyant personality, but she had never brought anyone before to their breakfast table.

Jake maintained a fluid conversation with Ingrid but pondered underneath the creation of a system of marketing the diamonds stored in his safe deposit box in London. Something compelled him to explore who this person was that was driving him around Manchester making strong flirtatious overtures.

"Ingrid, tell me about Ingrid."

"Jake, you're asking an open-ended question. Do you want it straight or embellished?"

"I don't mind if you add color."

"Well, Jake, I'm athletic, I jog, try to golf every week, even when I'm out of the country. I'm a microbiologist by training, but make much more money doing what I do. I enjoy my actual work evaluating gemstones, but the travel part I hate. My job description includes determining the carat value of gems and establishing the price. I'm buying my own flat here in Manchester and practice frugality, except when I'm out with an interesting person. My greatest weakness is entertaining myself by going out of the way to speak to strangers, like you, then, assert myself into his life in a way that keeps him wondering what kind of a person I really am. Now, Jake, is there a quid pro quo exchange in my catharsis? It's your turn now."

"Ingrid, let's make our topic about you and your work right now."

"You want to remain a mystery man just to stimulate my interest—don't you?"

"I'll divulge who I am later, but for now, let's talk about you. You say you don't like the part of your job that takes you out of the country. Is this a recent dissatisfaction or is it long term?"

"Jake, are you attempting to be my therapist? You're making me too serious, and I don't think our time together needs any of this. I have enough of this in my work. Yes, this dissatisfaction of overseas travel in my job is long term. I'm tempted at times to return to my work as a microbiologist just to get away from the travel. Most people who have my qualifications jump at the opportunity to travel abroad and earn my salary."

"Ingrid, do you ever think of setting up your own business, importing gems and becoming a wholesale producer of finished valuable products?"

"Many times. I already have the required licenses in the countries where I now go, and I maintain all the documents for importing them into this country. My extensive experience has connected me with many prominent wholesale outlets in Europe. The downside to all this is it takes a bundle of money to become established, and what I have won't reach very far in this effort."

"How much money do you need for this kind of venture?"

"This is difficult to say, Jake. There're many variables. One has to create the production system with a shop, enough capital for travel to the countries to purchase the gems, pay the gemologists, and all the other incidental expenses. Just to get started and run the production for six months will cost between four and five hundred thousand pounds. This doesn't include the outlay for rough gems.

157

"If you had a good supply of diamonds on hand, how long would it take with your knowledge and expertise, to get them finished and on the market with cash coming in?"

"Under those conditions, I could contract the cutting and polishing out to gemologists I know, and the cash flow could start within thirty days."

"Ingrid, it's my interest to establish a gem cutting and marketing business here in the UK. If you work for me, I'll guarantee a year's salary at your current level, and after twelve months of operation, I'll sign over to you thirty-five percent of the business, providing you meet all profit and developmental expectations. My attorney will draw up these arrangements in detail. Of course, this will still require your travel abroad to purchase gems; however, it'd be on a much lighter schedule."

Ingrid became quiet. She pulled the vehicle over to the side of the road and stopped. She sat motionless, her vibrant energy gone, then asked, "Who are you, Jake? There must be a reason for you not giving me your own background. Are you an engineer like you said? What were you doing in Africa? How long have you planned this proposition you've made to me? Have I made a mistake in meeting you in Freetown?"

Ingrid was serious in her rhetorical questions. She knew the diamond business well from top to the bottom. The bottom part included its dark side—she wanted nothing to do with it. *She thought something strange was going on. Inside her vehicle was a man who didn't look like a person who could command the money he offered her. Was he just an agent, a front man representing an organization from the underworld? It did occur to her he was in Manchester with her because of her own invitation.*

"Ingrid, I want to assure you I'm an Engineer, went to Africa for a one-year project for the government. It was after my arrival in Manchester this business proposition came to mind. In the States, I have a successful construction and land development business. My father manages the corporation. My reason for going to Africa was because my grandfather had served there as a mission doctor when he was my age. He meant a great deal to me. My religious background is much like yours, you know. However, I have walked away from it all."

"Jake, you've rocked my world today. You are stealth! I didn't think you had a penny to your name. Right now, I'm embarrassed. Everything up to this point makes me look like I'm interested just in your money. It's time for me to become the other side of myself—the shrinking violet."

"I think you should let the analytical section of your brain take over and the feeling part float away for right now. This is an opportunity for someone like you to create something that'll bring great personal and monetary satisfaction."

"I agree with your statement. However, in spite of what you think of me as an aggressive female with a showy personality, I'm a microbiologist and still use the microscope for important things in life outside the lab. Right now, you and your offer are on my glass slide for close inspection. I can't give you any indication of my interest at this time, but in a few days, I'll let you know."

"Ingrid, is your caution from your assertive or shrinking violet side?"

"Am I allowed a mix between the two? Let's talk about the city and the reason you came here."

The two of them spent the rest of the day viewing historical sites and visiting the old cemetery where some of

Jake's ancestors lay buried. Ingrid was helpful by taking numerous photos with Jake alongside the gravesites.

After arriving back at her parents' bed and breakfast, Ingrid looked away to avoid eye contact with Jake, saying, "You're invited to my flat tomorrow morning for breakfast. If you agree, I'll pick you up at seven-thirty. Eric can load your luggage in his vehicle when he comes by to take you back to London."

"I look forward to it," responded Jake. He made note of her subdued behavioral change.

The next morning when Ingrid picked him up, she had moved further into her subdued role. Everything was different. Her actions appeared distant and formal. It was when Ingrid was setting the table that she saw Jake's attention drawn to the slight tremor in her right hand.

"Mr. James, you'll have to pardon the tremor in my right hand. Some kids at sixteen get part-time jobs to earn spending money. I learned to be a gemologist at that age and with excessive repetitive use of this hand, I developed nerve damage in my wrist. The injury causes these shakes when lifting something of any weight. My gemological skills gave me part-time work when I went through the university but left me with some permanent wrist impairment. It's a nostalgic experience when I sometimes go to my father's shop and just watch the work going on. One gets a wonderful feeling taking a rough diamond and making it into something beautiful that everyone wants, and in some cases, are willing to die for. I created exquisite beauty at the expense of my hand."

"Your tremor is hardly noticeable, and I suppose this is a lesson for all of us in life. To create loveliness, we run the risk of being injured. We all bear those scars in one way or another."

The longer Jake sat at her breakfast table the more he came to understand this person was exceptional. All she needed was a push with capital and she could explode into success. It was up to him to convince her to make the right decision on his offer.

"Ingrid, I invite your investigation of me in the States by calling my attorney to confirm my identity and investments. He'll answer any questions on matters of my business. I do request your inquiry go no further than my attorney."

On the back of his business card, Jake wrote his attorney's name and phone number and handed it to her across the table, saying, "I'll call my attorney informing him to release any information about my financial holdings you request." She took the card and looked at the name. Her determined and exciting eyes he saw earlier had yielded to a passive resonance accompanied by an invisible barrier. Her changed disposition came from guilt after having displayed excessive flirtation with a person who would be around tomorrow, and someone who might also become her employer. Because of Jake's own eccentricities, only certain types of people with inimitable personalities could make the transition into his world with him in it. She was one of them.

Ingrid recovered her natural sparkle by the time Eric arrived to pick up Jake. They went outside together, she gave Eric a farewell embrace, turned to Jake, saying, "I have something for you to take as a token of friendship. Please wait a moment while I run inside and get it."

When she returned, he saw her carrying a rolled-up paper. "This is what an engineer looks like"

He took it from her hand, saying, "Thank you, Ingrid. I'll consider this a favorable expression of better things to follow if you know what I mean."

Ingrid gave a gentle smile when they drove off. After they moved on down the road, Jake rolled out the paper. It was her free-hand sketch of him with her name and date printed below. He knew she hadn't forgotten the drawing; she just managed to gain enough courage to give it to him.

Before they arrived in London, Jake bought a picture frame for Ingrid's sketched drawing, and when entering his one-room apartment, he found a special place for it—the kitchen table.

Chapter 11

Secret Revealed

THE NEXT MORNING there was a wake-up call at Jake's front door. It was a familiar rap. The way a person knocked on a door could sometimes act like a fingerprint; it identified the messenger. Sidney's rap was recognizable anywhere.

"Is that you Sydney?"

"It's Sydney."

"Just a minute!"

Jake opened the door without shoes and socks. Sydney stood facing him with a coffee in one hand, a newspaper, and bagel in the other. He placed the coffee and bagel on the table, then opened the newspaper alongside the coffee.

"Good morning Jake. The coffee and bagel are compliments of me, the newspaper is here at the suggestion of Siana. She called me thirty minutes ago asking me to be sure you had the morning paper. She thought the lead article might interest you."

Sidney pointed to the front page: *"Two Terrorist Suspects Killed Execution Style."* The article went on to say, *"The police believe these killings were a result of theft and disloyalty among some of the members. Execution was used as a way to enforce loyalty."*

When Jake finished reading the entire article his coffee and bagel were cold, but so was the riveting thought that sometimes poetic justice fell within the law and sometimes outside the law. Today, it was outside the law. He remembered the structured loyalty among Middle East people who were part of the long-held custom of consanguineous marriages: relatives marrying relatives. This institution prohibited marriage beyond the bloodline. For a woman to marry outside her clan could mean certain death. Today, the newspaper record showed that violence could reach even to the male clan members when loyalty was in question. Jake redacted the front-page newspaper story from his mind, replaced it with his memory of past events: events of violent attacks on innocent civilian victims. These two found dead were part of this violent movement. Their way of life had judged them sooner than later. The old adage, divide and conquer, didn't end with colonialism. It still served its purpose.

With a grimaced face, he turned to Sydney.

"Sometimes jurors aren't needed when justice demands a verdict."

Then he thought to himself, *these didn't require a stop at Siana's gas station for the partial tank of gas needed for the desert ride. Now, the portion designated for them could go to other more worthy travelers.*

Sydney interrupted his musings.

"Jake, Siana wants to come right over and meet with us here at your place about several matters."

"I'm quite embarrassed the way this room looks, but I suppose I can tidy it up a bit before she arrives."

Jake straightened his bed, moved some of the discarded empty boxes to the trash, then went to the bathroom mirror to improve his appearance. He realized the room was cold from sleeping with the windows open. He closed them, turned up the thermostat. There were three simple chairs at the dining room table. After removing

164

everything, Ingrid's hand-drawn sketch of him was left on the tabletop as a centerpiece. He was now ready for the barrister, but having to wait caused him to ponder why he should be so concerned about how his placed looked? He had never done this before for anyone—even for a woman.

Then came a knock at the door. Standing in front of Jake were Siana and her driver loaded with breakfast and a large thermos of hot coffee,

"Well, do I get invited in, Mr. James?"

He took some of the things from her arms, laid them on the table. Her driver entered, placed on the table what he had carried in, left, and shut the door.

Jake noticed Siana looking at the sketched drawing done by Ingrid. She leaned over to look at the name of the artist.

"This is new, isn't it?"

Because the sketch had a name and date, he didn't reply. She dropped the subject but saw her glancing at it from time-to-time.

"Who is Ingrid Spence, Mr. James?"

"Ingrid is a microbiologist in Manchester and may come under my employ. She's also an artist, a talented person, like you. Don't you paint mental and emotional pictures with your arguments in court? You do with me!"

"Let's not go there. We've had enough of that for a while, don't you think?"

What kind of work does an artist do for a Mr. James, who has no previous connections with Manchester?"

"Miss Siana, you underestimate my knowledge and connections I have in Manchester. It's a business venture. She's a highly reliable and capable person. That's important, you know, openness and reliability. She comes from a good family too!"

When Jake used the word openness, the conversation about Ingrid lost its inertia. The lawyer moved on to the reason for coming to Jake's place. She took from her handbag a small package and placed it on the table.

"Sydney, there are three thousand pounds in British notes here on the table. Take these and divide them between you and your people. This is payment for your expense and time in your successful work in the sting operation."

She handed the package to Sydney. He was pleased with the amount. She continued: "Now, for the more serious matters we need to cover. the post office and copied documents must carry a veil of silence among us. If we want to help my father back home, a code of secrecy is required with each of us. The information of the post office documents and luggage plant must never be divulged to anyone.

"Mr. James, you could qualify as a good CIA operative in the light of what you put together and pulled off, with the help of Sydney. It was brilliant and most important—it worked!"

"The success is because of Sydney. He deserves all the credit. Because of him and his people, success came our way."

"I must get to my office soon," said the lawyer, "I'm running late."

The three walked outside. Sydney left. Standing alone were Jake and the lawyer.

"May we talk for a moment in your vehicle," Jake said.

He thought she'd be more comfortable in her vehicle than speaking with him alone in his room.

"Sure, but just briefly."

Both got in her car, the driver waited inside his apartment.

"Siana, I've made a business proposal with someone in Manchester. If this person accepts my offer, she'll leave a large company that buys and finishes gems for wholesale markets throughout Europe. This person is a gemologist and purchasing agent for this large firm, and it's my hope she'll enter my employ. If this person joins me in the proposed arrangement, I'll have a production shop in Manchester. There's a need for another distribution store and shop here in London. Because of your interest in jewelry, experience in the artwork of design, and your contacts in the country of diamonds, I believe it might interest you to consider an investment with me in a gem-cutting shop and store. My person in Manchester will help us set up everything here. Your father can help you acquire a diamond export license, and we can use people of Samuel's quality to bring shipments to London."

Like a statue, the lawyer stared straight ahead, her facial expression unmoving. Jake knew inside she had confusion, anger, and a whole lot of excitement going on. These mixed combinations kept her still. She practiced her courtroom demeanor showing no emotion, then turned toward Jake. Her eyes looked like cold steel—they refused to sparkle. Just her lips moved.

"You are a high flyer! How do you do it? Is there anything you can't do? You landed in England a few weeks ago. Now, you have a new enterprise underway, a dangerous one, I must say."

"I seize opportunities by gambling and using the right people. These go together to make things happen."

"You must give me time to consider this. I can see my contacts in Freetown being an asset, and my skills here on this end can make things come together, but what kind of investment are you expecting of me?"

"What do you want it to be?"

"You're some clever person, aren't you? You love to play your game of chess in everyday life with me. You're trying to put me in checkmate. Let me turn it back to you. What do you want it to be, Mr. James?"

"Siana, I have all the money I'll ever need in my lifetime, unless I lose it in a big gamble. My investments are for the satisfaction of adventure. It's the scenic value of the train ride I enjoy, not the destination."

When Jake addressed her with her given name he saw eyes soften and a fixed image yield to the kinder person she was.

"Well, you sound like you enjoy life. It's the gambling part I have reservations with."

'If you choose to involved yourself in this investment, I'll make you an equal partner without any outlay of money, providing you draw up the legal documents for a bona fide partnership and do all the work of jewelry designs and shop management."

"Mr. James, I'm sure you know what I'm thinking. Out there in some dark corner are those contraband diamonds. My conscience and profession will not permit my participation with any of the contraband you have in your possession. If you can assure me they'll not be part of our business arrangement, I'll take the time to consider your proposal."

"You're a predictable person," said Jake, "I'll guarantee the business we create here in London will not process or sell any of those gems. Does your straight-and-narrow on this subject come from your religious teachings or your legal persuasions?"

"It comes from both, though you may not think so. It's my opinion that laws governing moral behavior are derived from the higher order of a religious and moral conscience, and its influence comes to us from the beginning of history."

"Yes, Miss Barrister, I know the history of Western law development. It goes all the way back to the Sumerians four thousand years ago in the Fertile Crescent. It's my understanding law was mixed with religion when Moses came along."

"Mr. James, when our ancestors left the Garden of Eden, they left with two things: the clothing of animal skins on their backs and a conscience knowing good and evil. Understanding the difference between good and evil was enlightenment given to man for the creation of moral laws that would govern human societies. Moral laws derived from the human conscience validate the biblical record of man's creation and explain why we have codified moral law today. The human conscience was the vehicle that produced natural moral law. The biblical religious tablets of law given to Moses confirmed what was already inside the human conscience. Therefore my straight-and-narrow comes from two dimensions: one, from civil law, the product of the conscience, the other from tablets of stone, revealed by God."

"Miss Coker, you're splitting hairs. You've chosen a different way to defend your religious persuasion, and I must concede this is the only kind of chess game you can beat me in—you put me in checkmate."

"I take no pride in doing so. But since you acknowledge your defeat, I think you should consider the winner taking all. If you consider our polemics a game, and me the winner, then you must allow me to choose the winning prize?"

"Does this mean I'm the one to put up the prize?"

"Yes, and I want the prize to be a promise that you'll go with me to my church for a service on a convenient Sunday morning."

"What! You don't know what you're asking. Do you know that if I go to church with you, it'll be the second time since I was sixteen years of age?"

"It's good to break a bad habit. Don't you agree?"

"I prefer breaking other kinds of bad habits. I'm attaching strings to the prize. When I return from the States, I'll go to church with you just once, providing you accept my business proposition."

The lawyer looked straight ahead, was expressionless.

"I'll respond affirmatively if you will join me on two occasions at my church."

"You drive a hard bargain, but you have a deal."

"You know dealing with diamonds, Mr. James is a slippery business, and I caution you to walk softly and discretely in what you do with people you know nothing about."

"Your advice is well taken. You can be sure my arrogance and self-confidence will not exceed reason. I want you to know it's my intention to take all the contraband diamonds and finish them in Manchester. Everything above expense will go to build a hospital in your country. Its dedication will serve to honor the memory of my grandfather.

"That's a noble cause, and I regret I cannot be part of it."

"Because of the contraband diamonds that will be used to build it?"

"You said it, I didn't."

"Tomorrow, I fly to the States to complete a real estate transaction of one of my shopping centers. My father, who manages my affairs, has sent me a message informing me they need me there to complete some legal work. It's been three months since I've seen my family. I flew my mother and father to my place in Africa. They stayed with me for two weeks in my humble dwelling up-country. It was a wonderful experience for them. I hope to have them at the hospital dedication to honor the memory and work of our patriarch. When they were with me, I took them to see the ruins of what used to be the hospital where my grandfather had worked as a physician and surgeon."

At this point, Jake saw agitation surfacing with the lawyer. She reached for her phone and called her driver.

"Samuel, please come to the car, I need to leave for the office." She looked away from Jake.

"Mr. James, I need to talk to you about something personal, but now is not the time. Perhaps, if you're free before you fly out we can get together before your departure."

"My flight leaves tomorrow at twelve noon for New York out of Gatwick. Let me know what you want to do."

When the lawyer drove away, Jake called a taxi and made plans to spend the day at the public library. After six hours of reading materials on the diamond industry and visiting two bookstores, he arrived back at his apartment with an armload of books. He absorbed as much information as he could about the gem-cutting industry. At six in the evening, his phone rang. It was Siana.

"Are you available to be picked up at seven-thirty in the morning? We can have breakfast together before you fly out."

"Why so early," he asked?

"There're matters I wish to talk to you about before you leave. They're important to me and significant for you

171

also because they involve the history of your grandfather in Sierra Leone.''

''You have a good approach in motivating me to comply with your request. I'll expect you at seven-thirty sharp. Goodnight Siana.''

Jake hung up, went back to his studies. The lawyer still held the phone in her hand thinking about being pleased to hear him use her first name in conversation. She felt he had avoided doing so in order to keep a cold distant business relationship with her. She knew he excelled in the business world because he took chances, could read people and probably never suffered remorse when others got hurt. Inside, she hoped the latter proved to be untrue. Now that Samir was dethroned, and her father secured in his role, she didn't need him to lean on. But she did owe him something: loyalty and honesty. Tomorrow, she would expunge herself of her guilt and be free.

The alarm rang at five in the morning. Jake dressed, went for a morning walk, returned, packed his luggage, and showered. He decided not to shave his beard, but let it continue to grow if, for nothing else, it provided disguise. After he placed the luggage case by the door, he sat on the edge of his bed waiting. From where he was in the center of the room, his physical world was minuscule. He could see everything. The large manila envelope the lawyer had given him caught his eyes. It contained old pictures of his late grandfather. Inside the envelope was history, a mystery world he couldn't see, or measure. Up to this point, he had avoided discussing the matter, waiting for the lawyer to bring up the subject. Opportunity had now presented itself for confrontation.

It had begun to rain. On schedule, vehicle lights made their way down the driveway. Samuel came to the door, carried his case to the car and placed it in the boot. The lawyer was in the back seat. He entered the door opposite her. Her dress was informal. Jake assumed her day's schedule did not include going to her office. After greeting her, they engaged in small talk, but he noticed she kept glancing down at the envelope he held in his hand.

"I see you found the photos."

"Yes. I've waited for your explanation of them."

"I'm glad you brought the photos because this was the reason I wanted to meet with you before you left for New York. I'll say nothing more until we arrive at the restaurant."

She valued confidentiality and was not free to discuss issues with the driver in the front seat. Jake knew this and avoided conversation that was personal or connected with business.

The driver pulled in front of the restaurant she chose. They hurried inside to get out of the drizzling rain. The host took them to a booth she had reserved because of its location. They sat down, ordered coffee. She was tense when she began speaking. Her eyes focused like a laser toward her soft, folded hands on the linen tablecloth.

"Mr. James, my discourse with you here this morning is the most difficult task I've ever assigned myself to do. Even after committing myself to it, I feel I'm walking on thin ice that may crack my psyche. I want two things to happen as a result of our meeting together this morning: the first is personal inner healing for me, and that we remain friends.

"Mr. James, I confess that I resented and disliked you from the moment my father called me to contact you. It had nothing to do with you, but it was everything about my total experience when I went away to the university where I met and socialized with hypocritical elitists. Emotional identity is a great force in a young life. I learned to resent the duplicity of those who moved around me, where in the classroom they espoused one thing, and in real life the ears of learning were deaf. In my mind, you carried the profile of those destined to be the leaders of society. Outside the classroom, these people rejected who I was. I came from a mixed marriage and just half of me received acceptance in academia. I was always wondering what half I was and what half they wanted to see and hear. Higher learning for me was the gateway for ultimate success but was also a seeding time for resentment and anger. I became as guilty as those I blamed. I'm broken this morning because I failed to prove to myself you were like others in my past. When you told me your grandfather's name was Baron, it registered in my memory of having heard my father cite his name on numerous occasions. I called him to confirm this. Then, he proceeded to relate the whole story.

"Your grandfather, Doctor Baron, came to my country with a missionary society after he'd finished his internship and spending time studying tropical medicine. He was the only doctor in the country with special training in this field. He served to help a number of patients who could not otherwise find effective treatment. My father was one of them. He was ten years old when he came down with a condition doctors throughout the country were unable to treat. Lying at death's gate, they transported him to Doctor Baron's hospital. My grandfather and grandmother stayed at the upcountry hospital for two weeks while he underwent treatment. My father owes his life to your grandfather's efforts. Therefore, had it not been for your grandfather I wouldn't be here today. This news from my father has broken me inside. It has brought me to this point of asking you to forgive me for my prejudices and ill-feelings against you. With this plea, I conclude by saying you can't know how difficult this is for me. I have practiced over and over

174

what I have spoken to you, and it has been like going to my own trial with no defense to speak on my behalf and you are the judge and jury. I have no excuse for my guilt and throw myself on the mercy of your court. Now, the photos inside that envelope need no explanation."

The lawyer's face looked withdrawn, showing pain, distress and helplessness, all punctuated with marks of loneliness.

"Mr. James, when I was a teenager going through adolescence, my mother said to me once, 'In the hospital where there's the greatest pain, there's also the greatest joy, and where do you think that is?' Nothing was rhetorical with her. She made me think this statement through before she said, 'Pain always precedes the joy of childbirth, and it's like a life experience with an unpleasant beginning, but in the end serves to give life.' I learned this principle as a teenager, and now, I've re-learned it as an adult. Because of what I was, and what I thought you were, the news of Dr. Baron and my father put me on a painful journey in my dealings with you. The pain that came to me also gave me life."

Jake sat silent and still. He didn't know how to respond. His emotive and affective domain never handled these kinds of issues well. When he was a child growing up, his moments of crying happened mostly when he felt pain from physical injury. Her cathartic confessions made him insecure. For a person who was brilliant on his feet in the discourse of polemics, he sat speechless and inept. Deep inside, he wanted to help in her pain, but he couldn't, he didn't have the tools. By this time, the lawyer's face had tears on her cheeks. Saying nothing, he got enough courage to stretch his arm across the table and gently patted her arm.

"You're a wonderful person, Siana. You make me look small in your state of humility."

175

The lawyer said nothing. She wanted her father there to hold her, to give reassurance that someone cared. If only her mother were here, she could fill her emptiness. She even wished Jake would embrace her as a brother, hold her tight instead of giving her soft pats and saying soft words. She didn't want to be alone.

Jake could see her lips quivering, forming silent words with her eyes closed. He knew she was praying. Praying was also out of his domain. Both remained quiet, saying nothing.

He took his two hands and covered hers on the tabletop, saying, "Siana, this story of my grandfather and your father is one I'll always remember, and your statements about your change of attitude regarding me are appreciated. However, my nature is adversarial and conflict comes naturally with me. I'll try to live with less challenge coming from your side of the aisle as a result of your journey, and I'll try to give you less adversarial challenge."

The lawyer gave a forced smile, and with an act of strength, took her hands from under Jake's and placed them over his.

"You'll never be without challenge if I'm around, Mr. James."

"Siana, is your grandfather's name, Lewis Coker?"

"Yes, and how did you come to find this out?"

Jake then went through his childhood experience of the metal box that contained all the letters written to his grandfather after he had returned to the States from Africa. He told her it was in that box he found three letters from a Lewis Coker.

"Do you think your family still has those letters?"

"I'm not sure, but I'll ask my mother when I see her."

Their conversation on the way to the airport was warm but stilted. The invisible barrier between them lifted, and by the time they reached the terminal they were like old friends talking and laughing. Samuel took the luggage from the boot, Jake shook his hand, then turned toward the lawyer whose arms hung at her side, embraced her with a hug she had wished for earlier, and up close heard a whisper coming from her lips, "Please be careful."

He walked away, and looking back he saw the last vestige of memory before leaving England: two people who came from the same country, two worlds apart, but were together in spirit for their land.

By the time he reached the departure gate, an announcement came overhead: "Due to weather conditions there will be a fifteen-minute flight delay." While waiting, his phone rang. It was Ingrid.

"Mr. James, this is Ingrid. I called your attorney as you requested. He answered all my questions and even more about who you are. From what he told me, you're further up the economic ladder than you implied. It's not for me to ask, but how have you achieved so much at your age?"

"By gambling, working night and day and being frugal, even among strangers I go out of my way to meet. Let's get to the point; you didn't call me to discuss my portfolio."

"After much thought, I've committed myself to accept your offer. Tomorrow, I'm flying out and will return in a week. I need to know how soon you want me to start and what your expectations are? My present company needs a two-week notice."

"Ingrid, here is my outline. A large quantity of rough diamonds already in England is available to me for immediate production. I want a plan to get these on the market first. Then, we need a system to keep the flow coming into the country and a production system for the wholesale and retail markets. I leave it with you to give me in writing your plan for the estimated cost and the time-frame to accomplish this."

"I'll keep in touch with you by email on a daily basis if necessary. You'll receive from me a step-by-step strategy of development that will include your inventory already in the country. Trust me, I know what to do and how to go about bringing all this together. I'm sure we can work together even though I'm a shrinking violet."

"Miss Spence, I employ top people to do my work and consider you one of them. After I receive your plan, my lawyer will forward a copy of an agreement for you to sign. It will state your salary and contingency of thirty-five percent ownership if expectations are met."

From overhead, the announcement of boarding came blaring through the intercom. Ingrid heard it.

"It appears you're boarding your plane, so I'll say goodbye—have a pleasant flight. You'll hear from me in a few days."

Chapter 12

Gemology

AFTER JAKE'S PLANE LIFTED OFF THE RUNWAY, all he could think about was his project in the safe deposit box in London. His flight was a time to reflect on where he was in life and what he wanted from it. The smuggled luggage case in London had changed his life's direction, had opened up a new world—one of challenge and new friends. He was already missing his conflicts with Siana. It took this plane flight to mirror his soul. He was not the same person. Events had changed him, and right now, he wasn't quite sure how and to what extent. Something was different.

When he arrived, his parents were there to meet the son they always ran after when he was a child. Now, as an adult, he was returning home after another adventure; the difference now was they could only watch and hope for the best. They brought along Jake's younger brother, Luke, who was completing his medical internship following in the steps of their grandfather. Luke was different from his brother. He lacked the wild spirited nature Jake possessed, was less willing to take risks. Jake felt Luke's quiet nature exuded far more admirable qualities than his. He loved his younger brother.

The next day Jake bought a new laptop and cell phone, called Siana, and left on her voice mail the message he had arrived after a good flight and everything was fine. He searched his family's attic, found his grandfather's box that contained Lewis Coker's three letters.

He and his father completed the real estate transaction. Together, they looked at investment property that had been researched by his father who was better at land assessment values and the tedious day-to-day management than Jake was. Details in paperwork were his specialty—he was a CPA. Jake was one who always saw the big picture and was willing to gamble with higher stakes. They went over the books. His father, being an accountant, gave an in-depth analysis of how well the company did. The books showed a net gain of over four million for the previous year. This didn't include the appreciation of property values. Then, his father showed him a newspaper article written in the local paper about his son's success as a land developer. It gave Jake's background as a local boy who made good and went to Africa for a project where his grandfather had served as a medical doctor with a mission. His father didn't tell him, but Jake knew he was responsible for the article because he was proud of what his eccentric, impulsive son had achieved at such an early age. These were his words coming from the newspaper. Tears came to the father's eyes as he watched his son read the article. It was on this visit Jake realized he and his father needed bonding, something long overdue. In all his father's perfection and goodness, he had failed to reach far enough down to his son when he was a child, and as Jake grew up, he never found the tools in himself to span the distance between them. Now, after many years, the distance between them had narrowed.

By the time he had his new laptop going, he found an email from Siana. She wrote:

I can say what I have to say by email better than by phone, especially after our last meeting about myself. When will you be back? I miss your adversarial friendship. My father couldn't believe you were Doctor Baron's grandson. He was hysterical. Also, Samuel sends greetings.

After he finished reading the email, the mission of building a hospital in the country where his grandfather had worked loomed as an achievable goal with the entire diamond processing done in Manchester.

Four days after he arrived in the states, Jake received an email from Ingrid:

Mr. James, enclosed are the steps I propose to take in creating a viable gem-producing business with the roughs in your possession and the eventual gem-cutting site and shop. The first step includes a two-stage approach. The first phase is processing the rough gems in your possession. We'll contract out the rough cutting and polishing to independent gemologists with my direct supervision. When the gems are finished, I'll market them with wholesale dealers I already do business with. My contacts will allow me to maximize the price we can get per carat. In view that marketing gems require direct personal sales, I'm requesting a five percent sales commission above my salary. I hope this meets with your approval. The second step is the broad matter of establishing a gem-cutting site with a central office for public relations and sales. When the time comes for this expansion, I have contacts with quality gemologists and experienced people in this field. The time required to bring this into full operation will be based on your investment outlay.

She continued in detail, showing her inexhaustible experience and knowledge she had in this field. Straight away, Jake responded:

Miss Spence, please prepare to act immediately on phase one upon my return. Regarding the second step, report to me on any findings of suitable property for the project as soon as you get any.

After ten days in the States, another email came from Ingrid:

Mr. James, I've acted on your last request and found a suitable site with sufficient space to develop our project. Its location is good for upscale clientele. They've given us the offer of buying or renting with an option to purchase. Enclosed is an attachment with pictures. I've already arranged for quality gemologists to start with your rough inventory on a contract basis upon your return to England. Once we tie this place down as a production site, I can have the cutting and polishing equipment in place within two weeks. To commence, we need two experienced gemologists. We can start small and build as everything settles in.

His response to Ingrid was:

Please act on this offer. I prefer renting with an option to buy, providing the selling party gives us a satisfactory purchase price. My lawyer will send you a legal document giving you the authority to act on my behalf. If you need a deposit, let me know and I'll wire you the money. Regarding your commission with direct sales outside the shop, I'll agree to the level of five percent, providing you sign a five-year agreement that you abstain from creating any similar competitive business. If you agree to this, my lawyer will get in touch with you.

Ingrid was quick to respond: *"I have no problem with that arrangement."*

Jake's plane was in the air on the way to London after two weeks at home. He was excited about returning to put into motion the new plans to grow the investment in the box.

For the two weeks he was in the States, he had sent Siana three emails and received three from her. There appeared less tension between them via email, but the true test for improvement between them awaited a trial outside her courtroom in everyday interaction.

The plane touched down on schedule at Gatwick. Jake was in first class. This allowed him to be one of the first off the plane. To Jake, an airplane was like a large cattle truck hauling its cargo to a sophisticated cattle lot where they handled large numbers of people instead of livestock and used signs to herd the masses instead of workers applying electrical shock devices. The shocking part came later, like lost luggage, finding your flight didn't arrive soon enough for a connecting flight, or that the airline had canceled it. He was in no hurry, so he lingered long enough at a small coffee spot to pick up a freshly brewed cup.

Jake needed two things done before leaving the airport: secure the luggage and purchase a sim card for his new cell phone. He drank his coffee and took his time walking to the baggage table to retrieve his two cases. Already, a crowd had gathered around the circular baggage table like a group of people clustered together for a cockfight. Everyone watched the action on the table and competed for cases. Jake wasn't in a hurry, so he stood on the outside perimeter until the crowd thinned. He cleared customs, moved to the area where family and friends waited for arriving passengers. At that point, he heard a voice penetrating the den around him—someone was calling his name!"

Looking over the throng of passengers, He saw someone waving frantically two hands high above the crowd, saying, "Mr. James, Mr. James!" It was Samuel moving in his direction carrying his typical look of warmth and joviality.

"It's wonderful you're back with us here in London. Miss Coker sent me to pick you up and take you to your place."

"How is it you know my flight and arrival time? I didn't give that information to anyone."

"All I know is that Miss Coker instructed me to pick you up. She gave me this letter for you."

He took the sealed letter from Samuel, opened it, and found the answer to his question in the first paragraph in Siana's own handwriting:

> *Mr. James, there was a Middle-East man observed moving around your neighborhood. I called your number in the States, and your father answered. I told him I was your business associate and needed to talk to you. He said you spoke of me, and he knew who I was, but you'd already flown out. They gave*

me your arrival time and flight number. I'm sending Samuel to pick you up with this information of the latest development.

"Thank you, Samuel. Please bring my luggage to the cell phone store upstairs. I'll wait for you there."

Jake's world was churning inside. *Who could still be in pursuit of him after the luggage plant—after the revenge killings? Their actions of executing two of their own had put to rest any question of him being involved in taking the contraband. It had to be rogue players operating outside the inner terrorist leadership.*

A tinge of momentary guilt swept across Jake. He didn't wish for violence but the path he was force to take by being made a victim had forced his hand. To escape the gnawing of his conscience, he forced across his mind the scenes of dead, limbless women and children, the result of underground illicit blood diamond trafficking in support of terrorism.

Jake was in a jungle created by his own making. Coming to his rescue, was his experience of being a loner camping out in the wild. This gave him a fighting edge. He would apply the principles of living in the wild to an urbanized setting. One of the first things he must consider is moving to a place where he can depend on himself. The problem now is different from before. Earlier, he had to use a network, now, survival required complete dependence on instinct.

At the cell phone store, Jake wrote at the bottom of Siana's note a message: *"Thanks for the letter from Samuel. At a later time, I'll discuss the matter of my permanence here in London in an upscale, gated community."*

When Samuel arrived, he was given Siana's letter to be returned to her with his written postscript, then took the two cases from him against his insistence. Jake was already in the survival mode. The weight he carried helped him focus on immediate plans.

On the way to the apartment, he rode in the front seat with Samuel and placed a call to Ingrid.

"I'm back from the States and here in London. I want to know how things stand there in Manchester."

"Welcome back! Everything here is set for action when you deliver the rough stones. I moved on the rental arrangements for the production center. They also accepted my reduced offer of ten percent below the listed price. The affidavit authorizing me to act as your agent is not valid to finalize the business transaction. Therefore you will have to be on call to come to Manchester when the papers are prepared."

"Ingrid, I'll call you tomorrow to set a time to meet with you in Manchester."

After Jake signed off, he thought how fortunate he was to have Ingrid on board in this new business venture— she was a mover and shaker. Silence inside the vehicle was broken when Jake asked Samuel a personal question.

"Of what ethnic group are you, Samuel?"

"I'm from the proud Temne tribe, Sir."

"I know some of the history of the hut tax war in 1898, when your tribal leader, Bai Bureh, led a fierce rebellion against the British forces and a lot of people died. Your ancestors were known as great warriors in those battles."

Samuel avoided the discussion of history, he wanted to address the current broader picture of Sierra Leone's problems.

"Yes, my people resisted foreign intervention and the imposed hut tax by the British. However, today there's another external influence forcing its way into my country from the Middle East: the influence of radical Islamists. The Christians and Muslims used to live side-by-side in harmony in my country until they came in and introduced radical Islam. It's like a foreign invasion, something worse than European Colonialism. They incite Muslims within the country against Christians, bring in money to corrupt government officials and sponsor radical Islamic programs. They use diamonds belonging to our people as blood money to pay for their expansion of terrorism. We Sierra Leoneans have displayed our independence with pride, but are still ruled over by a subtle outside influence with forces as great and more dangerous than colonialism itself."

A big picture came into view for Jake. From what Samuel had told him, he saw how time had become a healer of historical scars, even as in his own country between the North and South. His life had crossed the paths of two people from the same country that stood in contrast. Each represented a microcosm of a healed past: Samuel, a descendant of those who massacred a number of Siana's Creole ancestors in the Hut Tax War, and Siana, a survivor of Westernized Creole values. History measured them with distinguished diversity. but with equal parity of substance, like ice and snow. However, the heat generated by the present looming danger of foreign religious fanaticism was melting their differences, creating a blending for self-preservation in the spirit of building a better and more unified nation.

Everything looked normal when they entered the driveway of the apartment. Jake opened the door for Samuel who carried his luggage. He saw the familiar site where he had slept two weeks earlier. It bore the commonness of his home in Africa where he had lived for twelve months. He was sad he had to leave the small oasis.

"Samuel, stay a moment until I speak with Siana."

She was close to her phone when Jake dialed.

"Where are you? Is everything okay?"

"Slow down please...I'm at the apartment. Everything is fine. Samuel is with me, and before he goes, I want to get your permission for him to do some work for me tomorrow when you don't have the need of his services. In a couple of days, I'll purchase a vehicle which will require a driver until I get my UK driving license."

"You can use Samuel fulltime if you wish, because I have other trusted drivers I can adjust my schedule around. Samuel will pick you up after he drops me off at my office tomorrow morning. I want you to know we all missed you here in London. Welcome back!"

"Siana, I'm going out of London on some business. When I get back, I'll call you."

"Do you ever slow down?"

"Its full steam ahead for Manchester as well as our new venture here in London. Are you ready for it? I'd like us to get together this week and discuss some of the finer details of our new endeavor."

They agreed to meet later in the week. Jake called Ingrid early the next morning.

"Ingrid, this is Jake. I'm flying to Manchester this morning. Are you available to meet me at the airport?"

"Yes, I can be there. I have everything ready for you to review. If you can bring some rough stones with you, I'll give you an evaluation and set in motion the finishing and marketing process."

"I'll bring along a sufficient supply for this purpose."

After hanging up, he thought how this young, tall, attractive person had the commanding brilliance of a lovely violet flower, and not a shrinking one when it came to knowledge and ability.

Samuel drove Jake to the bank. He took from the safe deposit boxes a bag of rough diamonds and three hundred thousand pounds; the diamonds went into his briefcase, the notes into a new checking account. It was a small push toward a big project. After leaving the bank, Samuel drove Jake to the airport for his flight to Manchester.

"I'll call you later today to confirm my return flight, Samuel. My schedule brings me back here at nine; however, if something changes the schedule, I'll let you know."

Ingrid was at the airport waiting. Dressed in an appropriate manner, the jewelry she wore included a simple broach on her lapel. On their way to the building site, Jake reviewed the documents she brought along.

They finalized the lease agreement with an option to buy and paid a year's rent. Ingrid gave Jake a tour of the building explaining how the final layout would be when all the equipment was in place. There was a front section arranged for glass-enclosed showcases for the display of finished products along with other accessory jewelry.

"Ingrid, I suggest we go out for dinner and celebrate together your success in closing this deal."

"Did you bring the diamonds?"

"Yes, they're in my briefcase."

"Good, then let's go to my flat first. I have all the necessary instruments and equipment there to give you an approximate carat rating.

"That suits me just fine Ingrid, providing you have some good coffee."

Jake seated himself at her kitchen table. Ingrid came over with a gram scale and several other instruments she used in assessing gems. From his case, he lifted the single sack of rough diamonds taken from the bank box and placed them on the table. This was an exciting experience for Jake to see the first time. For Ingrid, it was just a perfunctory act done a thousand times before. She placed the bag on the surface of the scale, read the weight, wrote it down on a paper pad, then poured out on the table the entire contents of the bag and returned the empty sack to the scale. Now, she knew the total weight of the rough diamonds. She used her smooth inner palm to spread out the gems across the flat surface. Her eyes became fixed.

"These are excellent, high-quality stones. The average size is good too. I'll have money coming in for us two weeks after I get some of these delivered to my gemologists. First, for our records, we have to count and catalog every diamond."

For one hour, they sat segregating all the diamonds into three groupings: large, medium, and small. Because larger stones had a much greater value per carat, she paid close attention to these by examining each one with her special magnifying lenses.

"Mr. James, let's put these in zip-lock bags to keep them separate. I'll keep all the medium size and start the process of cutting and polishing tomorrow with my contractors. I've already made up a catalog of diamond-cut styles. I'll be calling on wholesale buyers presenting our products and taking orders. Until our shop is operational with a secure place to keep the diamonds, you should store these other two groupings at your bank. When these three bags of rough gems are finished and put on the market, their value will reach over a million pounds. Do you have any more roughs?"

Jake attempted to give the approximate quantity of diamonds that came in the luggage case, the two ebony curios, and the necklace made of shells.

"I have brought over only one-tenth of all the roughs I have in storage."

Ingrid's eyes gave a sudden silence. They registered what was going on internally, and like a computer, her response came up on the screen.

"You're going to be rich from all those, and at five percent commission, I'll do well myself. I won't ask how you came about acquiring all these gems, but knowing what your lawyer told me, I'm sure you're not crossways with legal issues."

Jake gave a cold stare, saying, "I might add, it is not in your purview to ever inquire. Rest assured, I didn't steal them."

The riveting thought of the diamonds being contraband moved Jake to justify why he kept them.

"The net profit coming from these will build a hospital in Africa, a special project I have. Now, we can go out and celebrate."

"First, I'm going to change into something else. The way you're dressed, I'll be able to pass you off as a poor artist seeking help from a patron of the arts. Perception is everything, you know."

"Ingrid, I'm sure you'll do a good job in playing that role."

Ingrid had put closure on the business at hand. She had a way of compartmentalizing her life and was now ready for a glamorous night out. While she readied herself, Jake drank coffee, and when she returned he was introduced to another world—her world: one of beauty and glamour. What he saw was what he expected: a beautiful face, black dress, sparkling diamonds, and high heels.

The restaurant was a popular establishment providing entertainment and live music. Ingrid sat across the table from Jake. When the waiter arrived, he asked, "Do you wish to order a drink?"

"Yes, please bring me a martini, said Ingrid."

"How about you, Sir, would you care for a drink?"

"Just bring me coffee, please."

Ingrid responded with a momentary dour look. "Mr. James, on occasions like this you should order something stronger than coffee. You don't belong to Alcohol Anonymous, do you?"

"Am I giving you a guilty conscience? There's a big evening ahead of me, and I have the need for caffeine, not alcohol. Besides, alcohol and I don't go well together."

By this time, he detected witty cleverness turning over inside Ingrid, her way of prying and getting inside someone.

"Mr. James, are you revealing something about yourself that lies hidden and out-of-reach of others?"

"Miss Spence, your arm isn't long enough to reach that far to uncover what's hidden inside me."

"Try me, and I'll show you."

"The dark spots inside me, Ingrid, are pushed so far down I have trouble finding them myself.

"If you have trouble finding them, then you must not have any. My dark spots float around on the surface, picked at by people like you."

"Ingrid, you're fishing for positive reinforcement from me, aren't you?

"Of course I am. I have the need for people like you to tell me how good I am."

"Miss Spence, let's get serious in the world outside ourselves. It's important for us to have a good informal professional business relationship, and I think what can help this along is working on a first-name basis. From now on, I'm Jake to you, and you're Ingrid to me. Is this agreeable?"

"Well, we started out that way between us until you cut my feet out from under me by telling me who you really were."

"It appears you still have your feet and are as quick and sharp as ever. In fact, the stage you perform on now is even bigger than before. You know you love the audience's applause."

"Don't we all? There must be some kind of stage inside you that demands a rhapsodic response."

"Oh, I have a bigger stage than you," said Jake, "and that's the reason I can see yours clearly. It takes one to know one: you perform to get action from other people outside yourself, my performance serves to generate action inside."

"Why are you always so blunt, and right? Sometimes you could speak around a subject instead of right at it. You know, some people call it tact. Anyway, I respect men who see the complexities of the person I am."

Ingrid was exposing the other side of her dual nature. She was good at mixing words and subtle mystery together under her shroud of sculpted beauty. Her eyes showed a special glint as she took center stage.

"Jake. I like that name. I've liked it in a special way ever since we met at the airport in Africa. It has a masculine ring to it. I bet many other women have thought so too. Especially, those who know you have money. Is this the reason you carry yourself as you do? I mean, excuse me for saying so, the almost scruffy impecunious look in your dress, and the way you're always silent about yourself. Is this what you do to escape the clamor from over-aggressive women, like me? If your looks matched the way you dress, I may not have introduced myself to you at the Freetown airport."

"It'd be my loss, Ingrid, had you done that."

She was enjoying herself with sparkle still in her eyes. Perhaps, it was what she had drunk that forced to the surface her exuberance and boldness.

Jake continued. "Ingrid, I'm who I am. Up to this point in my life, the only thing that turns me on is adventure and challenge. Women haven't reached the level of being strong enough competitors for my eccentric drive to gain my attention—at least with any longevity."

Ingrid removed her glamorous façade, the conversation turned serious.

"Jake, you're not alone in eccentricity. However, mine goes down a different path. I know other people think I'm bright, beautiful, and successful at what I do, but I'm not at that point of believing it myself. Therefore I'm always trying to prove it and gain acceptance by it. It's a tragedy someone can have so much and believe in so little. What has prevented me from becoming what I often act out, but not falling all the way into, has been my religious training at home and in the church. My personality is sometimes my curse. You're more than a challenge for me, Jake, because you see through me. Now, I'm talking to you as my counselor instead of my employer."

"Ingrid, I'll be both at any time; however, I'm qualified to be just one. Since I'm your employer and future partner, I think we should settle up on your salary and go over some business matters."

Jake gave Ingrid a packet containing detailed guidelines of accounting methods and accountability instructions. The Manchester shop would have its own bank account with Jake and Ingrid as signatories.

"Providing everything goes as planned," Jake said, "you will become a wealthy person when your contract of twelve months is up."

"It appears so. It still seems like a dream. I'm glad I got in your face at the airport in Africa even though you are a poor dresser."

"You love to rub that in, don't you?" Jake said.

"Well, you do come up short in that area and speaking of short, the length of your trousers should be longer; you look like you're wading water."

"I didn't hire you to be my valet."

"It's too bad you didn't because you could use one."

"There's one thing I can say about you," Jake said, "you're a lot like me—you say what you think."

Ingrid had all the tools to push her way into any man's space if she were interested; tonight she was interested. Her tools didn't end with her imposing beauty and personality, she used another subtle talent.

"Jake, what can I draw, or paint, that will capture the image of our business endeavor; perhaps, another sketch of you as the new entrepreneur in the gem business?"

Jake didn't answer Ingrid, but looked away toward the waiter in the distance and motioned him over to their table. It was Ingrid's business to interpret body language. She knew he was using the server to delay his response to her sketch proposal.

"Sir, what can I get for you," asked the waiter.

"Please bring me some ice cream and more coffee; do you care for something else, Ingrid?"

"No thanks."

The evening closed with two players on a game board. Ingrid was trying to get closer to Jake by using her artistic skills to appeal to his vanity; Jake was using her talent for his own purpose.

"Ingrid, you can do another sketch of me later when the business is a rolling success. For now, just give me a sketch of yourself. A sketch of you will serve that purpose well."

When the waiter brought his coffee and ice cream, Jake asked the waiter, "Who ordered the ice cream?"

"You did, Sir."

"Oh, I did, didn't I?"

Driving to the airport, Ingrid took satisfaction in knowing Jake had become so preoccupied about the sketch of herself that he forgot what he ordered in the restaurant. She was also pleased he wanted her picture instead of his own. Jake took pleasure in his decision; a drawing of her would create interest at his place in London.

On the flight back to London, Jake reflected on this being a much smaller business event than what he was used to dealing with in the States, but it was different, gave challenge and served his purpose of establishing a ready-made gem shop. Also, it gave a bright person a new sense of independence. The next day he returned the two zip-lock bags of diamonds to the bank as Ingrid suggested.

Within a week he had managed to acquire a UK driving license and a new deluxe BMW. The more expensive vehicle was atypical of his persona. At home, he always came across as a person who drove vehicles that characterized a conservative, non-conforming lifestyle. However, Jake always knew how to adapt to make business work. Getting into the gem business required a certain success image—the vehicle contributed to this. A more secure and upscale flat was part of his immediate plans. He called Siana wanting to surprise her in fulfilling his promise to attend church with her.

"Miss Barrister, I'm inviting you to go with me to your church in my new vehicle this coming Sunday."

"Mr. Engineer… are you for real?"

"I do keep my word, you know. Isn't there something in the Bible saying, 'Thou shalt not tell black lies?'"

"You took the wrong turn on that commandment. I hope on Sunday morning your driving is better than your knowledge of the commandments."

"If you'll come by my place, we'll leave from here."

Jake made this arrangement because up to this point she had kept her residence at arm's length from him; he was sure she would feel comfortable doing this.

Sunday morning, he remembered Ingrid's comments about his dress. He put on the best he had. It was a suit purchased when he was in the States. His thoughts about attending a church service brought back memories of childhood. He was always bored in church. When he became a teenager, it became worse—he never fitted with youth activities. When he reflected on those experiences, they told him he lacked self-awareness, though he didn't know it at the time. He acted and said things out of place. In the public schools, with a bigger social grouping, his awkward social interactions were less noticeable. Recalling his early church encounters aroused strong negative feelings about his religious upbringing. A soft knock on the door interrupted his thoughts. He opened the door. Siana stood in front of him in her church-going best.

"Good morning, Mr. James. Wow, you look different!"

He was mesmerized with her appearance. Her spoken words sounded like they were from a distance. It was her elegance that gave a mystery of enchantment. He could understand why he was unattached at his age with all his personality issues, but here stood someone who probably had to fight off qualified suitors. Beautiful and beautifully attired, she looked straight at Jake with a twinkle in her blue eyes, as if to say, now pay your debt.

"Do you wish me to be your chauffeur," Jake said. "If that be the case, you'll have to ride in the back seat?"

"I'll suffer great offense if I'm to ride behind you. I consider myself equal, and sitting alongside you in the front is just fine. But on the other hand, I prefer being a friend and an equal."

He opened the door for her on the front passenger side, saying, "You're great with words, Miss Coker."

"Not as good as you when you're on your bad behavior. Does going to church make you resent me?"

"Miss Coker, I'm not good at conversing about my feelings, and you, unintentionally I'm sure, do a good job fishing there. The affective domain of my life is well below the surface for my own self-preservation. What I'm doing today is honoring a request of a special friend."

"I'm pleased to hear I'm a special friend."

After entering the main roadway, she continued her discourse.

"In view we're going into business together, I want you to have a fuller understanding of a side of my life you know nothing about, and by experiencing it, I'll not have to explain it. Just consider it's a business experience when you visit my church today. Mr. James, you above all people should know what business is."

She was straightforward, like it was a prerequisite for working with her in a business partnership. Underneath, Jake had suspicions of ulterior motives.

"Miss Coker, I'm going to tell you something I never verbalized before to anyone. You're the first to hear this and should feel honored that I'm going to reach way down inside myself and become vulnerable with my feelings.

"My mother and father were ritualistic in their attendance of their formal traditional church back home. When I was a child, I learned to sing verbatim all the old hymns and could quote many of the Bible verses used by the clergy. Our home had a disciplined environment. The church we attended was an extension of that discipline. When I was sixteen, I didn't forget the secular discipline of my home, but my rebellious and adversarial nature made me forget the discipline of the church. I refused to conform to the rigidity of being a silent receptor for church dogma and platitudes. When I went to the university, the intellectual stimulation of conflict was what kept my attention. I submitted to the secular mold. My adversarial nature made me appear to be an iconoclast; however, most of it was for show, or eliciting a response for the sake of creating conflict. I used my energies and skills of argumentation in a creative way when I joined the debating club on campus. Everyone on campus knew of my debating talent. This allowed me to engage in a form of conflict that stimulated my brain with such a flow of adrenaline that it was like taking a drug. However, the church wasn't exciting enough to keep me in it. Had it debated me, perhaps I wouldn't be where I am today. My nature needed conflict. The church was everything but conflict. I was wild, adventurous and became a church casualty by dying the death of dormancy.

"Now, Miss Coker, you have my feelings story about the church in a nutshell. Do you sit to respond as my judge, lawyer, or jury?"

"Neither, it seems you learned a lot about the church and its culture but failed to learn about the Person of Christ who created the Church and gave His life for it."

"Miss Coker, it appears if I keep driving, I'll hear two sermons this morning. Your one sermon is enough for the day. Can't we just turn around and count it as going to your church?"

"If I knew you really meant it, I'd turn around, but you didn't, so I'll burden you to fulfill your vow by paying your debt. Was it my nearby fishing, or your weakness that uncapped your hidden feelings about yourself and the church?"

"My feelings may be hidden to other people, but I know where they are: they lie in the dark corner of my life where they belong. We all have formative years influencing what we become. You should count yourself lucky—I've never said these things to anyone else before."

"I am lucky, yes, very lucky."

When they entered the neighborhood of Siana's church, Jake could see that demographics included various ethnic groups. When the church came into view, it had an overpowering architectural appeal. It pulled one back into the late nineteenth century. It was Anglican, and Jake was already preparing himself for a somber liturgical service, looking at his watch and hoping for a benediction.

Jake and Siana walked together up the stairs of the historic church along with other adherents coming in good numbers. Siana moved closer to Jake, whispering, "I know you're a bit nervous coming here today, but just think of it being a new sound barrier you're breaking. Just add this experience to your laurels."

"Miss Coker, I know you're trying to put a good face on this, but don't spend too much energy on me and end up disappointed. Remember, it's just a business experience and not all business attempts are successful."

"You always enjoy using the cold water treatment, don't you?"

"Siana, cold water is refreshing when swimming in a pool of tepid water with fishhooks flying about."

"Don't be cynical, no one will hook you unless you allow them."

"If that's the case, that my free will is in control, then it is good news for me and bad news for you—if you know what I mean."

"Mr. James, I always know what you mean."

They were continuing their adversarial banter when they entered the church foyer. The imposing architectural atmosphere of the building faded. Instead of the cold, staid history of the church coming at Jake, he saw warmth and life. Greeters were everywhere at the entrance shaking the hands of every person coming through the door. Jake thought it had the sounds of a beehive buzzing with activity, the difference being the guards at the entrance were welcoming strangers instead of stinging them. The rebel Jake was, made him think that perhaps the sting came later. Back home, the person who shook hands was the pastor, and he did that when everyone left the church like he was glad to see them go.

One of the greeters came up to Siana. "Good morning, Miss Coker, and who is your gentleman friend?"

"This is Mr. James; he's visiting us today all the way from America."

Jake wondered why she chose to put it that way. After all, she could have said she brought him here because it was a bargain arrangement, and he was just fulfilling his obligation.

Someone in the crowd stepped up to Siana asking, "May I see you for a moment, Siana?"

"Mr. James, please stay here, I'll be right back."

She walked away. The usher leaned toward Jake.

"Miss Coker is an important person in our church. She serves on several committees and is a vital part of our music program."

No sooner had the greeter spoken that Siana was back at Jake's side like a mother hen. They walked together to an inconspicuous pew and sat down. She whispered in quiet reverence, "I'm going to assist in the musical part of the service. When I'm finished, I'll return to sit with you. Now, will you be all right?"

"Siana, I was born at night—but not last night. I'll try not to bite my nails while you're gone."

Her popularity showed when she walked down the aisle toward the front by the number of people who stopped to greet her.

Jake saw nothing of the traditional choir loft, the large pipe organ, and the ornate pulpit; instead, it was a scene that looked like a band concert. There were guitars, percussion instruments, and a grand piano. The church was almost full, well integrated, and was a good representation of the community. He had never seen this exuberance of free expression in a church before. Jake's depth perception of history and the science of cause-and-effect were always acute. *He thought half of these people here in this building had ancestors living elsewhere two hundred years ago responding to Anglican Church missionaries from the UK.*

Now, with England so secularized, the waters were beginning to flow the other direction.

Siana was playing the piano with the orchestra. Indeed, she was a pianist and a barrister. Jake was awestruck seeing a person of such a caliber associating with this level of informality in a public religious exercise.

Then, in stark contrast to the freedom of expression up to this point, when it came time for the clergyman to speak, everything became silent. Siana returned and sat beside Jake in the pew. The illustrations the pastor used in his sermon, along with his accent, made him aware he was from West Africa. He articulated his sermon in a thoughtful manner, and in closing, he led the congregation in singing Amazing Grace. After the benediction, Siana gave Jake her message.

"Mr. James, the reason I invited you to visit my church is to show you who I really am. These are my people and they're like my family. The church, as you see it, is my life and represents me. I feel comfortable around people who represent my total self."

"I'll try to read between the lines in what you're saying. Are you telling me you attend a racially mixed church to fulfill the double person you see yourself being? Shouldn't you feel just as comfortable if the church were all black, or all white?"

"As usual, you get right in my face, don't you?"

"Siana, I was brought up being told it didn't matter what one looked like on the outside, it was what a person was on the inside that counted. With my being white, do you feel uncomfortable around me when we're by ourselves?"

"Mr. James, there you go again, knocking at the door of my protected waiflike psyche. If this keeps up, I'll receive a bill for your professional counseling services."

"You've defined for me your comfort zone. I represent only half of it. If I'm just half of your world, and will always be that, then this puts a strain on us, and on our business agreements, and perhaps even our friendship."

"Mr. James, you should be the lawyer and I the gambler. I don't make logical arguments, do I, at least with you? Most lawyers don't when they talk about the emotional part of their lives. I was in my protected comfort zone until my father called me about contacting you."

"Siana, do you wish me to walk away? I could fade from your life as quickly as I entered it. I'm experienced in this; however, this is the first time the other party will wish it so."

"Mr. James, you're the brightest light ever to come into my life, and rejection is my greatest fear. No, I don't want you to walk away. I just want you to understand me. I don't have your towering strength or background. You may be eccentric and arrogant, but the world you walk in is your world. You possess and occupy it. If I'm to walk in your world, it will take me time and the use of crutches. Are you willing to go at my pace?"

"Siana, I'm here in this country for something important to me and will do whatever it takes to finish the project."

Jake was always quick to give himself clear, succinct responses. Here was someone single and unattached at the age of twenty-eight and was struggling to live in two worlds at the same time, avoiding the acceptance of either. Jake saw their business partnership sailing in troubled waters with canvas-frayed sails.

However, water always had a way of seeking and finding its own level. Inside Jake, the pooling and settling of the swirling currents from their discussion cause him to yield to the truth of his own nature: he was adversarial, had limitations in giving and receiving nurturing. He was an engineer, yet he couldn't design foundations to build relationships on. He had pointed a finger at her, yet was guilty of the same, but for different reasons. This conflict with Siana had opened into a large room he was unfamiliar with. He had never moved this far into a woman's life before. His relationships in the past with the opposite gender always suffered premature death.

Siana was distraught over what Jake had said; it all hung on her face. He wanted to apologize then, but crowds were still moving about and he wished to speak to her alone.

"Siana, I want to take you out to lunch if you're willing to go after what I just said."

"Mr. James, I'm delighted to go. Thank you for asking me."

With Siana giving Jake directions, he drove the two of them in his vehicle to a well-known restaurant. After they settled in at the table, Jake began his untraveled road of admission and confession.

"Siana, I apologize for what I said in our discussions earlier at your church. It was inappropriate and wrong for me to have said those things. I'm very sorry."

"Mr. James, it's out of character for you to apologize for anything. What has come over you to make you feel guilt?"

"It's you, Siana. You've turned my head in a way that makes me look at myself with a different perspective. This bothers me. It has moved me to a state of being less secure in myself. I'm not contrite today because of the insecurity I'm going through, but it's from the mirror you hold up in front of me; it shows my shortcomings and I'm responding to what I see. Perhaps, my confession of human frailty will help strengthen you in some way to understand me."

Courage evaded Jake. He couldn't look straight into her eyes while he gave his speech. His head and eyes hung downward; all he saw were his hands on the white linen tablecloth clenched in a stressed manner. It seemed both were negotiating their conflicts with each other from a position of weakness rather than strength. Raising his head, he saw her eyes glossy with tears. Then he became more insecure. It was his history and practice to shy away from emotional issues, even courses in college in the affective domain he avoided. He was the engineer, a person who lived in a world moving on wheels without feelings. Perhaps, what he had chosen to divulge to Siana about his negativity of the church was a door opened too wide for his own good. Then, he felt a soft, calm hand touch his that were twitching.

"Mr. James, you and I both mirror each other's opposites. The process seems to polish our own lenses to see beyond ourselves into other worlds that have meaning and purpose, and by doing so, we make each other better."

Jake had no history of having built bridges over which he could walk and meet someone halfway. But today was different. An energy inside him was giving strength and courage to take his first step. Under his hand was the unused soft linen serviette. He lifted it in his hand and touched the small tear about to roll down Siana's cheek. She smiled, saying, "Mr. James, you're a good friend."

Both left with the feeling they were friends, potential business partners, and better people. Conflict had given opportunity for personal growth.

The next day, the diamond industry was consuming Jake. He read everything he could get his hands on, even hired a gemologist in management and marketing to spend time with him. It was in his nature to know the facets of the industry, everything from the designer's mind to the nimble fingers that polished the stones. His approach was to reverse his engineering skills. Instead of starting with the foundation and build upwards, he would begin with marketing and the politics of diamonds at the top, then work all the way down to the source, the mud pits in Africa.

Siana had all the potential needed to make their plans a reality. He wanted the project off the ground, and this required Siana to move on it. She needed to see the potential she had with her contacts and connections in her country of diamonds. Being an analytical person, perhaps evidence would serve that purpose.

Jake was at the bank when it opened. He selected six medium-size diamonds from the safe-deposit box. After calling Siana, he arranged for dinner together at a place of her choosing, then hurried off to one of the diamond-cutting shops recommended to him. The shop itself was sandwiched in between two clothing stores. It had front windows with watch displays and a variety of low-line rings, bracelets, and necklaces. Inside was a large, typical, glass-enclosed counter separating the sales clerk from the patrons. Hanging on the wall was a posted sign, "We Do Customized Jewelry." There was an open, office-type room in the back of the store. Beyond was a closed metal door. He could hear a slight grinding hum coming from behind the door. The storage and processing areas were behind the metal door and accessed when activated with a magnetic door opener by someone inside. This provided security for the gems and the people who worked in the area. The best shops employed GIA diamond certified gemologists and didn't need to advertise outside their shops if their products were of high quality.

It was always Jake's approach to start at the top of the chain when technical questions needed answering. The woman behind the glass counter asked, "May I help you, Sir?"

"Yes, is the owner of your shop in?"

"Yes, he's in, but busy, may I get the manager for you?"

"No thanks." Jake began to walk away when she asked, "What do you want to see him about?"

"I have some rough diamonds and would like to know their value."

"One moment, please."

She went back to the middle section of the shop, just outside the metal door, lifted a phone and spoke to someone behind the wall. The clerk returned to the glass counter.

"The owner is coming to see you."

A man with a large blue apron with graying hair came from behind the locked door. He stood behind the counter where Jake was waiting.

"Are you the owner of the shop?"

"Yes, I'm the owner, what can I do for you?"

He pulled from his pocket the small plastic bag containing the six rough uncut diamonds, placed them on the glass tabletop.

"I want to know if you're in the market for rough diamonds and if you are what you will pay for these six stones?"

"Let's go back here."

He led the way to the middle room where he sat at a desk and removed the diamonds from the bag. He studied each diamond with a special optical viewer, then, weighed each stone separately. The owner of the shop knew the diamonds were of high quality but avoided telling Jake.

"These stones are fair quality. If you want to sell them in their rough form, I'll offer you six thousand pounds for these six."

"Thank you. I'll accept your offer."

"Wait here just a minute, and I'll be right back."

He went into his gem-cutting room behind the closed security door and later returned with six thousand pounds.

Jake was preparing to leave when the owner of the shop said, "If you have more like these, I'll make an offer on those too."

He left the store with the owner's card and felt everything went well. Now, he had physical evidence to place in front of Siana. The oft-repeated expression, opposites attract, never meant anything to him until now. They were two different people so far apart and removed from each other that common ground between them was so narrow that any future appeared doomed from the start. If the ground widened, it would have to come from the effort of each party. He was excited about seeing Siana to discuss the potential they had in their proposed investment.

Up to this point, Siana knew almost every step he had made: his drivers, the hotels he stayed in, and his business activities in Manchester. All he knew of her world outside her enclosed inner feelings were simple answers to his questions when she chose to respond. She hadn't spoken of her brother or talked about her place of residence. He was hopeful he wouldn't bring the worst out in her tonight.

They both drove their own vehicles to the place she suggested they meet for business. He had in his briefcase six thousand pounds from the sale of the diamonds and the three letters from Lewis Coker, Siana's grandfather. She had requested these letters when he went to the States, but was waiting for a special time to give them to her — tonight was opportune. She was already waiting when he arrived. Jake slid in on the opposite side of the booth and greeted her.

"Cusha, how de body."

He was greeted with a smile and a light touch of intended sarcasm.

"Mr. James, you're ten minutes late. I don't mind you being late, but we live under the shadow of certain peril and you should've called me."

"Well, Siana, with your soft stroke of cynicism are you volunteering to be my driver so I can be on time."

"Be careful, Mr. James, or you'll bring my bad side out.

"You're so perfect, so how can I bring out any bad part of you?"

"I'm not perfect, but you're becoming more so.

"How is that Siana?"

"Because you're learning to call me by my first name. I want you to know I prefer you addressing me that way."

"Does this mean I'll have a name change?"

"Mr. James, someday I'll call you by your given name."

"You're like my mother, Siana. I end up telling you everything I do or plan to do and it all seems to be one way. So let's allow history to continue by my asking you for advice in finding a well-secured, gated flat. I want my own furniture, housekeeper, and garage. I don't want to be around hotels, a lot of people, and one-room apartments like the one I'm staying in. Can you recommend a place fitting this order?"

"How many bedrooms and what floor level do you prefer?"

"Three bedrooms and the level doesn't matter. Gated security and quietness are my concerns. Okay, now let's get on with other matters. First things first. I brought you something special from the States."

Jake reached toward his briefcase; Siana's eyes followed his hands. Child-like excitement radiated from her beautiful expression of anticipation.

"Siana, I have here three old letters taken from the family attic at home. They are from a Louis Coker, written to my grandfather from Sierra Leone after he returned home."

"Oh my! you know how to overwhelm me with these letters. They will be delicate parchments as part of my family's history. I see the stamps are missing on the envelopes."

Her hands caressed the letters like they were something alive, saying to Jake, "You will never know how much these mean to me. They tell the whole story of my grandfather's connection with your grandfather. Thank you."

"If I had known the destiny of these letters twenty years ago, they'd still carry the original stamps...just for you."

She didn't open or read the letters in Jake's presence.

Jake took from his briefcase the six thousand pounds from the sale of the six diamonds. After placing the notes in front of her on the table, she looked at them.

"What's this about?"

"Siana, I want you to count it."

"Why do you make such drama out of life in matters like this?"

Showing a meek and compliant manner, she took the money in both hands and counted it silently.

"How much is there?"

"Do you have to be so deliberate and mechanical about this? There are six thousand pounds here."

"I just sold six medium-size diamonds for the amount you hold in your hands."

Jake saw a slight gasp on her face when she realized the full potential of a diamond business.

"Mr. James," she said, "I know law, but I don't know business like you."

"If you can fulfill your responsibilities as we agreed, I'll be your business manager. Draw up a partnership agreement between us, and I'll see that you become a successful entrepreneur, and you'll not lay out any up-front capital."

"If you promise none of the contraband or money derived from them is used to start our business, I'll do my best to fulfill my agreement with you; however, this doesn't mean you can't tell me how things are coming along in your hospital project. I'm very interested."

"You just want to see my guilt from afar, don't you? It's all right to look at my disreputable activity from a distance, but not up close."

"Don't say that. Do you prefer I not be interested? I'm not supposed to pray for someone with criminal intent, but I'm breaking the rule in your case because your intent is right. Can we now drop it?"

She lowered her head, turned her eyes upward. It was the cocker spaniel look attempting to elicit from Jake sympathy in the midst of her own guilt. He would always remember that innocent look—it showed the softness of her gentle nature.

Responding, he said, "You and I will use the diamonds we bring into this country legally. However, my goal is to build a good hospital with modern equipment and essential housing for the medical staff with the contraband diamonds, in memory of my grandfather."

"Mr. James, I can help manage a gem and jewelry business here in London in my spare time. Finished diamonds in jewelry settings will bring more than twice the amount per carat than what you received today from the gemologist. If this can work out, it'll be an extension and fulfillment of my greater interest. When the need in the shop demands more time, I can always reduce my caseload."

"Siana, in a year you'll claim ownership of a successful new business. You need to take measures to secure for yourself the necessary permits and licenses in Freetown and London to purchase, export, and import the rough diamonds. I'm sure your brother can help you with this. Leave it with me to develop everything necessary for our project. For your information, I'll be contacting the mission my grandfather was with to confirm an offer of building a new hospital in place of the one now in ruins."

"Mr. James, I'm reluctant to present this to you but I feel I must. The close ties my father has with some of the Lebanese allow him to hear rumors unobtainable elsewhere in Freetown. They're telling him Samir is moving about in the UK, and we should be careful."

"Does your brother have this information?"

"Yes, my father keeps in constant contact with both of us. My brother has added security outside his home and is taking his children to school himself."

"What about you?"

"My flat is in a well guarded and secure complex. The greatest exposure I have is when I'm out driving. I plan to take cautionary measures so as not to be vulnerable. Word is, Samir is carrying a lot of money with him and looking for a way to get back to Lebanon. He and his family had a history of violence in the Middle East before going to Freetown."

"How can the world be so big, yet so small, to have this kind of information reach here in a matter of hours?"

"It's my father's business connections with the Lebanese. Their loyalty to him helps prepare us. You know, Samir will get information about you eventually. It was rumored he murdered a family member in an argument over a business deal gone bad in Freetown. The Lebanese community despises him, and until now, they feared him because of his money and power.

"Before we leave, here's an address of a flat open and available. It may fulfill your expectations, but you must look into it right away because a big demand is always on these units. The party who owns the flat is going away for twelve months and will allow some of the furniture to stay if the right party leases the unit. I want to warn you though, I live in the area."

He took the address from her, saying, "After hearing the unpleasant news from your father, I feel I should drive behind you on your way home."

"Thanks, this is thoughtful and kind of you."

The drive to Siana's flat behind her vehicle gave Jake time to evaluate the news of the potential danger from Simir. Now, there were several parties exposed to this malevolent and evil-bent supporter of terrorism. His kingdom was gone in Freetown, his reputation damage among his own, and was now a wild cannon headed in their direction. After ten minutes of driving, he found himself processing information having more immediate concerns of life, like why did Siana give him an address of a rental flat near her residence?

There were two towers inside the walled compound where Siana lived. Jake followed her to the gate entrance and stopped. She told the guard he was with her. They pulled into the parking lot, Siana got out of her vehicle, walked over to Jake still sitting in his car with the motor running.

"Please wait here for a few minutes, and I'll give you a call."

She had parked near one of the tower units, but walked in the direction of the other tower and went inside. Soon after entering, his phone rang.

"Mr. James, the reason I wanted you to wait is that I saw the light of the flat for rent on, and I wanted to see if the party would permit you to go through the place."

They met at the lobby, used the elevator to reach the floor of the rental. Siana introduced Jake to the owner and his wife. She was acquainted with this couple through her church. The company the husband was with was sending him on a one-year assignment overseas, and they wanted to lease the flat instead of selling it. Everything was out of the flat except the basic furniture. There were three bedrooms with a small balcony overlooking the metropolis of the area. It suited Jake, he agreed to the deposit and lease amounts. Before he and Siana left, the husband spoke.

"We'll leave the keys to the flat with Siana. She's consented to have the lease prepared tomorrow for you to sign. This flat has an assigned garage parking space and a small area for visitor parking."

When he and Siana walked out to the elevator, Jake spoke first.

"How is it you recommended me for this flat?"

"Don't you remember me telling you that for me to catch up with your gait you'll have to give me time? I'm walking faster by allowing you to live nearby, aren't I?"

They walked together to the parking lot, said goodnight to each other. The lawyer went to her flat, and before Jake entered his vehicle to leave, he stopped, turned around, and looked up at his new aerie. Up there, he thought, he could live as an eagle in seclusion.

Several weeks of living in a separate tower than Siana's worked out well. They didn't visit each other except on business matters, and social events were always in restaurants over dinner; sometimes, they took in a movie. They called each other when security questions arose, and Jake noticed when she was in the enclosed area of the complex, she had a greater relaxed atmosphere about her. Together, they selected a store site in a good location in London. Jake paid the required annual lease in advance. They delineated job responsibilities. Jake was to supervise the creation of the physical site and everything involved in shop production. Siana would prepare the partnership agreement, take charge of jewelry design, and help manage the shop. Jake turned all the shop development over to Ingrid's father who had already completed everything at the store in Manchester. Siana's brother and father worked on their ends for the required export and import documents. Even before gem cutting was underway, Siana had immersed herself in her spare time creating assortments of jewelry configurations adaptable to various types of gems. She arranged with her father to employ and supervise trusted agents to purchase diamonds in and around the minefields. Couriers made deliveries to London as demand required. In the growth of their business, Siana was now comfortable at getting together with Jake in his place; however, it was always short-term and always business.

Ingrid was sending weekly reports of the progress of the business in Manchester. The last report came in the form of a package. She wrote: "Everything has come together with our own gemologists doing all the production of rough gems at our own shop. The stone-cutting volume has increased, and the designs you sent from the person you call Siana are very good, some of which have already been used in settings."

She enclosed a pencil-sketched drawing of herself. Jake framed it and placed it in his living room with other meaningful photos.

When Jake was in school, staying focused was always a challenge; however, he could get super focused on projects and never stop until they were completed. It was also like this with books he read. Once he started a good book, he never put it down until he finished it. Sometimes, this was to his detriment—it shortened his night. He was into one of these books one evening when his doorbell rang. To his surprise, it was Siana. He invited her in.

She was carrying some business papers in her hand to leave with Jake. The first thing she saw as she stepped in was the drawing Ingrid had sent Jake of herself. Siana had a photographic mind. She knew the precise spot and placement of every article in Jakes living room, especially, the photos. It was difficult for her to keep her eyes directed toward Jake— she kept looking off at the sketch of Ingrid.

"I brought over some financial reports and new design layouts to be reviewed."

Avoiding eye contact with Jake, she walked over where the photos were, and pretending to look at all of them, she stopped at Ingrid's picture.

"Is this your artist friend?"

Jake knew at that moment something had changed inside her about him.

"Is she religious?"

"Her family is, but I'm not sure about her. Am I religious, Siana?"

"No," but you're not far from it."

Her eyes remained on the drawing.

"Is the sketch troubling to you?"

"In some ways it is. It brings back memories when I was in the university and found rejection by the fellows. I was too white for the blacks and too dark for the whites. I guess I didn't have any competition here until this sketch showed up."

"How can she be your competitor when I'm not in the church?"

"You're right, but someday you will come back because your grandfather has marked you for that event."

She placed the reports and drawings on the coffee table, turned to go back to her flat.

"Good night, Mr. James."

When she walked out the door, Jake said to her, "Give me your photo, I'll frame it and place it alongside the others I have here."

She didn't say anything as she walked away. She was hurt seeing the portrait of Ingrid that Jake displayed in his living room. What she had denied, and now admitted, was that Jake had become more than just a friend; it took the picture of Ingrid to give her that message. The terms, "flight, or fight" came to her. In one way Siana felt rejected and needed to flee, yet she knew Jake was wild in his own idiosyncratic ways, but he wasn't wild over women, if anything, he was naive and lacked certain skills to understand women. Sometimes, it was these kinds of men who became vulnerable to aggressive women. She imagined Ingrid to be this type, having sent him a self-drawn picture of herself. The thought made her want to fight.

Jake went back to bed for the night and continued reading his book. Thirty minutes further into the story, the doorbell rang the second time of the evening. He thought, who could be at his door at this late hour. He slipped his robe on, and by the time he reached the door and opened it, he saw no one, was about to close it, when he looked down and saw a framed photo of Siana leaning against the threshold. She had decided to fight rather than flee. He picked it up, smiled, and placed it alongside his other photos, saying to himself, *this method of madness worked beautifully.*

The pencil-sketched drawing of Ingrid didn't appear to deter Siana. She went full steam ahead with the shop management in her spare time. She knew a lot about jewelry and enjoyed the process of interviewing recommended certified gemologists. Jake had brought over Ingrid's father to set up an adequate cutting and polishing shop and used him in the shop's initial startup. Within six weeks, the glass-enclosed cases in the front were full of retail watches and jewelry pieces. Siana brought in an experienced person to manage the front sales operation so she could come and go at will. The shop was processing cut and polished stones for the wholesale market. The display windows carried rings, bracelets, and necklaces designed by Siana. Sales were slow in the beginning but soon picked up.

Jake and Siana were both pleased with the progress. Siana was doing what she always had a talent for, creating designs for jewelry settings. She was staying close to the shop, even reducing some of her hours spent at the law office. Jake was working with the mission in the structural design of the new hospital. Modern technology provided him with tools eliminating most of the back-and-forth flying between London and the States. In Manchester, Ingrid received the volume of stones as requested every week. At the shop site in London, they had a special safe where they stored valuable gems. The same arrangements were made at the Manchester site. Every week Jake or Eric made a contraband diamond delivery to Ingrid. They installed the normal security of metal doors at both places. Ingrid had managed to cut and market one-third of the rough contraband stones with all the profits from sales going into the hospital account. With three of the sacks of diamonds processed and sold, the account balance had accrued to over two million pounds. Ingrid had brought her father into the shop to manage the cutting and polishing. Siana, in her continued fight mode, allowed Jake to move closer into her protected life by introducing him to her brother living on the outskirts of London. She continued to reduce her hours at her office, worked more at the shop, and was becoming an experienced inspector of gems. She came to know the standard of quality required in the marketplace and oversaw those standards in her shop. She and Jake were partners in ownership, but she was the genius who brought everything about.

After nine weeks of full operation, Siana gave Jake their financial standing.

"Mr. James, our shop has been in full operation for over two months, and the records show that next month we'll make a nice profit. From now on, profits are divided between us at every month-ending."

"Siana, I want thirty percent of all the profits going to me be placed in an account designated for the hospital project. The rest will go to you so you can devote more time to design and shop management."

"Oh that's not fair; I'll never accept that kind of arrangement between us. I've already cut my time at the office down to twenty hours a week, and I've never been happier. If we keep going as we have, I'll soon be full-time here at the shop."

"I insist on the profits of thirty percent," Jake said.

"You are very generous. I want you to know that you have brought great change in my life by starting this shop."

"It was the big picture I saw. You've made it a reality by your own talents."

Siana continued to use the formal "Mr." when addressing Jake, and it was still an issue with him.

"Siana, the title you give me of 'Mr. James' makes you sound subservient. I don't care for it."

"I hope you understand the 'Mr. James' title is your first name to me. Time will present itself when I'll give you a first name, and it won't be Jake. Besides, haven't you ever thought I might be intrigued by the idea of being subservient to you?"

After she said this, she knew she had stepped over the line. It was an impulsive subliminal thought that slipped out in the fighting stance; it was the need of being wanted and accepted; now, she wished she could flee. Jake came back hard.

"Siana, don't ever say that about yourself again. Willful subservience is weakness. You aren't weak, and you aren't subservient."

The first thing Jake did in the morning was to check his email. Today, he had one from his brother, Luke. He had just finished his internship and sent important information.

"Jake, I want a break before starting my practice here in the States. If you're open to my visit and willing to pay my fare, I'll pack my bags."

Jake had already told him the expense was on him if he wanted to visit, but he had to live in the hovel he lived in without complaining. Jake fired back an answer.

"Luke, come and visit me as soon as you can. We'll put together a trip to Sierra Leone and visit the site where our grandfather lived and worked as a doctor. I have a six-hour work day at the hospital building site getting the elevations and plot layout where the new structures are going. I'll call the travel agent and arrange your roundtrip ticket."

His reply was immediate. "My dear brother, I'll be on the next plane."

Jake emailed Siana's father asking him to reserve a four-wheel-drive rental for up-country travel. Thirty minutes later, his doorbell rang. It was Siana.

"My father tells me you're going to Freetown."

The tone of her voice sounded like she was upset.

"Yes, I need to do about six hours of elevation work at the mission building site. My brother is coming to join me. He just finished his internship and wants to visit me before he settles into his practice."

"I thought you would have told me before contacting my father. After all, we're business partners."

"May I read between your lines, Siana?"

"You always do."

"So, Miss Coker wants to go to Freetown with us, is that right?"

"That's right, I want to go to Freetown."

"How far do you want to travel?"

"All the way. I want to see the building site of the new hospital. I'll not be in the way because I'll have my own vehicle, driver, and my friend with me. She is a nurse practitioner and works at the Hill Station Hospital in Freetown."

"I'll agree to it on one condition: you act as our official interpreter and business manager."

"Mr. James, it fits into your nature to get others to do the small things for you?"

When she walked away, Jake saw her take a hard glance at her picture he had placed with the others. He made a mental note that it was because of Luke traveling with him she had the freedom to initiate this conversation. Three people created a safe zone for her.

Chapter 13

The Hospital Project

ON HIS WAY TO THE AIRPORT to pick up his brother, Jake became thoughtful of his family. When his younger brother came along, he received the biblical name of Luke and followed in the profession of the original name bearer. His family had also honored him with a biblical name, Jacob. He always wondered why his name ended up abbreviated or changed to Jake. He held the belief it was because of his ADHD symptoms of hyperactivity and the insolence that came with it. Looking back, he thought perhaps his family wanted a name that sounded less biblical, that perhaps his nature was deserving of a less biblical spotlight. This was his deduction because his family never told him that. His brother, Luke, was different. He was delicate, soft, and a pliable spiritual person. He always had friends around, and always kept them, was more of an introvert than he. He was always moving, and a friend today may not be a friend tomorrow. He saw himself without friends because he didn't need them. What he needed was action. Reflecting on his childhood made him think this was why he could always take the loneliness of camping by himself in the wild because part of him was wild. This wildness was the reason he had the smugglers' treasure trove in his possession.

He continued musing. He remembered school testing at the third-grade level. The tests showed he qualified for the mentally gifted program; however, because of his hyperactivity and short attention span, his parents thought it best he remained in the regular class. Teachers were always perplexed because he could never focus in the classroom but did well in tests. It was after entering middle school he settled down and was always at the top of his class. However, the energy for excitement was always there. Though people saw him different than most, they never thought he wouldn't succeed in life. If anyone thought otherwise, it was the members of his own family, except of course his grandfather. He always believed in him.

He was on his way home from Africa when he found illicit diamonds planted in his luggage. Choosing to use the contraband to build a hospital in the land of their origin changed his life forever. He judged his action as moral acts for the greater good; however, looking back on the event he wondered how much his need for adventure and excitement entered into his decision. Perhaps, this was what Siana saw in him: a certain wildness that frightened her. Jake's thoughts turned to his childhood and his grandfather. Whatever his shortcomings, his grandfather always believed in him and brought the best out in him. He also called him Jacob. He said to him once, as if it were fatidic, "Jacob, you're going to be like the Jacob in the Bible. Someday you will have conflict with an Angel and have a nature change, and people will call you Israel." Those words were now speaking to Jake like they were yesterday.

While waiting for his brother to come through customs, Jake reflected on the historic evening he'd have going to Siana's flat for a social event for the first time. He had been in her front room in a cursory way but just on business. It was an unspoken agreement that he observes rules of absolute propriety. However, things had changed with the arrival of Luke. She had invited him and his brother for dinner. Entertaining two gave her a sufficient comfort

225

zone. Again, there was her standard, the ever-compelling force in her life: everything had to be in categories of right and wrong, good and evil. Jake remembered when he was with her alone, whether in the car, at the shop, or in an office, she was quite nervous and anxious. Interrupting his thoughts was the scene of his wonderful brother coming with two pieces of luggage grasped in the hands of a skillful surgeon. Hands that were delicate and sensitive, hands used to touch pets, parents, even him, and all were left better from it. Now, those hands touched the sick and injured bringing healing to them as well. Jake pondered the differences between them. There were many, but their love f

or each was the same. Love was their common bond that never defined differences. They embraced, cried, and rejoiced. When Jake saw his brother's face with tears in his eyes, he said to himself, *someday I hope my face will carry Luke's innocence.*

"Luke, we're invited to dinner tonight at my business partner's flat near where I live."

"What I hear about this person is she is quite remarkable."

"That she is Luke, that she is! This may sound strange, but I've never entered her home for a social engagement before. She also never enters mine, except for business. Now you come along, and she can't wait to have us both over for dinner. It seems her religious scruples regulate her social interactions."

"Jake, this may be true, but part of it can be she's establishing her territory. Knowing you, you overpower her. You look too strong, always self-confident, and the stronger you appear to her, the weaker and less significant it makes her feel about herself when she's around you. Jake, try showing your weaknesses if you have any, and if you can't find any, make up some. When you do this, it's like putting dry wood on a fire. All this stuff you hear about women wanting to see strength in a male can be overdone. The need to show strength is for those who don't have any. Don't practice weakness; just show some now and then."

For the first time, Jake saw Luke, not only with delicate hands for surgery but a delicate mind in understanding human nature. They carried his two luggage pieces to his flat and placed them on the floor in the guest room.

"You have a nice flat here, Jake. I've wondered what type of unit you lived in, because you were always conservative and abhorred anything with the looks of affluence."

"Well, sometimes one does things for an image. We started a business requiring the image of success, so I drive a nice car, live in a nice flat and dress like I'm successful."

"Do you think you'll revert back to your old self in time when you no longer need the image?''

Unlike Jake's usual rapid-fire response, he paused, looked off in the distance, saying, "Luke, if no one is in my world when that time comes, the natural order of events will return me to my old traits."

"Jake, you're one-of-a-kind guy. Many people who changed history were just like you. Bottomless pits of energy and ideas. They have to go together. They go nowhere when they stand alone, but you brought them together and made things happen. People know you as someone who takes action on ideas.

"I haven't told you this before, but a lot of people thought you were crazy when you took granddad's inheritance and sunk it into blighted property. I was one of them. Also, when you took your profits from the first investment and unloaded it on undeveloped land for the shopping center and subdivision, everyone thought you would lose it all. Now, you have the last word and granddad is looking down, saying, 'I told you so.' He shaped and polished you to shine. He thought you had a special destiny in your life. You know, the family thought you were granddad's favorite, even though we all received an equal inheritance from his estate. The rest of the family has already spent their part of the inheritance, but you shined just like the star he knew you'd become. If I'm as successful a doctor and surgeon as you are in creating wealth, I will have served my watch well."

"Luke, our grandfather knew I was the weaker vessel. What you saw from a distance as polishing, were his surgical hands from his heart filling in the cracks and missing parts of my life. Luke, you didn't have any cracks in your life, you were born good. Anyway, we're too philosophical about life and ourselves! Let's go over and meet the Queen."

When Siana opened the door, she was beautiful and radiant, showing self-confidence and control.

Jake said to Siana, "This is my younger brother, Doctor Luke, and Doctor, here is the Queen of diamonds, Siana."

They both shook hands, Siana giving a momentary look of askance at Jake because of his reference to diamonds.

"Luke, I told you about all the qualities of this lady, except her skillful talent in designing jewelry. The beautiful piece she's wearing tonight was designed by her and manufactured right here in her London shop. It's in great demand and the fastest selling item in production."

"Please, Mr. James, let me tell your brother, that in spite of our differences, we're doing this together. Had it not been for your brother, Luke, we wouldn't be here tonight.

Now, you have the real record. Anyway, let's not use semantics to waste the evening away."

A woman helping Siana came to the living room where they were and told her the table was ready. Luke and Jake filed behind Siana to the wonderful outlay of West African delectable delights. There was joloof rice with chicken, fried shrimp, and plantain. Siana knew there was a greenhorn among them who may not like the spicy food of Africa, so she prepared two large steaks on the side.

After sitting down at the table, Siana said, "My home is my sanctuary, and my table is the place of thanksgiving. At my table, we always thank God for His blessings. Would one of you care to honor us with a prayer of thanksgiving?"

Luke responded. "Yes, I'll offer the prayer."

Jake didn't listen too well to Luke's prayer because thoughts kept coming at him that Luke had survived the onslaught of university life, unlike him, and didn't need to have a name change; it was already changed.

While Luke and Siana engaged in animated conversation, Jake saw her other side. A window opened up into a part of her life he had never seen before. Up to this point, he saw her as a stiff, religious, and austere church person, but tonight it was as if she had taken a mask off to convey her real self. The evening had its closure with Jake requesting Siana to perform some of her classical numbers on the piano. When she found out Luke sang in the church choir, she had him join her in singing a religious number.

"Mr. James, before you leave, I want to tell you some good news about our travel to the hospital site upcountry. My father has an interest in a mining company with a new helicopter in operation. He arranged with their pilot to fly all of us to the site and return the next day to pick us up for our flight back. There's sufficient room available on board to carry any surveying and overnight camping equipment."

"Please tell your father we appreciate everything he's done. This will expedite our work at the hospital site."

"Mr. James, I hope you have no objections with my friend coming along with us. Your work there will keep you and Luke busy, and she can keep me company."

"If you can pull strings to get us a helicopter, how can I object?"

"I'm sorry the flight robs you of all the pleasure you would get out of seeing me roughing it."

"Yes, your father has come to your rescue depriving me of seeing how much more beautiful you could be under the pressures of grueling overland travel and camping in the wild."

"It's not in your character to flatter me with all your eloquence. Is this another side of you I haven't seen?"

"It's the side I show when my brother is around."

"Then it's to my advantage he stays around all the time."

"Well," Luke said, "I can see I brought goodwill between the two of you by being here tonight."

"Yes, Doctor Luke, you certainly have."

After Jake and Luke left, Siana felt some of her fight instinct fade. Inside, she hoped Jake never saw that side of her; it made her appear weak and insecure. She didn't want him to see that. She would rely on her courtroom prowess: know the facts of the case, show self-confidence when presenting an argument, and when cross-examining witnesses, do so without offending the jury. Jake was her jury.

Freetown awaited their visit. Arrangements were made for Jake and Luke to stay at the Bientimoni Hotel,

Siana with her father. Mr. Coker would be providing Jake with a car and driver to use in the capital city. Each of them would carry ten thousand pounds of British currency inside money belts for the groundwork of the new hospital. Siana's father would be the fiduciary agent working with the representatives of the mission in charge of actual construction. Until the mission workers were there on the ground, Mr. Coker would oversee the dismantlement and removal of the ruins at the building site. Jake would complete the engineering phase after the mission in the States had finished its consultation with hospital architects. With Luke going along, he would become an informed observer of the project, and a valuable asset in procuring donated, expensive, up-to-date medical equipment.

Three days after Luke arrived, all three were in the air with a scheduled flight time of seven hours. Siana had scheduled the flight and made the seating arrangements. Luke sat beside Jake next to the window, Siana in the seat across the aisle from Jake.

Halfway through the flight, Luke was browsing a medical journal, Siana was working with a pencil and pad on jewelry designs, and Jake felt like he was inside an MRI chamber and it was time for him to be rolled out, but the table was stuck, or the technicians were trained sadists. He wanted to stand up and scream. Perhaps talking would help. Turning to Luke, he asked, "Have the designs of MRI machines been enlarged so there's less confinement than they were a few years ago?"

"To some extent they have, but they still create fits with people."

He reached over for his carry-on case on the floor, took out a couple of Doctor's sample pills. Siana watched what was going on between them.

Luke handed Jake the wrapped pills, whispering, "Now is the time to show your weakness. Let her see your humanity by taking these in her presence."

He followed the advice of his brother, held the two small pills in his open palm as a gift of life in full view until the flight attendant brought him some water, then gulped them down.

After downing the pills, Siana showed pleasure, saying, "Mr. James, the pills are more effective if they're taken before you board the flight."

"Miss Lawyer, I have no fear when I run with the bulls in Spain; however, I'm afraid of tight places. What does this make me?"

"I don't know what it makes you, Mr. James, but it tells me I can believe only half your story—the part that makes you take those pills."

"Someday, Miss Lawyer, I'll tell you some chilling and exciting adventures I've been through, some of which I'm not proud."

"I'll listen as long as they aren't criminal."

The plane was nearing the airport and descending in altitude. Jake recalled his last flight out of Freetown. One piece of luggage changed his life forever. This time, he was returning a different person, someone with a noble cause. Important people were now a part of his life; he sensed the need of being a member of that community.

Siana's father was there to meet them at the airport. After clearing customs, Siana ran to embrace him. When he saw Jake, he was welcomed like he was a member of his family. Siana's father looked older than when Jake last saw him on the bus going to the airport. All the stress of recent events had taken its toll on him.

After crossing the Sierra Leone estuary, they disembarked from the hovercraft and gave their money belts to Siana's father. Two vehicles were waiting to pick them up. Siana drove off with her father, Jake and Luke went to their hotel. Their room was on the second floor and overlooked the beautiful, cerulean-colored Atlantic Ocean. That night, the full moon highlighted from their belvedere the incoming and outgoing ships sailing past the lighthouse that kept them out of the shallows. It brought to their imaginations historic images of wooden ships with hoisted canvas sails flapping in the winds.

The next morning Jake and Luke stood out in front of the Bientimoni hotel waiting for Siana and the driver to take them to the helicopter pad. Siana and her father had put together everything needed for camping overnight. Jake brought his own transit and surveying equipment with him from London for the elevation work. The copter would drop them off for a one-night camp-over with the women staying in the local town while Jake and Luke slept with camping equipment at the ruins of the old hospital. By noon the next day, they would return to the capital city by copter.

When Siana arrived, the men were introduced to her friend, Loretta, who was a nurse practitioner trained in America. Here in Africa, she served in the position of a doctor. They were going to visit a place lying in ruins after several years of civil war. The old mission hospital complex was one of the causalities of that war. All the medical personnel had to leave, and because it lay in ruins, they never returned. Now that normalcy had returned to the country, construction was ongoing throughout the land.

News of the construction of a new hospital in the area created jubilant reaction. When the townspeople saw the copter come in, several hundred nearby people came running to view the sight. Everything was unloaded, followed by the protocol of meeting with the leaders of the community. The townspeople leaders arranged for Siana and Loretta to stay in secured block homes for the night. Jake and Luke went to the old hospital compound where it lay in ruins. They saw what was left of a cinder block home where their grandfather had once lived.

"Luke, this was where our grandfather lived before we were born, and it was from this hospital site he stored up all those experiences he told us about."

"He told you about them, Jake. He used action stories when he talked with you. Our grandfather always talked to me about what went on in the hospital. Perhaps, he was responsible for laying on me the burden to become a doctor. He discussed the operations and conditions of patients who came here for treatment. It was always in the context of this place."

They had sufficient daylight left for several hours of work before nightfall. First, they cleared a campsite area, then set up sleeping cots under protective mosquito netting suspended with rope.

"Luke, be sure to tuck your netting in under your thin mattress so snakes and mosquitoes won't join your company in the middle of the night."

"For peace of mind, you could avoid mentioning the snakes."

"Remind me to tell you later about my cohabitation with one during the night."

"Now, I know I won't sleep."

They spent the rest of the afternoon working on ground elevations. Local townspeople were hired to dig eight, four-foot-deep holes around the hospital building site for soil samples and compaction tests. Siana had already told them she and her friend, Loretta, would cook the evening meal. After Jake and Luke showered the old-fashioned way, with an overhead bucket, they relaxed in camping chairs.

A classical irony came into view as they sat in the shade under a large cottonwood tree looking down the roadway toward the town where the ladies had disappeared earlier. A cluster of villagers was coming up the road singing in their ethnic language. Included among them were the two Creole helicopter passengers: one, an English barrister, the other, a professional medical officer, neither having ever visited the hinterland before. Both were in national dress enjoying their experience.

Siana and Loretta had prepared a typical Creole dish without the usual hot pepper. The pepper was put on a side dish to accommodate Luke, the tenderfoot among them. Everything had been cooked together to form a sauce to be placed over cook rice grown and harvested from the nearby countryside. Everyone noticed Luke was examining what he was about to eat, when he said, "I'm not sure we should offer thanks for what we're about to eat, but somebody better pray hard over this."

Siana's blue eyes danced with mischief as she engaged in a psychological fencing game with Luke.

"Dr. Luke, I want you to know this critter in the pot was all we could get to make the meal. They caught it in the wild, penned it up for several days until we came along and purchased it from them. They agreed to dress it for us."

"Siana, please be reminded that before we left Freetown, I was the person who thought about bringing prepared food?"

"Luke, wouldn't that detract from the flavor of camping out?"

"Well, Siana, what are we eating here besides rice?"

"Luke, I suggest you eat what's placed before you without asking questions. Isn't this what the Bible says to do?"

"Listen, Miss first-time, know-it-all camper. Your argument is one-sided in my court of Epicurean propensities. The Bible also says to watch and pray. I'm doing both right now.

Everyone began to eat while Luke continued to prod the pieces of meat in the sauce until he got enough nerve to sample a small portion. He had worked all afternoon and couldn't restrain his appetite. His hunger pushed him through the barrier, and after the initial bite, quietness prevailed until he asked, "This is chicken, isn't it?"

Siana, still with the twinkle in her look, said, "Luke, let it be whatever you want it to be. If the flavor is right, you can create any delicacy you want with imagination. Up here in the hinterland, one is at an advantage if he has two things when eating: imagination and appetite."

Everyone but Luke was laughing inside. Here was a person who had never been outside the capital city creating table drama with jungle scenery and atmosphere for her own form of entertainment. Luke eventually found an identifiable piece.

"It's chicken!"

Everyone roared in laughter, except Luke. At the point of being embarrassed, he responded. "Siana, I'm going to remember this the next time you need my professional medical services."

Luke continued, "Why is the chicken so tender? Chickens allowed to run wild become tough and leathery?"

"Luke," she said, "Africans learned a long time ago tough leathery chickens can become tender by feeding them the fruit of papaya. In our case, they sold us a couple of village chickens fed papaya for several days; our bargain with them included dressing them for cooking."

Luke requested a second helping.

It was around campsites in Africa after a long day's work one would find some of the greatest storytellers. Without the noise of electronics, stories became sharper. Both, the storyteller and listener allowed nature to become the background music for good drama. When the evening meal was finished and the campfire glowed with burning embers, Jake's mischievous nature dreamed up storytelling entertainment for the purpose of scaring the novice campers: he'd tell snake stories. He was anxious to see how Siana would stand up after she had made everyone believe she was in command of herself and experienced in the rustic life of camping. He'd use nature's setting as the stage and the nocturnal jungle noises for sound effects.

There was a difference in telling a ghost story inside a cemetery at midnight and relating it at noon in a train station. The environment they were in was a natural theater for creating good mental pictures and feelings for stories about snakes before going to bed. Instead of the wolf howling in the distance under a full moon, there'd be close-by sounds of unknown origin coming from the darkened tropical forest. What the imagination was capable of in darkness was what gave good background sounds for a story.

"We have one night here," Jake said, "and I want everyone to remember to check their beds before retiring. Be sure you tuck your mosquito net under the edge of your thin mattress well, because sometimes snakes have a way of crawling around at night in search of prey. I failed to do this once, got in between the sheets and went to sleep. In the middle of the night, I thought I was dreaming when I awoke and felt something slide across my two feet under the sheet at the end of the bed. I remember saying to myself that it was just a dream, but why did it feel so cold and real? Somehow, those thoughts never had enough strength against the force of sleepiness, and I drifted off again. Later in the night, I was aroused again to a foggy awakened state, feeling something cold next to the length of my legs and back. It was then I knew I wasn't dreaming. I threw the sheet back, jumped out of bed and grabbed my flashlight. Standing on my bare feet with the flashlight in my hand, I saw a six-foot spitting cobra in the middle of my bed. It had placed itself in a coiled striking position. This kind of snake spits poisonous venom into the eyes of its victim to blind it before it strikes. The use of my flashlight prevented the snake from seeing my eyes, but he managed to deposit a large amount of venom on my hand that held the light. There were two things ruined that night: my bed with snake all over it after I beat it to death, and the rest of my night's sleep."

Siana acted frightened, and with gusto in her voice, whether real or pretended, said, "Mr. James, you're incorrigible! You love the power you have over us, don't you? You love to see us squirm under your control with these stories. You've had training somewhere on methods of interrogation by using snake stories. What kind of information do you want out of me, my dreams, because this is a wonderful nightcap for staying awake? If this story needed telling, an earlier time of the day would be preferred, like this morning, so it wouldn't be so fresh in our minds before bedtime."

"Siana, you know this actually happened to me— don't you? It's authentic, it actually occurred!"

"Yeah, just like the story about you running with the bulls in Spain."

Luke was trying to stay out of the line of fire because he was cracking up, and poor Loretta was as serious as Siana, but was letting Siana do all the talking.

"Well Siana, it's better to have a fresh story before bedtime than to have a fresh snake. If the snake story came earlier in the day, you might forget to tuck your net in tonight before retiring."

"Mr. James, I'm going to get even with you someday and you will beg for mercy when my justice comes down on you."

"Siana, I plead with you. If you promise you won't take measures to get even with me, I'll not tell you about the snake the locals call the two-step snake."

There was a lull. Quietness. Then, Luke jumped in and said, "Is that the snake that prefers dancing over sleeping with you?"

Everyone roared in laughter, except Siana. She fought back any sign of a smile, but couldn't hold back, and buried her face in her hands in an attempt to conceal giving in.

"Mr. James, how long did you and Luke practice the snake line before delivering it?"

Everyone continued to laugh as Siana took center stage. Either she was playing her own game of ignorance for her contribution of humor and entertainment, or she lacked information on the Horned Gaboon Viper, the most deadly of all snakes. Victims bitten by this snake died after taking two steps.

They all retired for the evening in good spirits. Jake and Luke were in bed on their cots under their mosquito nets. Because of their parents, both of them came up under strict discipline. The discipline included being in bed and lights out by a certain time. The experience of going to bed early revisited them. They had no power for reading or seeing, just talking. It was like the days when they were kids at home, talking with the lights off.

"Luke, do you think I offended Siana tonight?"

"She came out of her blocks ready for battle. She knew your snake story was a setup. She was prepared for that moment and expected you to pull something out of the hat to make the midnight adrenalin flow. What she liked most was you taking the time for her benefit. Really, I think she got the best of you because she put on a big act, an act of being scared so she could tease you."

The conversations turned to their younger years about people they knew in high school, where they were now, and what they did.

"Luke, you're twenty-eight years old. Are you interested in anyone for marriage?"

"I'm glad you brought this up because I wanted to tell you before I returned home that there might be a wedding within six months. I met someone of special interest when I did my internship. We're planning a marriage date as soon I settle in a practice. I have several offers with great opportunities because of spending an extra year specializing in surgery. Her name is Gloria, a year younger than I and is a pediatrician.

"Jake, what's going down with you there in England? Why are you loafing about in London without any big projects going on? Big projects are what you're known for."

It was a temptation for Jake to tell him about the diamonds, but he chose the nobler thing by practicing silence.

"Luke, Siana and I are in business together, and it's doing well. There's something productive and rewarding on a huge scale coming down the pike, and I'm not at liberty at this time to discuss it.

"Luke, after Dad was well compensated for his work, my company netted over four million dollars last year. If it were just about money, I'd be in the States compounding the profits. I sought something different by going to Africa and remaining in London. Up to this point in my life, what I'm looking for still eludes me, but there may be a ray of light coming my way, but only time will tell. Congratulations on your engagement! I wish you the best."

The next morning they were all up early. While having the customary coffee and bread for breakfast, Jake asked Siana, "Did you sleep after my snake story last night?"

"Do you think you can frighten me with a snake story? I slept well, thank you."

"I want to apologize. This is the bad side of me coming out."

"Was it an actual event?"

"Oh yes, it was a real experience. I embellished the story to give it some color. The snake just crawled across my feet, it didn't lie alongside me. Even the bull running in Spain is part of my history."

"I think you add a lot of color to your stories. The jury is still out on whether I believe any of them, with, or without color. However, I give you an A-plus on your histrionics."

Jake and Luke had finished their work at the construction site and were putting their equipment away when there was heard loud yelling and clamor coming from a distance. Down the roadway was seen a group of townspeople running in their direction. The one leading the group came up to them yelling in Krio, "Wan pekin don fordom nar dry well." By the time he finished telling them what happened, Siana had run over to get the complete story, then turned to Jake.

"A child has fallen into a dry well and needs help."

"Siana," Jake said, "get some men to take us to the well site."

Jake's camping history prepared him for most eventualities. Rope was always part of his inventory. The villagers led him to the site of the well. It was an old well and hardly visible with all the forest growth around it. Now, It was a pit acting like open jaws swallowing anything slipping over the edge. They managed to push the overgrowth back enough to use a flashlight to penetrate the dark chamber below. At the bottom, there appeared a motionless, limp form of a small child. Jake managed to tie the rope around himself in a way to make a safety, harness-type connection. Four men held the rope and began letting him down slowly. The farther he descended from the surface, the darker and narrower the hole became. Halfway down, he looked up and saw somber faces staring at his descent. The one who meant most to him was Siana. In this emergency, all his physical and psychological powers had to be fused together to counter his claustrophobia. Confinement was his enemy. The adrenalin acted like a sedative, enabling Jake to continue the descent without distraction. The light coming from the flashlight held in his hand was all he had to show where the child lay. The stench and odor at this depth snapped his brain into knowing gas from decaying organic matter was present, robbing the cavity of any life-giving oxygen. No sooner did he realized this, he began to fade. The flashlight fell from his hand alongside the unmoving child. With all the strength he possessed, he reached for the child.

"Pull me up, there's gas down here!"

He faintly heard Siana's voice, "Hold on Jake! please hold on! we're getting you out!"

Jake was always proud of his physical agility and athletic qualities, but in this dungeon of dark death, he had to reach down inside himself for strength he didn't have to grasp and hold the child until they reached the top. His consciousness ebbed. He saw the light from his dropped flashlight at the bottom of the well fade in and out like a lighthouse beacon competing in the distance with swirling fog. His rigid torso scraped the wall of the hole as they pulled him up to the surface. The open mouth of the dark pit of death was regurgitating its swallowed victims. While still dangling over the pit with fastened rope, they pried the child loose from his frozen hands and arms. Luke and Loretta took the child while three of the men lifted Jake out. Unable to stand, he collapsed. Loretta and Luke were administering CPR to the child while Jake gave himself a mind threshing for overlooking scientific facts: gas created by decomposition of organic matter, whether plant or animal, was lethal in these conditions. Time was lost to Jake. He lay in a spinning world of nausea caused by noxious fumes. With a doctor and nurse at the side of the limp child, he made no effort to get up. The tragic saga ended when the two medical professionals stood to their feet over the lifeless frame. In the old days of mining, canary birds were the samplers of subterranean air for gas before miners descended. Today, one small innocent canary took his descent never to return to his nest with others.

Cool gentle strokes of a damp cloth across Jake's heated soiled face opened his eyes. He looked at the beautiful face of Siana that carried a worried expression in her soft blue eyes.

"Mr. James, do you feel better now?"

He navigated himself into a sitting-up position.

"Siana," he said, "I can't bear to look upon the child's face. The child has the face of God. I'm afraid of God, afraid of Him because of what I am, what I've become. They'll wash the child's body, won't they, before they bury him?"

He struggled to stand upright on his feet. Luke came over to talk to him and put closure to the signature of death. He had done this at home with others in his medical training.

"Jake, Loretta and I did everything we could to revive the lad, but most likely, he was already gone when you brought him up."

"I hope they wash the body of the child before they bury him. What will they do with him?"

Siana saw that this grave tragedy had brought the best out of Jake. It had removed the veneer from his staged show of resolute hardness. For the first time, she saw the real person of the man who was trying to come into her life. Taking his hand, and looking into his eyes, she said, "They'll take the child, wrap his body in some cloth, place it in the ground and life will go on with sadness."

The mother and father of the child were alongside their lifeless son. The mother was weeping. Jake and Siana together walked over and looked into the lifeless face of the child. Jake had never seen death like this before. Death was supposed to be for the old and infirmed. He took from his pocket, two twenty-pound notes, gave them to Siana, saying, "Please give this to the family, and tell them to wash the body of the child and buy clean, white cloth for his burial."

Siana turned to the mother and father. Speaking in Krio, she said, "Dee Pa say, 'for wase dee pekin ein dae body en go buy kansake wit dis money for berr de pekin wit am.'"

Luke and Siana knew his instructions about the cloth were for his benefit in dealing with death.

"Jake," Luke said, "I saw Granddad's nature coming out in you back there. I must say my brother today demonstrated some of his nurturing and care."

Hearing those words from Luke validated Jake's sense that something mysterious was going on inside. The big universe he lived in was reducing in size. He was now seeing pieces to a smaller world—details shrouded with feelings.

Siana and Luke held both of Jake's arms as he staggered back to the hospital worksite. He was brought a clean shirt, a blanket was arranged for him to rest on under the shade of a tree, and for an hour the four spent time trying to move from the recent tragic memory. Their therapy included learning Krio and telling humorous life experiences—was better than a coffee shop in London.

The party of four arrived back in Freetown late in the afternoon with all the fatigue and weary look of a hard day's work in the tropical heat. They were met by Mr. Coker who was relieved to hear that everything went well. When they drove by the Lebanese travel agency where Jake had purchased his airline tickets and luggage case, a market was in its place. The agent, a member of the smuggling group, either had fled or was in custody.

"Mr. Coker," Jake asked, "what are the latest rumors on Samir.?"

"What we hear is that he's still in England moving about in his community, but even they are wary of him now because he seems to have suffered a mental breakdown. It'll be wise of you to be careful. He has given out threatening statements of retribution on my family and me. He has money to move ahead of the law. I'm sure he'll attempt to re-establish his network again in diamond smuggling, but his proven connections with terrorism will always give him

245

fugitive status here in this country and in the UK. His safety is in some Middle East country where he can hide. In his community of crime, a person has to control people to get loyalty. He's lost control, so he doesn't have loyalty. You see, smuggling diamonds as he operated, requires a whole network to make it work well. It's like a chain interlocking together; one is dependent on the other and each gets his part when the action is over.

"Samir was a courier for the terrorists. He fed information about their activities to London and distributed the same to their cells in West Africa. He collected contributions from terrorist-leaning Middle East business people, made sure it reached the underground movement in London. The extremists had two sources of money when they were in operation: what they collected as contributions and the enormous profits from smuggled diamonds. Because of Samir's power, the flow of both went through him. What the police found in London broke this chain apart piece by piece. However, Samir will not give up. It was rumored his biggest operation was taken by some of his own people in London, and the terrorist cell took action against them for disloyalty."

Siana and Jake looked at each other but said nothing.

After a good night's rest at the hotel, Luke and Jake went to a beautiful beach on the coastline, a place called Two Rivers. The locals provided a cover from the sun and freshly cooked lobster from the sea. The snow-white, sandy beach welcomed them under the hot tropical sun as clean blue waves lapped at their feet. It was a paradise for two brothers in search for what was best and honorable in life. Luke enshrined it to memory.

Saturday morning, Mr. Coker and Loretta went with the departing trio to the airport. Since the departure of his archenemy, Samir, it was evident the public saw him as a victor, and respect exuded from people wherever he moved. The Sierra Leoneans even considered it an unspoken national victory. In this country, the masses always listened to the unprinted, word-of-mouth information for the real story. Just before boarding the plane, he came to Jake, and they talked about Siana.

"Mr. James, I want you to know my daughter thinks you walk on water. Since she's met you, she's a much happier and settled person. Since her mother passed on, life has been difficult for her; however, now she tells me her anger of the past is resolving itself. Also, I'm pleased she's cutting down on her hours at the law office. She's a religious person, and working with criminals in defense cases brings conflict to her sensitive nature."

"Mr. Coker, your daughter is a remarkable person. We banter a lot in friendly conflict, but we get along."

"No one gets more of that from her than I. It runs in our family."

The three walked across the tarmac to board the plane, turned around halfway to the ramp and waved bye to Mr. Coker and Loretta watching them fade into the distance.

Luke leaned over toward Jake, saying, "It must be hard for a father to have one of his children in England and the other slipping from his presence like the lights of a ship leaving a port for an unknown destiny."

"Luke, you speak true words of the father, but I think he knows her destination."

They were in the air with the same seating arrangements. Siana asked Jake, "Did you take your medication for your claustrophobia?"

"No, I forgot."

He looked at Luke who appeared to be asleep.

"Before we boarded the plane, I got some for you from Luke."

She opened her closed hand and there were two tablets ready-made for him to unwrap and take with water. Jake thought this lady, who was his lawyer and business partner, was now becoming his nurse. Perhaps, this was what he needed in life, someone to take care of him.

"Sometimes, I can be nurturing," said Siana, "but you don't need any of that, do you?"

"Siana, you should be careful in what you uncover in me. I could turn out to be a bottomless pit of need, and speaking of a pit, I remember you calling me by my first name when I was down there."

"I do have my moments of weakness. In fact, I have a lot of weaknesses I'm uncomfortable discussing at this time."

"My grandfather is speaking to me now, Siana. Something in his vision for me in this life has something to do with you."

They both became silent when Jake spoke these words. It was the silence that had a peaceful mystery to it, like a closed door hiding the unknown and unexpected. Something was in the air and they both felt it. They allowed the somber, respectful silence to continue.

When they all arrived in London, it was late Saturday evening. Samuel was at the airport to pick them up and when they reached the driveway of the towers where they lived, Jake spoke.

"Siana, are you going to church tomorrow?"

"Oh yes, of course."

"Do you mind if Luke and I go with you?"

"Only if you promise to go with me after Luke returns to the States."

"I promise I'll go with you every Sunday morning I'm here in London"

She said nothing, just smiled and walked toward her tower with spring in her steps and her head lifted high.

The next day, Luke and Jake were dressed and ready to go when Samuel came by and rang the doorbell.

"Mr. James, Miss. Coker is ready and waiting downstairs.

The four rode to church together. Knowing the service would be a shocker to Luke, Jake attempted to prepare him for something different from what he would expect in an Anglican church.

"Luke, this church isn't as liturgical as what you're used to back home. It's quite different, you know."

"I'll measure the whole service by what the rector has to say."

Siana had gone up and taken her place with the musical team. When the singing was halfway along, Luke leaned over and asked, "How long has it been, Jake, since you attended our church for a service at home?"

"Fourteen years."

"Well Jake, our congregational singing is a lot like here, perhaps not so demonstrative, but we do have three or four people leading the worship accompanied by varied musical instruments."

Luke made Jake aware that the culture of communication in the music of the church had changed and he was lost to that change. He would also learn he was lost to the message as well.

When it was time for the pastor to speak, Siana returned and sat with Luke and Jake. The pastor's sermon carried the theme of the pillars of the Christian faith, that man was a fallen creature on a journey of self-destruction, and that God had made a provision for the road of self-destruction to be reversed through His Son, Jesus. He emphasized the struggle of faith was the struggle of the heart to believe even when things in life didn't go right, that God wanted to work in us to restore what was damaged, whether by self-infliction or by events of chance. He had thrown everyone a rope, and those who reached and held on could find help in their fallen state. When the pastor cited the rope, and calling for help, Jake saw himself, not in the pit in Africa with the rope holders, but in the pit he had created for himself by leaving his faith in making himself the sole person in charge of his destiny by putting human reason and natural order in place of God.

When the pastor closed his sermon, he invited those who wanted to pray to kneel at their pew. In life, Jake had allowed his experience of rejection and negativity in childhood to drive him from the culture and teachings of the church. It was on those skids at the university he slid into sophistic unproven scientific theories. He knew he was a good engineer; it turned out his best design was the one he had built to enclose himself.

The words spoken by Mr. Coker came to him, "I was the Prodigal, and someday I would return home and my family would welcome me." But he thought himself different from the Prodigal in the Bible. The Prodigal traveled a great distance to another land to leave his father; he only had to travel to a nearby mind-altering university. The Prodigal lost his friends when he ran out of money; he lost his when he gained a lot of money. The Prodigal spent his life on riotous living; his was on riotous thinking. The Prodigal's rebellion was in the way he lived; his rebellion was in the way he thought. Foreign forces used the Prodigal's greatest weaknesses to break him; nearby forces used his greatest strengths to pull him into his prison. The Prodigal had yielded to his weaknesses. He had yielded to his strengths. Both reduced its victims to a state of poverty. He wasn't hungry, shoeless, poor and in rags like the Prodigal, his deprivations had a façade, a cloak of erudition because his poverty and need were inside. He wasn't the Prodigal who needed to return home; he was home, but lost being so near—yet so far.

Jake leaned over to Siana and said, "Please pray for the restoration of my childhood faith." Then, he repeated the same words to Luke.

Jake knelt at the altar in front of his pew to pray that what he had damaged Christ would restore, and what he had thrown away, he would find. That the fulfillment of his grandfather's expectations of him would happen with a new name and a new nature. He knew if he could take blighted, disfigured property and put up new modern neighborhoods with large shopping centers, God could take his blighted life and do the same with him.

Jake felt two hands touch him on each shoulder as he struggled to come into life, like the chick he incubated when he was a child. It was a struggle into life he would complete by dismantling the shell he had built. He could hear the sounds of the chirpings of life going on inside. The dead boy he had taken out of the well in Africa and carried inside himself was no longer dead, but now had a face of life. When Jake stood and sat in the pew, he was somber, quiet, and still. He wanted to weep, but his brother and special friend were there. Luke and Siana placed their arms around Jake. She used a handkerchief to clear her eyes of tears. He remembered that human life begins with two cells, invisible to the naked eye and silent to the human ear, nevertheless, life was present with all the inherent DNA components to build an organism with design in its plans. Today, Jake chose to let his life move forward in that design. Then, tears ran down his cheeks, and he wasn't embarrassed.

Siana, still teary-eyed, took Jake's hand with both of hers, and held it, saying, "I prayed for you every day that you would return to your faith. God will help you fulfill your grandfather's vision for you."

Her words reached his hearing as if spoken from a distance in a darkened room. For a moment, his sensory reality disconnected. The external world of words coming at him faded into muffled sounds by the energy of change. It was a defining moment for his cognitive powers to register the proximity of two parallel worlds now living in one person at the same time. On their way back to his flat from the church, he only responded in conversation and never created any. His life had taken on new meaning and purpose.

Chapter 14

Checkmate

THE NEXT DAY JAKE ENTERED a new world. It was a world containing identifiable parts and pieces. Siana had used the term details, and now he understood what she was trying to say: that meaning in life came from small important things. His faith now burdened him with personal growth in self-discovery by recognizing the worth of small things in life. He had allowed his brain to be entrenched with deep pathways of addictive behaviors. These behaviors were as compelling as drugs. The strange irony of this was that the public from afar admired the end result of his addiction: his driving entrepreneurial success. Those nearby knew different. His success had created a barrier—it hindered him in understanding who he was, and the importance of others. He had become narcissistic, creating a world evolving around himself to the exclusion of others. Had early failure been his lot in life, perhaps he would have reached this point sooner. These conditioned pathways inside his brain needed re-routing toward new creative ends that responded to life in a different way. At this point in his life, he was like an addict who had walked in from the street into a drug treatment center for help. But he was different from the drug addict. The drug addict's helplessness came from the abuse of external chemicals; his disability came from within. Though he and the drug addict had different causes for their addictions, they had common solutions: both needed help from others. Jake was willing to make the journey knowing withdrawal pains awaited him.

Siana and Jake had scheduled an early work morning at the shop. She arrived at his flat at seven, Monday morning. When the doorbell rang, he opened the door and they both stood and looked at each other saying nothing. Then Siana spoke.

"You're a different person, aren't you?

"And you're more beautiful than ever. You have the most beautiful skin I've ever seen."

Siana looked away. "You're embarrassing me, and besides, Luke may hear us.

"I love embarrassing you," and putting his arm around her, he said, "Please come in and have toast and coffee before we leave. I've arranged for a catered breakfast for Luke at nine o'clock. He'll occupy himself with a book while we're out this morning."

On the way to her shop, Siana found it difficult to focus on conversation. She was gripped with the riveting memory of Jake's arm around her earlier describing her as beautiful. He had reached into her guarded fortress of loneliness, and it was something she welcomed. Then to her surprise, he pushed further into her bastion. "Would you be interested in going to the States with me to visit my family and look at a bigger retail market?"

Now, the man she'd allowed to enter her front gate was knocking at her front door. Her world was spinning. She'd never been tantalized by a man like this before. And the irony of it all was that she welcomed it. But so much was coming at her so fast. Jake was in her world here in London. Now, he was moving her into his—in another land. A sudden latent fear of rejection surfaced. The emotional energy given to pleasant memories faded.

"You make me frightened by asking me this. I'll have to leave my safety for your world. But I'm honored to go and meet your family." *Anxiety lost its hold when she remembered Luke, his brother, who was already a friend.*

"Good, I suggest you get your passport and visa prepared for the trip. We can also take some of your newly designed jewelry pieces to some high-end, wholesale outlets while we're there and see what the market will do."

After leaving Siana at her shop, Jake went to the bank and picked up a delivery of stones for the shop in Manchester. He and Ingrid were meeting for a business breakfast in a London restaurant. By the time he arrived, she was there waiting with a reserved booth.

"Good morning, Ingrid."

"And greetings to you, Mr. Entrepreneur. You've come a long way since you first arrived here in London."

"It's all because of you Ingrid."

"Jake, we've increased local retail sales. Our shop is now capable of finishing off all the roughs you bring over. The demand from the wholesale market and the sales in the front store keep us busy. We can finish all your stock on hand in a short time and keep it in storage. However, to maintain our profit margin, it's best we proceed as we are now because it allows us to design and target the demand market. I need to know how many more roughs you have here in London so I can plan my future purchases for our operation."

"Ingrid, at your present rate of production, the roughs in storage will last for another five or six months. Until then, traveling abroad will not be required. Eventually, people indigenous to the country of Sierra Leone will collect and import the stones. When we reach this point, your foreign travel will be minimal.

"Now on to another subject. In view that you finished the renovations on the property six weeks ago and are continuing to make it a success, I'm going to make a transfer of funds from my account in the States into the Manchester account. You are to use these funds to make the purchase of the property at the agreed price. When you finalized this, we'll own everything outright. If you fulfill your agreement, in a few months you will own thirty-five percent of the property and business."

"Jake, you crossing my life's path, or might I say, mine crossing yours, is the greatest thing ever to come my way. You changed my life. In one year, I will have earned more than I did in five years with the other company. I know money can't make a person happy, but it has given me a feeling of owning my life."

"Ingrid, it's a milestone in a person's life when one finds that money can't buy happiness. It's also an achievement to learn certain forces can be as powerful as money when attempting to find happiness. For me, life sought fulfillment with big dreams. This way of living is as meaningless and empty as an obsession with money. In my experience, when one project was finished, I had to create another on the horizon. I always needed something big with action to escape myself. However, I reached a time when I realized I was using busyness and success to escape God. Last Sunday morning I turned myself around by giving back to God the part of me He had when I was a young child."

"Jake, that sounds strange and hard to believe coming from you. For once, you thought with your heart instead of your head."

Ingrid had not lost her beautiful composure. Her magnetic personality radiated in her conversation with Jake. Everything she did or said was always at the level of excellence. He knew it would be difficult for a suitor to match her ambition and elegance. Perhaps, this was the reason she hadn't found anyone—they all failed to reach her level. Was this the cause of her flirtatious flippancy, a form of play-acting, knowing when the curtain closed for the evening she would still be the lone performer on her stage?

"Ingrid, we're going to have a longstanding business association and I want you contented and the relationship between us in its proper place. I hope to see you in social connections with others who have similar religious moorings as those of your parents. Doing this would benefit yourself and our business dealings. You may never find anyone that comes up to your level, but this doesn't mean you shouldn't try. Sometimes we run across people who don't display strengths on the surface, but down underneath they have admirable qualities."

Change came over Ingrid. Instead of cowering in the presence of her boss, her fighting spirit that had made her what she was came to life in a burst of zest: "Jake, though you're a special person to me, I take great umbrage in what you said. I don't think my social life is any business of yours! Just because I over-step the line with you doesn't give you the right to act parental!"

"All right, Miss Beautiful, and you know you're that. Every moment I spend with you I consider pleasurable, honorable, and challenging. I'm sorry I invaded your privacy. My temperament causes me to act like this sometimes when I need conflict to get stimulated. Some people respond to love, praise, fear, or coercion to get motivated in life. My nature, unfortunately, has used conflict, and it comes in subtle forms, sometimes unobservable by others. I can sometimes be obnoxious. Time allows me to understand myself better, and I'm working at trying to change."

"Jake, you can sometimes be challenging. I emulate confidence on the outside. Everyone sees this, but you can see I need more of it inside. I won't hold what you said against you and I'm sure our business together will fare well.

"Let's move on to the financial reports," said Ingrid. From the sales of cut and finished rough diamonds, minus our overhead expenses, I've deposited in the hospital account at the bank three and one-half million pounds. Upon your direction, these receipts went into your hospital account over which I have no fiduciary responsibility. My records and the written reports show the total receipts of sales and disbursements. They also include the operational overhead, my salary, and the commission of outside shop sales. You can see in the financial overview we're keeping within our budget and are seeing sales increase at the shop in the retail department. It's apparent when all the roughs in storage are on the market you'll have enough to build your hospital and some left over."

"Ingrid, there's no such thing as leftovers because of the ongoing operational overhead of the hospital. Any leftovers will always be in demand. When the physical plant is completed, the front of the hospital will bear a nice bronze plaque honoring the person who believed in his grandson.

"Before we break up our meeting, I want to tell you something personal. For the first time in my life, someone has seriously interested me. I've known her for several months. She's the person that does the jewelry designs for our shop in Manchester."

Ingrid's eyes turned away from Jake. The slight movement of her hands over the table stopped. Ingrid was fast and efficient at everything she did. Today, she was true to form. She had processed what Jake said quickly and adjusted accordingly.

"Well, congratulations are in order, Jake. It's with honesty I say I'm jealous, as you may well know. However, life goes on, doesn't it? I won't have to ask you her name, because it's on the designs you send me. I look forward to meeting her sometime."

"There's a personal request I wish to make, Ingrid. I want you to purchase for me in the market of uncut gems a diamond that will finish out with at least a four-caret rating. Also, include in this purchase four smaller one-caret size diamonds. These are not to come from any inventory I deliver to you at the shop in Manchester."

"This will present no problem at all. I'll get it done right away."

"Thank you, Ingrid. I appreciate it."

Jake and Ingrid departed on good terms. He knew the information of his friendship with Siana would force her to get on with her own life. He had left her the supply of diamonds needed for another week and had taken with him the well-prepared financial statement of the accounts at Manchester.

It took Jake thirty minutes to reach Siana's shop where he earlier had dropped her off, entered the side door all employees used and found her standing near Sarah, the sales manager. Sarah was chosen for the position because of her experience in working with jewelry. She not only knew jewelry and gems as well as anyone in the field, she had exceptional public relations skills.

"Good morningl Sarah"

"Good morning, Mr. James."

"How did things go last week while we were away?"

"Everything went well; the sales are continuing to climb. The new wholesaler who came in a couple of weeks ago has placed a big order on Siana's new design. There was a strange man who came in on two different days displaying weird behavior. He pretended to be shopping, but kept looking toward the back room."

Siana gave a quick, sudden stare at Jake, then asked, "What did he look like?"

"He looked a bit scruffy—Middle Eastern," she said.

Before Jake and Siana left, he took the security camera and tape home to review at his flat. After getting in the car, he said to Siana, "Do you remember the net income of the business for last month?"

"Now, Mr. James," she began, "you and I both know what it is. I know where you're going with this because I can read you like a book, a well-read book. Friday is my last day at the office and they want to schedule a farewell for me. I told them I would agree if you could come with me. They agreed. Will you consent to go with me for this celebrated event?"

"Siana, I'll give due diligence to this invitation if there's compensatory consideration by cooking African food for Luke and me before he returns to the States."

"Is that as far as you can reach? I have already made these plans anyway."

"I know, I'm just reminding you."

It was one o'clock by the time they reached their parking garage. On their way up to Jake's flat, he picked up his mail. They found Luke doing his favorite pastime: reading a book out on the verandah overlooking part of London. Jake glanced over the mail he just collected and saw a letter postmarked from Manchester without a return address on the envelope. After opening the envelope, he found it contained a formal announcement with an invitation to an open house at the shop he had purchased in Manchester. A hand-written note was enclosed that read: *"Jake, please forgive me for not consulting you about the open house. I wanted it to be a surprise for you. There will be important wholesale people I do business with in attendance. Please bring Miss Coker, the person who does the designs, and remember to look your successful best. Also, prepare a short speech. Best wishes, Ingrid."* A surprise it was. Ingrid had written this a few days before their meeting today.

Ingrid was a mover and shaker and continued to prove it. There was no end to her energy and drive. Jake gave several moments of silent pause as he thought through this information. Ingrid knew about this when they met together today and said nothing. She had planned this for several weeks. He turned and faced Siana.

"Siana, I'd you like to meet Ingrid?"

The vibrant world Siana was in came to an abrupt stop. Swift, cold hush etched her entire face—sparkling eyes stopped shining—lips became fixed like the face of a statue. Her universe of sealed comfort was threatened. She looked like the grim reaper was about to make a large swath across her secure world. Ingrid's sketch of herself was still resting beside Siana's photo on the shelf. Jake saw her glance at the pictures before she replied.

"Under what circumstances are you suggesting I meet her?"

She hadn't seen the invitation. He wanted to keep her hanging in suspense and use it for as much mileage as he could. To get her attention, he had already set the stage with Ingrid's self-drawn sketch of herself. It had worked, and now he was pushing it further. This was part of his old addiction—creating conflict for amusement. But now he was in the throes of trying to change that nature, and today had fallen off the wagon. The invitation he held in his hand was extended to her with him saying, "Would you like to attend an open house at my shop in Manchester?"

Siana's world was spinning. She tried to get in control of her feelings by pushing them up inside her barrister cap; she wanted to be rational, not emotional. She knew Jake played mind games, and she tried to be ahead of him when it came to her. She also knew he suffered from emotional dwarfism, but so did she—in a different way. She took the time to look at the invitation. Her world stopped spinning when she saw Ingrid had invited her.

"Mr. James, how many pictures of women do you have on your shelves in the states? Is this your form of playing the game of chess? Are those two pictures of Ingrid and me just pawns for the preservation of the king who lives on excitement and adventure?"

"You have posed three difficult questions, and I'll try to answer each one in their order. First, I will confess that I do have two pictures of women on my shelf at home. People tell me that they are lovely women, very photogenic. The reason I keep them around is because they're like my best friends, I've known them for several years. Is there something wrong with this? A lot of men keep pictures of women they know or have known.

Siana's jaw almost dropped when she heard Jake describe his two women in the States. She thought even if it were true, most men wouldn't admit to it. She had intended these questions to be rhetorical, but he was dramatizing each one.

"Now, you asked me, 'If my pictures of women are part of a chess game?'"

With a scowl on her face, she responded, "That's the best analogy I can use to describe what I see going on here."

"Since you put it like that, let's carry on with that thought. Of the two photos here, one is the real queen, the other is a pawn dressed like a queen. The king has used the pawn dressed like the queen to safeguard the real queen. It's left for you to guess who the real queen is."

"You love to play games, don't you, Mr. James?"

Jake walked over to the two pictures. They sat side-by-side. He took Siana's picture in his hand and placed it on the top shelf above Ingrid's photo.

"Siana, the one on the top shelf is the real queen, the other, a faithful and loyal pawn I used to get the attention of the real queen. And by the way, those two beautiful women I have photos of at home in the States are of my older sister and mother."

She was in a standing position when Jake finished. A weakness came over her. He had pulled her into an unexpected world of surprise with his drama. She sat down staring at her tightly clasped, delicate hands resting on her lap. She felt disarmed, there was no fight left in her, and was at a loss of what to say or do. Embarrassed, she asked, "Mr. James, if I'm the queen, then where is the king?''

"The king is in hiding. He's fearful the real queen will put him in checkmate with rejection. The question is, will the real queen defend the king on this board and keep him alive?"

"You flatter me when you say you fear my rejection. Your actions would have embarrassed your grandfather if he were with us."

"My grandfather would have frowned at me on the outside while he laughed on the inside, then, he would have leaned over and asked me in a whisper, 'What move was that in your chess game?' I was just trying to put some challenge in your life for my own benefit!"

"You certainly have done that!"

"I believe I asked you a question and have yet to hear a reply."

"Mr. King, if you come out of hiding and promise to be upfront with me, I won't reject you and will be glad to accompany you to meet your loyal pawn in Manchester."

For the next two days, Siana was busy in her legal practice and shop management. Jake and Luke went about London visiting historical sites and trying to find good places to eat.

On the day of Ingrid's open house, Samuel dropped Luke, Siana, and Jake off at Gatwick to catch a forty-five-minute flight to Manchester. True to form, Siana made provisions for Jake's flying issues by bringing his medication, then reminded him, "Mr. James, I can do three things better than you: practice law, design jewelry and remember your medication."

After landing, they picked up a rental and found themselves arriving early enough to be among others in attendance. The building Jake and Ingrid had purchased was a two-story structure made into a jewelry store and gem manufacturing shop. The upper floor had a large open room that served as a lounge and came equipped with a modern kitchen. With Ingrid's remarkable talents, it remained an interest with Jake how she'd accommodate all the guests.

Siana was nervous when they entered the front door. She leaned toward Jake and whispered, "You won't go off and leave me alone, will you?"

"If I do, Luke's here to prop you up."

"With my status, I prefer both of you, if you don't mind."

"Just pretend you're in court with your usual self-confidence giving arguments for the defense."

"If I had a choice of going to court knowing I'd lose the case, I'd prefer the loss over this."

Ingrid had contacts with important people in the diamond industry. Many were here today milling about the shop in the front part of the store. Jake and his party were looking at the display of jewelry arrangements inside the cases when he heard his name called from behind.

"Mr. James! Mr. James!" It was Ingrid. She was pushing her way through the crowd of people making her way toward him. She looked her usual beautiful self, acting as if she could conquer the world.

"Ingrid, meet Siana, my business partner, and my brother, Luke, from the states."

They shook hands in a warm formal manner, then Ingrid said, "Please excuse me, we have a lot of guests with a luncheon to serve upstairs. Perhaps, we'll have time to visit later."

Ingrid had hired a first-class catering company to provide a beautiful outlay of food of every description. Round dinner tables with white linen tabletops and serviettes graced the hall. Enlarged photos of jewelry configuration sets hung on the walls on three sides. Smaller pictures showed the step-by-step process a rough gem went through to become a finished diamond, a woman's best friend. There were at least fifty guests present, and when it came time for Jake to speak, Ingrid introduced him.

"Friends, thank you for coming today to our open house. We want each of you to know that the quality of our products is of the highest order and created by the most gifted and experienced gemologists in the market. With us today are two important people who make our products the success they are. First, thank you, Miss Coker for coming. Siana is a practicing barrister in London, also one of our

265

designers. Seated beside her is Mr. James, the owner of our company here in Manchester. Mr. James, please come and greet us."

Jake went to the small lectern and proceeded to speak citing Ingrid's expertise and experience, then moved into a short dissertation of his hospital project.

"In some countries, gemstones, such as diamonds, are exploited; they make a few wealthy and impoverish others. Miss Coker and I have created a non-profit foundation to raise funds for medical services for African countries that export diamonds to Europe. The people of the countries themselves are deprived of the benefits from this natural resource, and those who profit from this industry in Europe should return something back in a tangible way. These countries are in need of hospitals, clinics, and a support system to maintain them. It so happens, our first project is the construction of a hospital where my grandfather served as a mission doctor. We want this information disseminated among anyone who derives wealth from diamonds. Ingrid will send you a brochure with information detailing our mission statement and objectives. Thank you."

He returned to the table where Siana and Luke were and was surprised the group responded with applause. Luke was first to speak.

"Jake, what a splendid concept! Returning diamond wealth in the form of medical services to the country they came from. This may catch on and end up being something big."

A new world had opened up for Jake. Guilt hung all over Europe because of the wealth derived from the diamond industry, and it waited for someone to knock on that door to assuage the guilt. Jake thought perhaps he could be the one knocking at that door. The right exposure, promotion, and open financial records with specific projects would create an atmosphere favorable to large gift donations. Jake turned to Siana, saying, "What do you think?"

"This is something you alone could think up, and it will succeed providing you don't get caught in checkmate."

Now it was Siana's time to use the chess-game analogy knowing it would pass over Luke's head, he being uninformed about the contraband in Jake's possession.

"Checkmated by you, Miss barrister?"

"You know what I mean. Evil has a long memory. You just hung up a sign advertising yourself. Some people who deal in diamonds in Europe buy smuggled diamonds. Honor among thieves is alive and well. Do you remember the question you asked me, 'Will the real queen defend the king on the chess board and keep him alive?' I will do my best, Mr. James, I will do my best."

The open house was a great success. Ingrid was jubilant. After everybody had left, she came over where Jake stood.

"Jake, there was positive feedback from several here today who thought a foundation like you described would receive good response, especially when donations go where they're designated."

Before they left, Siana and Ingrid were at a table going over some of the new design arrangements when a tall, well-dressed man entered the room. Ingrid got up and went over to greet him. She introduced him as Cliff, her friend who came to pick her up. With his arms filled with some of her personal things, she said, "Please take these to the car Cliff, and pick me up in front."

When he left, Ingrid turned to Jake. "Jake, I took your advice. Cliff is someone I knew in our church when I was a teenager. He is a CPA, although in this country, it comes with a different title. It might please you to know he is going to take me to church Sunday, the first time I've been to church in a long time."

"Ingrid, I'm pleased. I know you'll find in your heart what is right for you."

"Jake, may I see you for a few moments in my office before we all leave? I want to give you the diamonds you requested me to purchase."

They excused themselves and went to her office where she took from her safe the diamonds he requested her to buy. They were placed on her desk in a small open box. He took them out, looked them over well.

"Impressive! These are perfect."

"I'm pleased you like them, Jake."

"Ingrid, these are special diamonds I want you to oversee when they're cut, polished, and finished according to Siana's new single-ring design with the accompanying four smaller stones. After finishing the cuts, the large centerpiece should be about four and one-half carats. Siana is to know nothing. I leave it with you to keep it confidential. After it's finished, insure it at market value and get it to me by special delivery."

"I'll keep this in the strictest of confidence. I believe the diamond will turn out to be larger than you stated."

Jake wrote something on a piece of paper, handed it to Ingrid. "Here is a brief script I want to be engraved on the underside of the ring."

"When the stone is finished, Jake, it will astound you in its beauty. I'll oversee the special care it needs in the shop. How soon do you want these finished?"

"Two to three weeks will be fine."

When they arrived back at their flats, the three of them went to Jake's place. It was still daylight outside, and

Pizza was on the menu. Luke had settled himself on the balcony with a book; Jake and Siana were in the front room. From where Jake sat, he could see Luke. Luke was always the little brother in age and in physical stature. Jake's thoughts about his brother took on verbal form with Sana who sat next to him.

"Siana, my brother is such a sensitive and considerate person. He was always younger and smaller than me. As we grew older, we morphed inside. He became the big brother and I the smaller. The most important things that mattered in life grew in him. When I was a kid, I used to go off and cry because I could never be good like him. I wanted to be good, but I couldn't. I remember praying once, asking God not to take him. Because Luke was so good, I was afraid God might want him to be with Him. I always did things that annoyed my parents when we were children, really crazy things, and poor Luke, my brother, would follow me doing the same things. When my parents uncovered the truth, I lied. I was a good liar. But Luke never lied."

Tears were in Jake's eyes when he said, "You're so much like Luke. You should have a close friend like him— someone who's unflawed."

Jake had crossed over into the affective domain, a place rarely frequented. Siana welcomed the exposure he was giving himself in the sunlight of her presence. The exposure made her feel like they were true friends.

"But you're looking in your own mirror. God has a mirror too. His mirror shows you what you can become. Most of us are not good. Luke's a special person and the person he marries may fall short of him, but this doesn't make the other person inferior to him. There are strong people, and there are weak ones. It's for the weak to know

269

they're weak, and the strong to know that it's for them to help the weak."

Silence was the closure to their conversation. Jake went to his office thinking of the picture she had painted of the two of them—he was the weak one in need of someone of her strengths. She knew he was weak, and he knew she was strong. He wrote out a check for his brother, returned and found Luke and Siana talking together.

"Luke," he said, "here is an early wedding gift for a down payment on a home. You and Gloria pick one out after you decide where you will take up your practice."

Luke took the check, and when he saw the amount, he grabbed Jake with a bear hug and wept.

"Siana," Luke said, "did you know Jake paid all my expense through medical school? Today, I'm debt free. I'm going to call Gloria and tell her about the down payment on our home."

"Tell her it's a payment for my sins against you when we were kids."

"Siana responded, "Mr. James, you did a wonderful thing for your brother, and did I hear you say you were not good?"

The evening before Luke was to fly back to the States, Siana prepared West African food. She served a connoisseur's epicurean delight. It was an informal relaxing time.

The next morning they saw Luke off at the airport. He gave Siana and Jake a big embrace and they wept together as he left to board his plane.

Returning to their flats, they prepared for the evening function of Siana's farewell at the law firm. Their busy schedules had prevented them from viewing the security tape taken from the London shop. Jake had installed the system himself and had used it to study clientele and security weaknesses of the store, so it was easy to activate the tape and review chosen segments. He connected a printer that would allow him to print out still frames of any scene. When he came across the scene Sarah referred to, he made a copy and faxed it to Siana, then called her.

"Siana, please check the photo I just faxed you. This is the picture of the man Sarah mentioned who came into the shop last week."

She called right back, and Jake noted the fear in the sound of her voice.

"This is Samir, the man my father talked to you about! We must be careful of our steps. He's a violent and dangerous person. I'll call the police and alert them of his presence at our shop."

They managed enough courage, acted on caution, and attended Siana's farewell together. She introduced Jake to each associate. Later, each gave a short speech with praise and commendation for her competency and skill in her work as a criminal defense attorney. It was an evening of fete for her service and contribution to the firm. In response, Siana stood to her feet without notes and forethought, proceeded to go through all the expected formalities people say at such functions. To Jake's surprise, she included him in her speech.

"I have with me tonight a special friend who has become part of my life and has helped me become a better person. Because of him, I'm able to do something I've always wanted to do for a long time. He made it possible by believing in me and showing me the bigger picture in life. I'm not leaving the practice of law, but am adding enrichment to my life with new Interests."

She continued with the emphasis in her speech that everyone had periodical finalities when a chapter of one's life closed to give way for newness, growth, and the inclusion of others. Jake was glad to be one of the others.

Chapter 15

Samir

THE ACTIVITY OF BUSINESS at Siana's shop gained momentum each day. The quality of finished diamond sets she had put together placed a big demand on production in the wholesale market. The gemologists sometimes had to work overtime and on some Saturdays.

It was early Monday morning. Jake drove to the shop before the sales department in the front had opened for the public. After going through the security door and greeting the workers at the tables, he proceeded to check the existing inventory of diamonds in the safe. He closed the door to the safe, returned to the front and noticed Siana's car had just pulled into the outside parking area. She had arrived before her sales manager. When she approached the door, he moved in her direction to open it. A figure emerged from the side of the building just as the door opened. A man with a gun in one hand and briefcase in the other lunged pell-mell with his whole body weight through the door forcing Siana inside with himself behind her. His eyes were fiery and wild. Jake, at first, thought he was a regular thief, but when he saw the man's full face, he recognized him: it was Samir, the infamous criminal kingpin who had escaped the authorities' net. He was unshaven and wore a wrinkled outer coat. In contrast to his disheveled appearance, he sported large, diamond-studded rings on both hands. The worst of all fears had come to Jake and Siana.

The sudden burst of unexpected terror narrowed Jake's cognitive skills to a laser-like beam; he needed to find a way to alter the circumstances.

Samir was yelling, "Where are they? I know you took them. If you don't produce the diamonds, I'll use this gun! I put too much effort getting them into this country to lose them now!"

It was evident the man was deranged.

Jake said, "Look, just take what you want here in the display case."

He leaned over, took some pieces of jewelry out of the case and offered them to him.

"Don't insult me with this pinchbeck stuff. You know what I've come for. I want those diamonds you took from us at the airport. You caused the death of my two cousins by planting a piece of luggage in their vehicle. My people won't believe me, but I know the truth because their families told me what happened."

A sheet of cold ice covered Jake. Samir had come for two things: diamonds and revenge. Jake continued to play ignorant, saying, "I don't know what you're talking about."

Siana had recoiled in fright. Her strong will forced her delicate frame to appear calm; the hysteria was inside. Her eyes darted back and forth from Samir to Jake. She recalled his known reputation in Freetown: violence and corruption. Now, she and Jake stood in his court already stained with the blood of his victims.

If only one of the workers would come from the back room or the shop manager through the side door. Perhaps it would distract him enough for him to seize the gun.

"I want the diamonds now!" Then he reached and grabbed Siana demanding, "Get me the diamonds, or I'll shoot this lady!"

Jake never knew how much Siana was a part of his life until he saw her fragile form pushed and threatened with a gun. He felt helpless, forced to walk over this tightrope balancing someone who had become part of the fabric of his life, and one slight mistake would rip her from him. Her face, filled with fear, had a look of powerlessness. Now, the odds moved in the favor of Samir by threatening Siana. Opportunity to react by someone coming into the shop evaporated.

The reputation of this person flowed through Jake's mind like the muddy water in a river from torrential rains. He could see the debris of old logs and garbage pulled from the banks. It all floated in front of him in its ugliest forms: killings, diamond smuggling, and complicity with terrorists who paid suicide bombers to kill innocent people. This was the real Samir. He had arrived to collect what he robbed and killed for. His physical appearance told the story of his lost empire. Powerful people didn't dress or look like this person, even the violent ones. Now, he was a mere fugitive from Freetown. The identity of Siana, the daughter of Mr. Coker, the person he was holding and threatening with a gun, must remain unknown to this intruder.

"Let Miss Jones go, and I'll take you where the diamonds are."

Moments earlier, Jake had wished for someone to come through the door, now, he hoped and prayed this wouldn't be the case. This man had once sat in an office of power and given orders for others to do his infamous acts. Now, his hands were empty, though he held a gun, his power was gone, his cohorts had fled. His banishment was to the lone island of the insane, trying to survive by running from the law. This kind of person was the most dangerous and unpredictable.

Jake fell into a state of remorse. Siana wouldn't be in this situation had he returned the diamonds. Then, a classical irony of life came to him: it was keeping the diamonds that had brought them together.

The man yelled again, "Where are the diamonds?"

Jake looked at Siana, then toward Samir. "The diamonds are in a safe deposit box at a bank, please let Miss Jones go, and I'll take you there."

Jake could tell he believed him as he started to calm down. Then demands were made he didn't want to hear. "Bring your car to the side entrance here. The three of us will go together, and this woman will remain, my hostage, while you are in the bank getting the diamonds."

What Jake heard was not what he wanted to hear. Samir had detected something in his voice that told him this person was someone special to him, and her being along as a hostage would better serve his purpose.

To change the odds of looming danger about to befall Siana, Jake's brain sought pathways to change Samir's advantage in the law of probability. Samir must not find out Siana was the daughter of Eben Coker of Freetown. He knew once he got the diamonds they would be of no value to him, and he would do to them what he had done to others. Madmen thought rationally and clearly when self-preservation was forced upon them. Jake knew when Samir's operation was over, the police would only carry the news event that they were missing persons. Knowing everything was stacked in Samir's favor, Jake had to put everything down on the table for the biggest gamble of his life. There were three parts to his roll of the dice. First, Samir must sit in the front passenger seat next to him.

When he slid into the driver's side of his car, he leaned over and moved the passenger seat as far back as possible, then pushed the driver's seat as far up near the dash as it would go. His tense hand reached over and turned on the key. With the key on, he switched off the front-seat, passenger airbags. From his front pocket, he took a black pen marker and marked over the seatbelt warning light. Everything he planned rested on Samir sitting in the front passenger seat. If he didn't choose that seat, there'd be no hope of survival.

Jake pulled the car up to the side entrance. He was in a state of fright, not for himself, but for Siana. She had become the victim of his actions in keeping smuggled diamonds. The contraband had changed his life forever—now he awaited his fate. His conscience often took time to mull over the memory of guilt, but today he would entertain only the guilt of endangering the life of Siana, an innocent victim.

Samir pushed Siana out the door as he held his gun on her. Passing the driver's window, he yelled, "Open the boot." Jake reached down and pulled the latch for the boot of the vehicle. In the rearview mirror, he could see two figures pausing behind the car. There was a slight thud in the back part of the car, then the sound of the boot door closing. When they came to the passenger side of the vehicle, he was without his briefcase. Jake knew ominous events awaited them: he intended to take the car with him wherever he was going—without them.

He opened both doors on the passenger side of the car, shoved Siana into the back seat, slammed the door shut and jumped into the front passenger seat opposite Jake. With

Siana in the back seat and Samir on the passenger side in the front, the second part of the trilogy was in place. Samir refused the restriction of the seat belt; it lay silent as he attended to holding his gun and watching Jake's movements. Restraint was never a part of his aggressive lifestyle and refused to accept it now even in his dethroned status as a fugitive. He got what he wanted by unbridled restraint and passion. Because he held his gun in his right hand, he leaned toward the dash on an angle facing Jake.

In the midst of this life and death moment, seeing the gun in his right hand caused a picture to flash in Jake's mind of a page from a book he had read on the topic of Middle East customs. They discouraged left-handedness. It was unacceptable for children to learn to write with their left hands. With his gun gripped in his right hand, it revealed compliance with that custom. When Jake pulled out onto the roadway, he saw in the rearview mirror someone getting out of a car watching him drive away. If it were the store manager, he wasn't sure he wanted her to call the police with the state of mind Samir was in.

Siana sat behind Samir in the back seat while Jake's eyes darted about the roadway, at Samir alongside him, and at Siana using the rearview mirror. When their eyes met, they communicated as if words were spoken. Both knew after the diamonds were in his hands, he would never consider their survival. The gun remained pointed at Jake in the front seat.

For what Jake was about to do, Siana needed to move over behind him in the rear seat. On the busy roadway, Jake swerved into the outside lane of a fast-moving car coming from behind. The driver laid on his horn.

"Miss Jones, I'm not used to driving on this side of the road here in London, can you move to the other side of the seat so I can see more of the roadway?"

Samir said nothing. His eyes kept looking at Jake with the gun in his hand. As she moved over, she gave a forced smile of anguish. She knew what Jake had planned because she knew Jake; he was a gambler. Now, she was gambling with him.

When Jake saw Siana's forced smile, he couldn't prevent the thought entering his mind that this smile may be her death smile. She buckled her seat belt quietly in slow motion, Samir heard nothing, his belt remained unfastened. Jake's math and science backgrounds never allowed him to believe in or explore mental telepathy. However, the intensity of their mental and facial energies, compressed together into such a small segment of time, gave clear messages between them what they were about to do. Jake had second thoughts about the theory of mental telepathy.

Gambling in real estate with everything on one number with your own money was a lot different than gambling with another person's life. Jake was losing his self-confidence. Someone else was now a part of his life. His instinct for adventure faded by having to think about someone outside himself.

Now, instead of one gambler in this car, there were three: Samir, that he would get the diamonds and elude the police, Siana, and Jake, that they would survive a planned auto crash. Jake considered the odds of survival in a vehicle collision were better than the alternative after giving the diamonds to Samir. Now, the last words to the gambling trilogy were about to be penned.

The man holding the gun blurted out, "How far is it to the bank?"

Jake reluctantly said, "It's about five miles."

"Just remember it's your life and the life of the lady back there if you're leading me astray."

He glanced at Samir's hands. His right hand clenched the gun, his left formed a clenched fist. His tightened hands held in front of him looked as if he were holding on to something he'd die for, like monkeys trapped in the wild with clenched fists. Outside civilization where monkeys were part of the diet, captors would use an age-old device to procure them. A hole was cut at the top of a coconut just large enough for the monkey's hand to fit inside unclenched. A rope held the trap, and grain was placed inside the coconut to attract the monkey. When a monkey found the grain, he pushed his unclenched hand inside the coconut. After filling his fist full of grain, the monkey refused to release it. Its clenched hand, now full of grain, was too big to slide back through the hole. His hunger for the grain was greater than his capacity to understand that freedom required the release of the grain in his closed fist. Samir had both of his hands clenched, full of grain, not knowing the captors were moving in to take him. The difference between him and the monkey was the monkey attempted to steal a necessity of life while Samir stole life itself.

Jake moved into the outer lane next to the shoulder. He needed an object off the side of the roadway to provide the highest safety margin for other vehicles. With his gun pointed at Jake, Samir's eyes glowed with hate and revenge.

Coming into view about a half mile in front was an overpass. It had a large supporting cement buttress on the side of the roadway beyond the moving traffic behind them. The impact had to be at the right angle at the point of the left front fender on the passenger's side. Jake slowed to sixty-kilometers an hour, then veered quickly over into the cement wall hitting the abutment on the planned glancing angle. The noise of screeching metal crumpling and tearing was horrific...then only silence—silence like an eternity. Time stood still. The airbags had activated all around, except where Samir sat. Jake lifted his head, pushed the airbag away from his face, looked over at Samir. He was motionless. His head had hit the windscreen. Blood covered his face. It wasn't Samir's blood Jake saw running down onto the dash of the car. It was the blood of innocent children and mothers he killed by sponsoring terrorism with smuggled diamonds. His gun had fallen on the floor. He yelled, "Siana, are you all right?" There was silence. Then came her voice, "I'm fine." He reached over to feel for a pulse from the gunman. His slumped-over body was as lifeless as those he sentence to barbaric cruel deaths.

Stored inside man was a natural reservoir of human compassion that exudes sympathy at the sight of death. Today, Jake's reservoir was empty for Samir. By this time, Siana was out of the vehicle dialing for emergency assistance. The driver's door where Jake was still sitting required effort to force open. Soon, they heard sirens blaring.

Through all the ordeal, Siana had held up but now caved with bitter sobbing. Jake held her tight and offered what strength he had. Soon, she relaxed, regained her composure leaving his shirt stained with her tears.

The paramedics came, extracted the body of Samir from the crumpled and twisted chamber of justice. They placed it on a stretcher. The white cover they laid over his body could not conceal the black record of his crimes and pain inflicted on others. For Jake and Siana, the final verdict of true justice today bore the dignity of permanent silence. In Samir's legal case of public opinion, *justice was delayed, but it was not denied.* The portion of gas going to him to make the desert run would now go to a more worthy traveler.

Siana and Jake gave the complete report to the police starting from the time Samir entered the shop. They took his gun and wrote in the report that the cause of the accident was from the driver losing control. When the police left the accident site, Siana called her father, then her brother. Each received a detailed report of the event. Her final call was to the manager at her shop.

With a weakened voice, Siana released her feeling to Jake. "At last it's all over. I never told you this, but his threats gave me many sleepless nights. The week we spent in Africa outside the UK was the only time I rested well." Jake put his arm around her and they waited until Samuel came and picked them up.

Samuel followed the tow truck to Jake's garage. The truck backed the mangled vehicle into the garage and the door was closed. It was out of sight, but the tragic memory would linger. Later, there would be extensive inquiries into the accident. With Samir's fugitive status, along with surfaced reports filed by Siana about the threats Samir had made against the Coker family in the UK, the case would quickly close.

Both went to their flats. When Jake entered his, he did so with great relief. His phone soon rang. Ingrid was on the line.

"Jake, I'm sorry what happened today. I called your shop there in London to talk to Siana about one of her designs and the manager informed me of the incident. Is there anything I can do?"

"Yes Ingrid, there's something you can do. What's the news on the ring project?"

"Jake, we just finished it. I was not going to mention it because of what happened. It's the loveliest ring I've ever done. When you see it, it will please you."

"Ingrid, send it special delivery after you insure it for its value."

"I'll do that, Jake, and I know it'll not disappoint you. I'll see it's delivered to you first thing tomorrow morning."

It was four o'clock in the afternoon. Siana was alone by herself in her flat. Something came over Jake he never experienced before. It was a sense of guilt for neglecting a person who had suffered emotional trauma, a person who had led him into deeper waters of the affective domain and introduced him to a spiritual order and dimension he knew as a child. He was at a loss on how to use new untried tools in a relationship. He always exuded confidence with insightful business ventures at home, but now, in this one-on-one venture with a soft and delicate innocent person, he lacked the blueprint on how to proceed. His history was a record of subjecting other people's feelings to the more measurable and tangible dimensions of his own self-fulfillment; it was all one way—his way. Now, the waters needed to flow in the other direction. He was not sure it was his brain reaching into his affective part, or his emotions leaping upward to the control center, or both acting together in concert to create a conscious decision to help someone else.

Siana was in her flat, recoiled in lonely, confused thought, lying on her bed with her face sunk deep into the pillow. It was her only friend; it was soft and welcomed her tears. Loneliness, her common enemy, had lost its loud whispers since Jake came into her life; now, they had surface as in old times. With everything coming down as it did with Samir, her mood swing left her bereft of inner strength. Her friends she had kept at arms' length were of no help. She was tempted to take a sedative to help relieve her pain when her doorbell rang.

Her mind registered the sound of the doorbell, but her will lacked the energy to respond. It kept ringing. When she thought it could be Jake, she jumped up, looked into the mirror, and wiped her eyes. She couldn't remove the redness, but she didn't mind. She thought it strange she didn't care he saw her blurry red eyes. She walked to her front room, saw his figure through the window, wiped her eyes once again and opened the door.

"Siana, be ready to go out in thirty minutes. We're making ourselves busy for the rest of the day and evening. I want your mind relieved of what happened today."

She welcomed the succinct sharp demands made on her. They were words with open arms, words that gave her a sense of belonging—something she needed.

"Are you sure you want to do this?"

By this time Jake was walking away. Turning around, he said, "I'm going to order us a taxi and return in thirty minutes. Don't be late."

"Yes, Sir," she replied in a teasing compliant manner.

They spent the whole evening together as an effort to suffocate the events of the day. It proved to be successful. For injuries to heal, it required time. However, pain medication administered at right intervals could alleviate the agony of waiting.

When they returned after the evening out, the taxi let them out at the gate of their enclosed towers. Jake said to Siana, "May I walk you to your flat."

"Mr. James, I'd like that a lot. Tonight, you lifted me from despair by sharing your strength."

Jake reached over, took her hand, and walked her to her flat. When Siana went to bed, her pillow was still damp from earlier tears. She turned it over, and before going to sleep, reflected on the two sides of her pillow: one, tear-stained, the other dry. She was glad her day ended without the pain of tears.

On his way to his flat, Jake pondered how both of them were lonely in their own special ways. Jake's bed looked inviting. He got undressed, turned off the lights and slid under the sheets. Dreamland was opening its wide door when he sat up in bed and almost yelled. *The briefcase! I forgot about the briefcase in the boot of the car.* He clothed himself, found his keys and went downstairs where the wrecked car was stored, unlocked and raised the door to the garage. He reach up, turned on the light, and staring at him was something that looked like a space capsule having crashed on one side upon reentry. He walked by the mangled side of the car, looked once more at the chamber of the jaws of justice. The door of the trunk opened with his key, he lifted the briefcase out and shut everything up.

Jake found the briefcase locked after placing it at his feet in front of the sofa. With effort, he forced it open. Inside were maps, passports, airline tickets, and four cloth bags filled with uncut diamonds. He took the bags out and placed them on the coffee table. Collecting smuggled diamonds had kept Samir busy. Jake and Siana's shop was his last stop. It was the smuggled diamonds Jake had kept at Gatwick that became bait to catch the biggest fish of all. Now, the whale lay beached. In his last gasp, he had coughed up messages of life. The diamonds that brought death to Samir would bring life to others in a hospital in Africa.

Jake went to his computer, wrote a letter to Siana, and made two copies. He signed one of the copies, enclosed it in an envelope, and put it in the drawer of his nightstand by his bed.

Eight o'clock the next morning his phone rang. "Mr. James, this is security at the front gate and there's a Miss Ingrid Spence who wishes access. Can you give me approval for her entry?"

Jake was waiting with his front door open when Ingrid arrived.

"Good morning, Ingrid. You must consider my package of ultimate importance to bring it yourself?"

"Jake, you must remember I work for you, and besides, I can't have someone else deliver this to you after doing most of the work myself."

"I appreciate that, Ingrid."

She opened her handbag, took from it a small package, saying, "Jake, you will find the finished product exceeding your expectations."

He took the package containing the diamond ring and opened it. She saw Jake's face register astonishment.

"It is most spectacular and unique, a beautiful piece of work."

"The large centerpiece is five carats, Jake, the four smaller ones alongside are one carat."

He looked at the inside of the ring to check the inscription. It read, *"Siana, My Name Changer."*

"Ingrid, I'll give you a bonus for your excellent work in this important project."

"Oh, you don't have to do that. I took pleasure in doing the project."

Jake prepared both of them tea and made it a point not to discuss business as they chatted about their families and themselves.

"Jake," she said upon leaving, "you showed me it's possible to return to one's spiritual roots after wandering away. Even in your state of rebellion, God allowed me to cross your path for this purpose."

"Ingrid, it's been, Siana. Her quiet spiritual life possessed the tools to make the difference in my life. The inscription on the ring's underside carries that record."

After Ingrid left, he took the box containing the ring and went to his bedroom. He placed the ring inside the large envelope containing his written and signed letter to Siana. After writing her name on the front of the envelope, he returned it to the nightstand drawer by his bed, then took a taxi and picked up a car rental.

The bank assisted him as before in getting into the box where he kept the diamonds. All four bags of uncut diamonds found in Samir's briefcase became part of the other contraband. The sound of the safe deposit door closing was like the music of the doxology being sung in church, the closing note of good conquering evil. After arriving back at his flat, the phone rang. It was Siana.

"Good morning, I called you earlier, and you had already left."

"Why didn't you call me on my cell?"

"Well, after the recent event, I didn't want to expose you to Murphy's Law with your use of the phone while driving."

"Siana, as you know, I'm flying out to Freetown tomorrow to confer with a building contractor who works with the mission. I want to discuss some of the plans with him. I have with me here at my flat Samir's briefcase from my wrecked car. I want you to inspect it and keep it for me while I'm away."

"Bring it over, and I'll show you some of my new designs of bracelets and necklaces."

Before Jake had rung the doorbell, she opened the door. "Come over to the table and look at what I'm working on."

Two things stood out to him: she invited him into her home without reservation and had no interest in the briefcase he held in his hand. It was as if another world had come into existence and she had invited him into it. He left the case near the front door intending to take it back to his flat when he left. It possessed no power in its present form, and its symbol of the past would fade in time. Jake would let the sleeping dog lie.

It was Siana's artistic creative designs that increased the sales at the shop in the beginning. With the popularity of her pieces of jewelry being in greater demand every week, it placed more challenge on her reservoir of talent for newer and bigger creations.

She went through her folder piece by piece indicating the details of those ready for production and those in the planning stages. This was her world of creativity, and Jake realized he'd never be part of it. It was like his attendance at the opera: he enjoyed the beauty and talent but was doomed to stay a member of the audience. Samir's briefcase had lost significance, and Jake picked it up on the way out and handed her a key to his flat.

"Please keep this key in a safe place for me while I'm gone."

Reluctantly, she took the key as if it were an invasion of privacy. He never mentioned Samir's briefcase to her again.

Jake spent the afternoon going over hospital building plans. The next day he was scheduled to fly out to Freetown to confer with the contractor who had already arrived from the States. While there he would transfer to Mr. Coker sufficient funds to underwrite the first phase of the hospital construction costs. He called Samuel, asked him to be at his place at five o'clock the next morning. Then he called Siana.

"Siana, I'm leaving tomorrow morning and will not have an opportunity to say my farewells then, so I'll do them now. Besides, I don't do departures with you very well anyway."

"Take care of yourself, and since I'm not there to help you do that, take special care."

Jake went to bed early. By four o'clock he was up. He showered, dressed, and carried his single luggage case downstairs where Samuel waited in the car with the boot already open. Jake placed the luggage inside, closed it, went to the passenger side and opened the front door. He saw Siana coming toward the car.

"Good morning, I wanted to say, bon voyage on your flight. If you see my father tell him hello for me."

"I will, and you take care. Don't put too much into your schedule this week."

"Did you remember to pack your medication for flying?"

"No, don't you remember, I forget the small things."

"Well, as long as I'm around, I'll remember for you."

She handed him a small packet, saying, "There's enough here for your flight both ways. Be sure you take it before you get on board."

"Siana, you make me not want to go with all this care and attention."

When he said this, she turned around so he couldn't see her face, walked away, saying in halting speech, "I'll be here when you get back." She didn't want him to see tears in her eyes.

Jake ran after her, took her by the arm, and turned her around. The light was dim, but he could see the sparkles in her moist-ridden eyes. He wiped the trickles of tears from her cheeks and embraced her, saying, "You will never know how much you've changed my life." It was the memory of Jake's embrace that would weigh on her mind that day—not her work at hand.

Jake and Samuel drove away with Jake saying, "How de body, Samuel?" With a chuckle in his voice, he responded, "I'm fine, Mr. James."

The flight landed in Freetown. The contractor the mission board had sent over was at the airport to meet Jake.

"Are you Mr. James?"

"Yes, I am."

"I'm Owen Bent with the mission."

Jake saw a person in front of him who carried the appearance of a rugged outdoorsman. The man's rough, gnarled hands showed scars and calluses from hard work, work he'd been successful in, else he wouldn't be here in this country. His dress was consistent with his rugged-looking image—looked like he just came from a work site. Jake saw part of himself in the man who came to pick him up.

"When did you arrive here in the country, Mr. Bent?"

"Two weeks ago. Yesterday, I returned from the hospital construction site. They did a good job in demolishing and removing all the old debris.

"Has information reached you about a Mr. Coker who is to act as my agent in handling the funds coming into the country?"

"Yes, I have. It's a generous gift you're making to the mission hospital project."

"Mr. Bent, have you done any building in Africa before coming here?"

"Yes, I supervised the construction of two mission schools in Liberia."

"Good, you'll have no problem understanding what your issues are. Mr. Coker is responsible to oversee the disbursement of funds for building materials and labor alone.

Anything falling outside this requiring funding, you're to contact me or go through the mission. In addition, I recommend you build at least two of the homes housing the medical staff before starting the hospital. This will provide living quarters for yourself and others who may come over to assist you."

"Yes, I've already thought of this."

"Do you have a family, Mr. Bent?"

"I'm married, but we have no children yet.

"Are you married, Mr. James?"

"No—not yet."

"May I ask why are you giving such a large amount of money to one project?"

"The money coming to this country for the hospital is given because a special person believed in me when I was a kid, and what I am today is because of him. His name was doctor J. Baron. He lived and worked at the old hospital for several years. The new hospital will honor his memory and dedication to the people of this country."

"This is a remarkable story."

"Mr. Bent this is just part of the story, perhaps someday I'll give you the last chapter."

On the second day, they were on a first-name basis. Jake found Mr. Bent was well experienced in the building trades and had done well in construction at home. He had investments to supplement the reduced income he received from the mission.

Jake's top priority was to meet with Siana's father. He called Mr. Coker and he agreed to have dinner at seven in the evening. It was important for Owen to meet and know the people who made things happen in Freetown: Mr. Coker was one of them. The meeting was going well, and Jake could tell

Mr. Coker had connected with Owen. Then Siana's father began talking to Jake by addressing Owen.

"Mr. Bent, my daughter's life is changed. She is now contented and happy. She's become a successful businessperson in her own right. Do you know who is responsible for this, Mr. Bent? It's the person sitting next to you. He did for my daughter what his grandfather, Dr. Baron, did for me when I was a boy—he gave me life at the hospital we're rebuilding. This is why I'm interested in seeing the hospital built and dedicated to the memory of Doctor Baron."

Siana's father looked at Jake with a face that carried the image of what he had been in life: a faithful husband, father, and an honest businessman. "Jake, without your grandfather there at the hospital at that time, Siana wouldn't be in London today."

"Mr. Coker, I feel unworthy of the words spoken about me tonight regarding Siana. This is a two-way street. Your daughter helped fulfilled my grandfather's vision for me by being the instrument of creating a spiritual change in my nature and life. My grandfather saved your life as a child, and the debt you owed him was paid in full by your daughter saving mine by leading me back to Christ. The bread he cast upon the waters at that hospital many years ago has washed up on my shore."

Tears welled in Mr. Coker's eyes—he couldn't respond. The three sat in hush. It was like a fog had settled in around them sealing off the outside world. The silence demanded a spokesman.

Owen broke the silence. "What I've heard tonight, I'll remember forever. It has inspired me to make this project my special mission."

The rest of the week was spent in researching the inventory on hand in the various supply stores, studying and adjusting plans to accommodate recommendations from a team of Architects in the States specializing in hospital design.

The hovercraft took Jake back to Lungi Airport. Owen had wanted to accompany him, but he insisted to be alone because he had special business to take care of before the flight. His flight would leave in an hour. Before he left London, he had requested Siana to be at home for a call before he boarded his return flight. What Jake was about to do was the most meaningful and important decision ever made in his adult life. He called Siana. She was expecting his call. He controlled the conversation.

"Siana, I want you to use the key I gave you to my flat. Go into my bedroom and take from my nightstand an envelope with your name on it. The envelope contains two things you must inspect and read. It's imperative you go as soon as you hang up, and I want you to be alone when you open the envelope. Now, please repeat to me what you heard me say."

She repeated verbatim what he requested her to do, then asked, "Are you all right, you sound tense?"

"I'm fine and everything is normal."

Her last words spoken were, "Don't forget your medication for your flight."

He found the medication she had given him in his briefcase. Using a bottle of water, he downed the tablets. It came to him that apart from his mother, no one ever watched over him like this since he left home. In the hot, humid climate these words coming from her felt like a cool breeze blowing across his brow.

He boarded the plane and found his aisle seat, then checked his briefcase for the copy of the letter he had enclosed in the envelope with the ring. Siana would open and read this letter at any moment.

> *My dearest Siana, I'm asking you to join your life with mine in marriage so we can make this voyage in life together. I'll live in your world if you're willing to live in mine. The box inside this envelope expresses my promise and commitment. I have two tickets on a flight tonight to the States departing within an hour after my arrival at Gatwick. One ticket has your name on it, the other mine. If you choose to accept my proposal and are willing to join me on this flight in visiting my family to announce our engagement, please meet me where I clear customs. If you choose not to come, I'll fly on knowing you've made me a better person. PS: The diamonds in the ring are not part of the contraband. Love, Jake.*

After reviewing the letter, Jake didn't think it was necessary to tell her the tickets were first class. The bottom of the letter indicated the airline and flight number.

The plane landed on schedule. Jake moved into the aisle ahead of other passengers. For the first time, he was considering how someone else thought of him in a permanent relationship. Chess games hadn't been part of his life recently, except in the drama of real life. Right now, the game he and Siana were in had few players left on the board. He just made his last move. Win, lose, or draw, he would soon know his fate.

After clearing customs, Jake moved toward the receiving area where passengers had families waiting, and among them, he saw a special person standing alone, someone prepared to make the biggest journey of her life.

She was waving her hand in a way that made the diamond ring sparkle with splendor. Siana was crying when they embraced. The chess game of life was over between them. The judges ruled the game a draw. Jake had discovered a profound truth: this was the only game played in real life where it was honorable, and preferred, that it end in a draw.

Still wrapped in his arms, Siana whispered in Jake's ear, "I'm so excited, my love, where and when will our wedding happen?"

"It will be the date you choose, and if you approve, the ceremony will be here in London."

They walked together hand-in-hand to the gate for their flight to the States, she with the thrill of excitement never experienced before. It was a new world alongside someone who had become a new person. It came to Jake that when he was growing up he had heard sermons on how the third and fourth generations inherited the sins of the father. Now, he was hearing another voice reversing that axiom. It was telling him, *because of the righteous act of a doctor in Africa many years ago in saving the life of a boy, he had passed down to his grandson, the third generation, an Angel, who was the instrument of change in his life.*

Jake took hold of the ring hand of the person responsible for the fulfillment of his grandfather's vision for him.

"That's a large diamond. Do you think it might fall off your finger?"

"No," she said, "it will always be safe in the strong hand of the person now holding it."

They faded down the corridor to their gate, and Jake leaned over and whispered in Siana's ear, "I'll let the thousands of patients treated at the hospital in Africa be the jurors to decide my innocence in keeping the diamonds, and

I'll place myself in the dock of public opinion among the survivors of the bomb victims to declare my guilt."

Jake's Lawyer looked at him and affirmed his statement with a smile. Then she said, "Jacob, I have your claustrophobic medication for flying with me."

Jake squeezed her hand tightly, saying to himself, *she called me Jacob. Not only has my life been changed, but I've been given a new name, just like my grandfather said it would be.*

Therefore if anyone is in Christ, he is a new creature; the old things passed away; behold, new things have come.

www.ingramcontent.com/pod-product-compliance
Lightning Source LLC
Chambersburg PA
CBHW051412170626
46809CB00006B/2124